BAD TIMING

Also by Nick Oldham from Severn House

The Henry Christie thriller series

CRITICAL THREAT
SCREEN OF DECEIT
CRUNCH TIME
THE NOTHING JOB
SEIZURE
HIDDEN WITNESS
FACING JUSTICE
INSTINCT
FIGHTING FOR THE DEAD
BAD TIDINGS
JUDGEMENT CALL
LOW PROFILE
EDGE
UNFORGIVING
BAD BLOOD
BAD COPS
WILDFIRE

The Steve Flynn thriller series

ONSLAUGHT
AMBUSH
HEADHUNTER

BAD TIMING

Nick Oldham

This first world edition published 2020
in Great Britain and the USA by
SEVERN HOUSE PUBLISHERS LTD of
Eardley House, 4 Uxbridge Street, London W8 7SY.
Trade paperback edition first published
in Great Britain and the USA 2021 by
SEVERN HOUSE PUBLISHERS LTD.

British Library Cataloguing in Publication Data
A CIP catalogue record for this title is available from the British Library.

ISBN-13: 978-0-7278-8960-7 (cased)
ISBN-13: 978-1-78029-731-6 (trade paper)
ISBN-13: 978-1-4483-0452-3 (e-book)

All Severn House titles are printed on acid-free paper.

Severn House Publishers support the Forest Stewardship Council™ [FSC™],
the leading international forest certification organisation.
All our titles that are printed on FSC certified paper carry the FSC logo.

Typeset by Palimpsest Book Production Ltd.,
Falkirk, Stirlingshire, Scotland.
Printed and bound in Great Britain by
TJ International, Padstow, Cornwall.

This one is dedicated to the memory of John Bent

ONE

The man had come to torture and to kill, but he'd had those pleasures, those tasks, taken away from him because of the fleeing, terrified young woman who had run straight into his arms.

Despite the moorland fires which were devastating this section of north-west England, he had trekked his way across the fields in darkness with the aid of night-vision goggles and a disposable face mask to cover his nose and mouth and prevent him inhaling the smoke. He had trudged up through the hanging, acrid atmosphere, knowing that when he had completed this job, leaving by the exact same route would cover his tracks effectively. Even if the cops put their dogs after him, he knew their sense of smell would be obliterated by the smoke.

Not that the cops would do so anyway. He knew that by the time his crimes were discovered – which could be days or even weeks, bearing in mind the isolated location of the converted farmhouse in which his targets lived – he would be long gone anyway.

He was looking forward to these killings. This was going to be one of those rare jobs where he could take his time in its execution. He could dawdle a bit, savour it, enjoy it. This would not be like his usual ones, often on city streets or down dank, dark alleyways, which mostly consisted of stalking, waiting, then picking the right moment when the target was isolated. He would appear behind them like a shadow, put a gun to the back of their head and pull the trigger twice – a double tap – always twice; then he would disappear before they'd even slumped dead to the ground and finished twitching.

Tonight he would have some time to play with. It would be much more laid-back but, ironically, more intense and frightening because of it.

And, of course, he would be doing it for love.

As he picked his way carefully through the darkness – even

with NVGs and a torch, there was still the possibility of breaking an ankle in the rough terrain – the man was already visualizing a chat, maybe some torture, even a rape, although he was wary of such extravagance because of DNA; no matter how careful one might be when committing rape, there was always the possibility of leaving a trace. Not that he had ever been arrested and had to provide a DNA sample, but his idiotic twin brother – estranged, not seen for five years – had been convicted of rape, and the man knew all about family DNA connections and how the trail might lead to him eventually.

So, maybe not rape. That was him just daydreaming; sexual assaults were not his thing, anyway.

But definitely torture. That was a given.

Probably basic stuff. Cigarettes stubbed out on faces and tits, making great sizzling noises. Fingers snapped like twiglets. Stuff like that. Nothing over-complicated because there was no need to force a confession as such. The two targets, a husband and wife, were as guilty as sin and proving this wasn't the problem. Extracting some information from them would be nice, though, so all he really had to do was have a bit of fun before putting a gun to their heads and – obviously – making the husband watch the wife die first.

And seeing that look of horror on his face.

Pure gold.

These thoughts had already been jigging around in his mind on the journey up from London on the M1, then the M6, finally leaving that motorway at the Lancaster north exit and driving east to wend his grim way along winding country roads to his parking spot in Azers Wood, on the northern edge of the Forest of Bowland.

He'd parked his very clean – 'clean' in a criminal sense – and unremarkable Dacia Duster on a narrow logging track, then changed into his walking gear before embarking on his chosen circuitous route, with the intention of dropping down behind the farmhouse where the couple lived a fairly discreet, under-the-radar existence, then killing them.

He had lived and imagined this journey several times on Google Earth and Ordnance Survey maps, and checked on the state of the moorland fires on news reports, but actually working his way through the smoke was more difficult and disorientating than he could have imagined, even though the fires were burning several miles away to the east; at least he'd had the foresight to bring the face mask along.

He was no nature lover or outdoorsman as such, but even he could see the fires had taken a terrible toll as they'd spread and raged remorselessly back and forth, dependent on wind direction, all the while being pursued by exhausted firefighters trying to beat them out, only to have the flames reignite again.

So he had locked his car in the woods and begun to walk as the night drew in, easily vaulting over low walls and stepping across ditches, until he reached the foot of a steep hill, on the opposite side of which was the farmhouse. It had taken him an hour of slow progress to reach this point, and under the cover of a dry stone wall he unhitched his rucksack and settled down on his backside for a swig of water from the plastic bottle and a chocolate bar for an energy boost.

Here, as he munched his Snickers, he rechecked his equipment.

It was a handgun job essentially, so he had brought along the very nice, trusted nine-millimetre Browning Hi-Power semi-automatic pistol he'd acquired from a dealer in Belgium. He had simply paid a woman to carry it back into the UK for him via a ferry ride. Another person brought in ammunition for him: two fifteen-round magazines, fully loaded, and ten further boxes of shells – probably more than he would ever need. One of the magazines was inserted into the weapon and the other was in his zip-up jacket pocket. He had a roll of duct tape, a length of clothes line, a piano wire, a ski mask and several pairs of disposable latex gloves. In much the same way as he thought of DNA, he didn't want to leave fingerprints either. There were none on police record; even so, he would have been idiotic to leave any behind. It was just asking for trouble.

All in all, he wanted to keep it fairly simple, and as he sat there eating the last of the chocolate, he was reconsidering the chat/torture thing.

Simple, fast and away was always the best.

He fully expected the couple to be sitting at the kitchen table for their evening meal, or maybe watching TV in the lounge. He'd knock on the door – lightly, innocently, friendly – one of them would answer, and now he decided that whoever it was would be shot dead where they stood, no chat, no preamble. He would step across the body, enter the kitchen and murder the other occupant, then be back out of the door seconds later, job done.

Probably the best way.

A couple of minutes at most, then make his way back over the fields to the car where another change of clothing awaited. He'd get into the clean set, bag up the used clothing and be away.

Yes: simples.

He scrunched up the chocolate bar wrapper and shoved it into the bottle which he pushed into one of the side mesh pockets of the rucksack, taking everything with him. He always tried not to leave anything behind. He took it, destroyed it.

He stood up, slid a ski mask over his head in place of the face mask (which went into the rucksack), refitted the NVGs and walked up the steep incline towards the ridge from where he would have a view downwards about a mile or so to the rear of the farmhouse in which his unsuspecting victims awaited.

They hadn't expected her that afternoon, but when she knocked on the side door, the one they always used in preference to the main front door, and stepped in with a happy shout of 'Guess who?' the first to rush and greet her was the dog, almost bowling her over with his ecstatic welcome. He was a huge, lanky, gentle-mannered Great Dane called – obviously – Scoobs, after Scooby Doo the famous cartoon dog; then her parents rushed to meet her, crowded her, flushing with pleasure at the surprise visit. Despite their effusiveness and fussing over her, she instantly detected something amiss.

Yes, they were clearly overwhelmed by joy to see her, their only child home from university in Manchester – she'd arrived by taxi for the extra surprise – and though they hugged and kissed and clucked over her in the vestibule and helped her get her coat off, there was something lurking behind the joy, which, for the moment, seemed extremely odd.

Maybe, she thought fleetingly, she had interrupted something a bit kinky going on. And actually she quite liked that thought – people who'd been together for twenty-five years still 'digging' each other. And even when the two of them stood in front of her a bit awkwardly, blocking her way into the kitchen, that was what she still believed it was: something a bit embarrassing.

They didn't budge.

'What?' she asked, grinning. 'Have I interrupted something?'

Painful expressions crossed their faces.

'I have, haven't I?' She laughed. 'Come on, let me in. Can't be that bad. Like, what's the worst it can be, guys? Blow-up dolls?'

She shouldered her way gently between the two people she loved most in the world and, with Scoobs at her legs, stepped into the kitchen where she came to a grinding halt.

'What on earth?' she said as her mouth fell open.

Her parents came in behind her.

'It's what we do, darling,' her mother said.

Her father said, 'You'd find out one day, I suppose. We've kept it hidden from you, but you're old enough now, so we might as well tell you. Let you into our dark secret.'

The daughter was completely dumbfounded, speechless, overcome by a feeling of shock and dread.

It wasn't the two bowls containing salad and the two glasses of white wine on the kitchen island that stunned her.

She walked leadenly across the room, skirted slowly around the island to the worktop underneath the back window, her eyes criss-crossing what she was seeing, trying to make sense of it all.

Eventually, she put a hand to her forehead and whispered hoarsely, 'Oh my God!' Then she spun aggressively to her parents, whose faces were still displaying the exact same expression of having been caught.

'I thought you were a chartered accountant,' Beth York demanded of her father. 'Or something.'

'I am,' he said, affronted.

'And you – you!' she pointed sharply at her mother. 'I thought you were a financial adviser, and both of you regulated by the Financial Conduct Authority, or whatever it's called.'

'I am . . . we are,' her mother answered.

'This is just a—' her father began, then faltered in his explanation.

'A what? A sideline?'

'Well, a bit more than that.' He looked pained.

'Explain. I'm listening.'

Her parents exchanged a troubled glance, then her father took a deep breath. 'Love, do you remember that businessman, a fellow called Jack Carter?'

'Businessman? Complete rogue, more like.'

'Yes, yes . . . well, be that as it may,' he continued. 'Well, you know we used to do his books and then he sold his haulage business?'

'I remember him well.'

'Yes, well, you know he came to us and asked if we knew of any way of his keeping the money out of the taxman's hands?'

'I seem to recall he didn't have all that much.'

'Mmm, well, he might have had a bit more than we let on.'

'I thought he had hardly anything.'

'Um, about two million, actually – give or take.'

'What? Hang on . . . as I recall, he sold the business and got next to nothing for it.'

'On paper, maybe,' her mother said.

'You cooked his books – is that what you're saying?' Beth demanded.

'Sort of simmered them. Anyway, that's by the by,' her father said dismissively as though it didn't matter. 'The thing is he asked us if we could somehow keep the money out of the taxman's sticky fingers. The other thing is it was all cash, every bit of it – other than the stuff we put into his actual accounts. He'd sold all his vehicles and equipment for cash, even the stuff he had on hire, so it was all untraceable and we put the sale of the company through the books at a loss . . .'

'And there he was with two million quid burning a hole in his pockets and he came to you and you went, "Yes, of course, Jack, we'll help you hide this money."' Beth could feel a spittle bubble frothing on her lips. She sucked it back and said, 'Tell me you didn't.'

Again, both looked to be in pain.

'Well, I knew a way of getting the money out of the country so he could keep the majority of it, earn some interest, and we would make some commission as well,' her father said.

'Which wouldn't appear in the books either,' her mother added helpfully.

'Spain,' Beth guessed. She knew her parents had spent a long time on the Costa Blanca a few years before.

'We'd met a builder,' her mother said.

'We invested in property and land,' her father said. 'And that way Mr Carter paid some commission to us . . .'

'How much?' Beth demanded.

'Five per cent.'

'So, what, a hundred grand?'

'Give or take,' her father said. 'If we'd have done it legitimately, even with legitimate expenses, Mr Carter would have lost about three hundred thousand on each million to the taxman.'

'Paid in lawful tax, you mean?' Beth said harshly.

'Well, yes,' her mother conceded.

'Anyway, anyway, that is not the point,' her father said, flapping his hands as though trying to bat away the unpleasantness of it all. 'The point is we were able to invest the money abroad and get a healthy return from it. We still receive a tiny commission, and his money has grown.'

'And Mr Carter is a very happy man,' her mother added.

'Well, whoopie-doo for Mr Carter,' Beth said. Then formed her lips into a tight, disapproving line before saying, 'Which doesn't even begin to explain what the fuck is going on in the kitchen!'

'Bethany York! Language, please,' her mother uttered, shocked to the core.

What was going on in the kitchen, what had frozen Beth York in her tracks as she entered, was the large military-style holdall on a worktop, sagging open and revealing itself to be jam-packed full of bank notes in about a hundred vacuum-sealed clear plastic packs; further along the top was a machine as big as a desk printer which vacuum-packed the money, and next to that was a stack of about twenty more sealed blocks of money. On the kitchen floor was another holdall jammed full of loose bank notes. Further along the worktop were several supermarket bags filled with even more money, and then a cash-counting machine.

Beth, surprising them by coming home unannounced from university, had obviously interrupted a very long money-counting session.

'Well, darling,' her mother – Isobel York – explained, 'it turned out that Mr Carter had an acquaintance who was suddenly interested in what we had managed to do and inquired if we could do the same for him.'

Beth blinked and joined the dots. 'You launder money for the mob?' Her eyes shot from one parent to the other and back again, repeatedly.

Her father – John – shrugged. 'Well, it's not really the mob here, is it? That's a very American phrase.'

'Organized criminals, then?'

He shrugged again, accepting that definition.

'How much is in there?' Beth demanded, pointing accusingly in the direction of the kitchen.

'We're not quite sure because we haven't finished counting it,' Isobel said.

'Oh my fucking God – I remember that snivelling shit Carter coming round here four years ago, before I went to uni. Have you been laundering money since then for the mob?'

'Organized criminals, dear,' her father corrected her.

'Semantics!' she spat. 'Fuck me!'

'We looked upon them as a very cash-rich London-based company who wish to be as tax-efficient as possible. And stop swearing. It really doesn't become you.'

Beth snorted contemptuously. 'So how much is there?'

'Maybe three million,' Isobel estimated.

'And how much have you laundered in total?'

'Nine, ten,' John York said.

'Million,' Isobel added for clarity.

'Jesus wept.'

'And don't blaspheme, dear,' Isobel admonished her. 'Not seemly.'

'You pair of fucking hypocrites.'

'Beth!' they exclaimed in unison.

'And me' – Beth tapped her own chest – 'me. I thought you were successful. Legitimately. Legally. Off your own hard work.'

'Darling – nobody's that successful legally,' her mother chided.

'How on earth do you think we can afford all those classic cars outside and in the garage?' John asked. 'They cost millions. You don't get that sort of money selling mortgages and life insurance in Kirkby Lonsdale. I mean, we did OK from that, but this little sideline has helped.'

'Sideline? Fuck me,' Beth said again. 'I thought your cars were just a passion, a hobby?'

'They are – but they cost lots.'

'And it does help that we scam them, too,' her mother admitted, then very quickly covered her mouth with her hand, realizing she had blabbed too much.

Beth's already shocked face grew even more incredulous. 'You scam gangsters who pay you commission to launder from them?'

'They'll never know. They're quite dim,' John said. 'The money literally turns up in plastic bags and cases, stuffed in, not counted. They've no idea what we do with it.'

Beth sat back in the armchair, hardly able to compute this. Her heart pounded and her breathing became laboured as though she was having a panic attack. She was only twenty-two years old, as fit and healthy as a person that age should be, but she was convinced her heart was about to explode. She tried to keep calm, but it was a struggle.

'I don't know anything about gangsters,' Beth said, 'except for one thing: they *know* when people are stealing from them, or conning them, because they're professionals at those games. And when they know, they take steps to rectify the situation. Well, all I can say is this – you are idiots. For getting involved in the first place and then for stealing what is probably drug money or money from people trafficking. Mark my words, it will all come around to bite you on your fat, lardy arses. You need to get out of it now.'

'Well, actually,' her mother began to say, but snapped her mouth shut when Beth held up a hand.

'Stop! I don't want to hear another word.'

Beth marched into the kitchen and wrenched open the cupboard where the booze was kept, snatched an almost full bottle of vodka and stormed upstairs. On the way up, she was already necking the vodka neat.

In the lounge, Isobel turned to her husband and said, 'We'll tell her our plans when she's had a bit of a rest, shall we?'

The house, which for many years had been a farmhouse, had been bought and renovated by the previous owners who had acquired it from a farming dynasty which had owned the place for almost 200 years. It was now divided into three levels – ground floor, first floor where the main bedrooms were located, then the second floor – a wide-open attic space turned into a games room with a full-size snooker table. It was also on this level that Beth's father had his gun cabinet, which was secured to the stone wall and contained his shotguns.

Beth's bedroom was actually a former hayloft accessed from the first-floor hallway, a space she had claimed when she was much younger. It could only be accessed from an electronically operated drop-down hatch and extending ladders, but it was large and spacious and had a self-contained bath/shower room and loo.

It had been her own private haven as a kid and teenager, and it was now the place to which she retreated to escape the horrible discovery that her parents, who had been dutiful role models to her, or so she thought, and whom she loved dearly, were now little more than criminal masterminds.

She pressed the button on the wall and the hatch opened, the ladders extended and she clambered up into the hayloft, pulling the ladders up behind her and closing the hatch. She needed to be alone.

Actually, she knew her father had sailed close to the wind a few times over the years, had been investigated by financial regulators and, she seemed to remember, the Fraud Squad. That was a long time ago, and he had emerged smelling of roses with nothing ever proved against him. Beth recalled the incidents only vaguely – the urgent, whispered conversations that ended with guilty looks from her parents when she walked into the room, tense times when their marriage had seemed brittle.

Beth sat on the edge of her old bed and tipped more of the vodka down her throat. It burned and blossomed warmly in her chest, blunting some of the shock.

So she had kind of suspected her dad had a 'chancer' streak in him, but that her mum kept him in check in her support role in the little business they ran together from a tiny office over a newsagent in Kirkby Lonsdale, just across the hills in North Yorkshire.

Thinking about it now, with the vodka sluicing down her gullet, she wouldn't have been surprised to learn her dad hid money for clients, but she would have expected it to be a few quid here and there for local businesses and individuals.

Not the fucking Cosa Nostra.

She wiped away tears that trickled down her cheeks, took another mouthful of vodka and climbed into her night things.

Finally the bottle was empty. She allowed it to slither out of her fingers on to the floor, started to cry and buried her face in the pillows, finally falling into a deep sleep assisted by tiredness and too much neat spirits.

When she woke up, it was dark. Her face was still pressed into the pillows, and as she raised it, groaning, she left a deep indentation and damp patches stained with mascara where her eyes had been and dribble from the corner of her mouth.

She felt terrible as she slowly pushed herself up and sat on the edge of the bed again, her shoulders drooping miserably as she chastised herself for being naïve and stupid.

She had been attending a degree course at Manchester Metropolitan University over the last three years and never once stood back to question the fact that while so many other students struggled to make ends meet, lived in grotty accommodation, had to find part-time jobs, she lived in a lovely one-bedroom studio apartment on the southern edge of the city, and received a healthy wodge each month from her parents. Of course there were others like her, but not many.

'Idiot,' she chided herself, 'I've been financed by the friggin' Kirkby Lonsdale mafia!'

A two-person business in a Yorkshire market town does not have that sort of cash to splash around – certainly not enough to buy an array of classic sports cars. A new four-car garage had even been built to house some of these vehicles.

She rubbed her eyes. They squelched. She stood up unsteadily, wondering how long she had been asleep – hours, it seemed – surprised at how quickly the alcohol had got into her system to wipe her out.

She blew out her cheeks, wobbled unsteadily to the en-suite and filled the long, wide bath with hot, foamy water. She undressed, slid in with a long sigh and closed her eyes again, falling into a light slumber, jerking awake twenty minutes later in the tepid water.

Heaving herself out, she perched miserably on the edge of the bath for another five minutes, head hanging low, with a large fluffy bath sheet draped across her shoulders as she debated internally what she should do.

The way she saw it, she had several options.

She could metaphorically clamp her hands over her ears, go 'blah-blah-blah' and pretend nothing was happening, that her mum and dad were not involved in a huge money-laundering operation, skimming money from the villains behind it all. She could deal with it by cutting herself off from the two people she loved most in the world. Or she could just go along with it, enjoy the money, pretend she knew nothing about it, live the high life and hope it didn't all come back to bite arses, as she had earlier predicted.

She did not know – she just did not know.

One thing for sure was that she had to get out of this place, head back to Manchester and think long and hard about it. First, though, maybe have it out with her parents again.

She towelled herself dry, pulled on her short pyjama set, cleaned her teeth to get rid of the vodka sheen, then went towards the hatch in the floor and pressed the button which lowered the ladder silently down into the hallway.

The man mouthed the words, *What the fuck?*

He had made his way up the hill and was dropping carefully down the opposite side towards the farmhouse. In the darkness, and in spite of the NVGs, it was fairly treacherous going and his progress had been a little slower than he'd anticipated. He'd stumbled once or twice, but not seriously, though he did finally find himself kneeling in a ditch and very annoyed with himself as he rose back to his feet with sodden knees, only to feel the impact of another human being crashing into him and sending him flying backwards into the grass, tipping the NVGs off his head.

The man fought back instantly, fearing he was being attacked, his instincts kicking in.

It took him just moments to subdue what turned out to be a young woman, who he pinned face down with one knee on her spine between her shoulder blades. One hand held her head down and the other took a grip of her slim wrists and held them tightly behind her back.

She fought, but he was bigger, stronger, had the power, the experience.

'Keep fuckin' still,' he hissed between his clenched teeth close to her ear.

Finally, everything seemed to deflate out of the woman – breath, strength, resolve – and through the man's hand, which muffled her speech, she said, 'Do it, kill me if you have to . . . I might as well be dead anyway . . . you killed my parents.'

'Fuck are you talkin' about, lass?' he said. He had adjusted his position now, kneeling on both her hands while he fumbled for the NVGs in the grass, found them and placed them back on to look at exactly what had flattened him and what he'd then caught.

He had no intention of letting her go, so he trussed her up with duct tape, and she lay there, almost catatonic, and complied without a word or move of defiance as he bound her wrists and ankles and smeared a short length of tape across her mouth to keep her quiet. He left her by a jagged outcrop of rock as a marker so he would know where to find her again.

A couple of minutes later, he was crouched behind the stone wall at the rear of the farmhouse lawn, still unable to comprehend what the girl had told him, what she had described.

He raised his head.

From his position he could see along the gable end of the farmhouse where the side door was. He could also see the rear of the recently built four-car garage in which, he already knew, the girl's father kept some of his classic car collection. Other cars were usually parked at the front of the property.

The side door of the house was open, light flooding out.

The man inhaled, sniffing a different kind of smoke to that of the wildfires. He knew what it was – that peculiar reek of cars on fire – yet from where he was hidden, he could not quite see what the origin of the smell was.

He heaved himself up and slithered over the wall, landed soft-footed on the manicured lawn, drawing the Browning from his waistband as, still crouching but moving swiftly, he made his way across the short grass to the rear wall of the garage where he flattened himself and edged along to the corner, quickly peering around initially, then, sure no one else was there, taking a proper look from this position.

Diagonally across from him was the open side door of the farmhouse; looking further down to the driveway, he could see the asphalt parking area and an old, short-wheel-base Land Rover parked up.

The man frowned, did not move, listened, then slowly emerged from behind the garage in a combat stance, his pistol held out in front of him, safety off, finger on the trigger.

He moved slowly along the edge of the garage and came to the next corner, almost directly opposite the side door of the house, and as he rotated, he saw the body of a young man splayed out, mangled even, in front of one of the garage doors.

The man crouched, crabbed sideways and quickly inspected the body. Yes, it was definitely the body of a young man, crushed as if he had been hit and run over by a car – and he was definitely dead. Next to him was a shotgun with a bent barrel, which also looked as though it had been under car wheels.

The man looked along the front of the garage. It had four separate roller doors, behind each of which was one of John York's classic cars. The first door was fully open and the bay behind it was empty. The next two doors were fully closed, but the fourth door along was open. He looked inside the garage along its length and saw the three remaining cars in place.

He looked at the body again. The young man's face was almost removed, the limbs on one side of his body crushed flat.

So dead.

The man twisted and ran to the front of the house to the Land Rover. The driver's door was open; he could see bullet holes in all the windows and that the vehicle was resting at an unusual angle because both rear tyres were deflated.

Along the front of the house he saw four more classic cars and now knew the origin of that burning smell: all four cars had been set alight and were now just four blackened, smouldering shells worth nothing.

'Not good,' the man said to himself, backing away and then going into the house, stepping into the vestibule, entering the kitchen cautiously, combat stance again.

His eyes and weapon traversed the room. He emitted a little whistle at the sight that greeted his eyes.

Money.

The reason he had made this journey: to talk money, to kill because of money.

He remained rigid at the kitchen door, not completely understanding the scenario but trying to put together the things blabbed hysterically by the girl on the hill – who had identified herself as the daughter of the man's targets, John and Isobel York – about money in the kitchen, stacks of the stuff, and her parents' bodies upstairs somewhere – hacked, she claimed, to pieces.

The man stepped in, kept to the edge of the kitchen and shuffled his way to the big hallway, behind which was the generally unused front door of the farmhouse. Again he paused, wondering if there was anyone actually alive in the house.

He checked the rooms on the ground floor – all empty – then went up the stairs to the first-floor landing, already noticing smears of blood on the walls and carpets. He crossed directly to the doors opposite him, avoiding blood where he could.

He glanced into the first one – a large white-tiled bathroom.

And swore, backing out quickly, then checked the other rooms, which were empty.

Next, he went up a further set of stairs which he knew would take him to the attic level, following a trail of even more blood into a wide room with a full-size snooker table at its centre.

Once he'd seen what was up there, he didn't dawdle – first because he did not want to be involved in any of this, and second because in the distance, but approaching quickly, was the screaming noise of an engine.

He sprinted back down to the ground floor, dashed past the money to the side door, stopped and peered around the jamb with one eye to see a big four-wheel-drive SUV, fitted with banks of headlights on the bull bars and roofline, tearing up the driveway.

He ducked and ran for cover behind the garage, passing the dead man without a glance, and backed off into deep shadow next to an unrenovated barn some twenty yards behind the garage block, from which he could see the side of the farmhouse and down the driveway where the SUV drew up behind the Land Rover. Two men carrying guns jumped out and jogged up to the house.

Their first port of call was to inspect the dead body in front of the garage. One went down on to one knee next to the corpse. The pair had a hurried discussion. They seemed young guys from where the man was watching, but he couldn't really make out their features. Then both entered the house.

No doubt to collect the money.

The man in the shadows had to decide on a course of action.

In the end, he chose to stay and watch proceedings, especially when it became obvious the two had definitely returned for the cash; he watched them carry out the holdalls and other bags he'd seen in the kitchen and toss them into the back of the SUV. Just before leaving, one of the men poured liquid from a can over the Land Rover and flicked a burning match on to it.

As the SUV spun away and accelerated down the drive, the Land Rover went up in a whoosh of flames which rose high as the accelerant took grip and destroyed the vehicle.

The man turned away, refitted his NVGs and made his way across the lawn, over the wall and up the hill towards where he'd left the young woman trussed up, all the while wondering what the hell he'd just stumbled across.

When he reached the point where he was sure he'd left the female, he wondered if he had miscalculated his bearings. But he knew he was correct. She should have been here, where he had left her.

She wasn't.

She was gone.

TWO

Four weeks later

Henry Christie awoke slowly, aware that his left arm was numb from his elbow down to his fingertips, caused by the weight resting on the crook of his arm. His eyes flickered open as he flexed his fingers and turned his head slowly to look sideways at the woman sleeping soundly alongside him; her head was wedged on his arm, blocking the flow of blood.

Henry cursed his stupidity, caused by a combination of male weakness, ego and excessive alcohol – that volatile, heady mix – and, as carefully as he could, extracted his arm from underneath her, hoping desperately not to rouse her. He'd made a big error, gone back on his own promise to himself, and he wanted to be out of here as swiftly as possible without causing or having to face an unpleasant scene or, God forbid, an awkward breakfast of tea and crumpets.

The woman – her name was Maude Crichton – rolled gently away with a murmur but did not wake up, or at least pretended to be soundly asleep.

Whichever, Henry was grateful.

As the blood rushed back down his arm, making his fingers tingle painfully, he sat up on the edge of the very expensive and expansive bed, manfully holding himself together as a shooting pain – much, much worse than a migraine, he guessed (although he had never suffered such a thing) – seared across the top of his skull like an axe being imbedded.

Normally, he would have emitted some kind of pitiful wail, plus all the other noises a man over the age of sixty might make, but he kept his silence, not wishing to disturb Maude.

He scooped up his clothing. *Just how did my underpants get there?* he wondered as he retrieved them from the top of a free-standing lamp. Clutching everything else, he padded barefoot to the bedroom door which opened with an agonizing creak, making him stop instantly, cringe and look back over towards Maude who had not moved.

Then he was into the hallway where he dressed quickly, not bothering to test his sense of balance by putting his underpants on, just shoving them into his jeans pocket together with his socks. He tiptoed quietly downstairs and let himself out of the front door wearing only jeans, a short-sleeved shirt and espadrilles, and trying to remember if he had arrived at Maude's wearing a windjammer or not.

He wasn't sure.

The day was already warm, the tail-end of summer having arrived following a week of torrential downpours that had caused flooding in many areas, in complete contrast to the weather before that, which had been sweltering hot, tinder-dry and had caused weeks of dangerous wildfires on the moors – now, at last, extinguished.

Henry paused briefly on the front doorstep of Maude's rather magnificent house, situated on the outskirts of Kendleton on the opposite side of the village to The Tawny Owl, the country pub and hotel where Henry actually lived; Maude's house was quite close to the detached police house occupied by the rural beat bobby, PC Jake Niven.

It was a mile-long walk for Henry that morning. He took a deep, steadying breath, hoped that as usual the village would be almost deserted at this time of day, and began what he hoped would not turn out to be the walk of shame.

His luck was out. Everyone he could possibly have met on the way home, he met.

The postwoman – a pretty lady who gave him a knowing smirk.

The milkman – who still delivered using an electric-powered milk float – gave a double thumbs-up.

And a couple of other smirkers. But what he thought would be the final nail in the 'shame coffin' was hammered home by Jake Niven who, incredibly, was out on patrol at this early hour and was driving by in the opposite direction. He slowed down almost to a stop, slid open the window on his old Land Rover and gave Henry a lecherous, tongue-out expression, to which Henry responded, 'Fuck off.'

That, however, was not quite the end. To cap his embarrassment, as he walked across the rickety footbridge spanning Kendleton Brook, there was a rustle in the trees and a red deer stag which frequented the area, and which Henry had named Horace, emerged from a thicket and gave Henry a baleful, knowing, disappointed look before bounding back into the woods with a snort of hot air from its wide nostrils.

'And you, mate,' Henry grumbled. He was still shaking his head at his bad luck as he crossed the car park at the front of The Tawny Owl and trotted up the front steps, hoping to make it into to the owner's accommodation unobserved. He had inherited the business from his deceased fiancée, Alison Holt, and now ran it fifty-fifty with her stepdaughter, Ginny – who was the next person he bumped into.

Somehow he got the impression she was waiting to pounce.

'Morning, love,' he greeted her, trying to fool her into thinking he was just returning from an early-morning stroll. He was, however, totally aware of the contempt she was trying desperately to keep out of her eyes. He loved this young lady as if she was one of his own flesh-and-blood daughters, and although Ginny was not blood-related to Alison, she seemed to have inherited quite a few of her traits – not the least of which was how she could see right through Henry and would not tolerate any of his bullshit or inefficiency.

Her mouth turned down. 'I thought you said you would never succumb to any of Maude Crichton's advances.'

He blinked, swallowed with awkwardness, gave her a stupid smile.

'Anyway, none of my business, I suppose,' Ginny said haughtily.

'No, probably not,' Henry retorted harshly, then immediately wished he could turn back the clock about five seconds to reconfigure what came out of his mouth.

Ginny looked hurt. 'Whatever . . . anyway, you said you'd paid those invoices to Mitchells, but they've been on the phone screeching at me already – in a nice way. Plus there's an email from Courthouses about another late payment, which you said you'd sort for those blinds in the annexe.'

'I thought I had.'

'Clearly the opposite applies.'

Henry took a breath. 'Right, sorry.'

'I've paid both now by bank draft, so at least we're back on side with two of our best suppliers.'

'Point taken.' He pursed his lips and walked past her.

'You dropped these.'

Henry turned to see Ginny bending over to pick up something from the floor between thumb and forefinger, which she proffered distastefully. 'And don't forget Tom Noonan's picking you up at ten.'

He snatched his underpants from her and made his way into the private accommodation which was accessed via a secure door with keypad entry to one side of the main bar.

He needed a shower – fully aware he reeked of body odour mixed with Chanel No. 5 – a change of clothing and time to clear his fuzzed-up brain.

Henry was growing increasingly concerned about his mental state. And his drinking. And his attitude.

All stunk.

All three things seemed to have ambushed him in the last

month or so and he was slowly coming to dislike what he had become or was becoming.

He pinpointed the beginning of this notable deterioration to the murder of John and Isobel York, a couple who lived in a plush converted farmhouse on the moors high above Kendleton.

At the time of the Yorks' deaths, the moors had been ablaze with uncontrollable wildfires sweeping across them, obliterating everything in their path. Henry had volunteered The Tawny Owl – known locally at Th'Owl – as a focal point for the community to keep abreast of developments and a place where exhausted firefighters could retreat for food, drink and respite; each day a 'ring-round' was made to all outlying properties most at risk from the fires to check on welfare. It was during one of these ring-rounds – a service carried out by Maude Crichton – that the Yorks failed to respond to phone calls or messages on the WhatsApp group established for everyone to keep in touch.

Without suspecting anything untoward, Henry had volunteered to drive up to Hawkshead Farm where the Yorks lived, only to make a gruesome discovery. Henry had then become involved in the police investigation into the couple's deaths.

Being a retired detective superintendent who had been an SIO – senior investigating officer – with Lancashire Constabulary until a few years earlier, Henry had been cajoled into assisting the investigation as a consultant. In a short but sometimes terrifying burst, Henry had managed to bring about the arrests of the offenders quite quickly, all of whom (with the exception of one who died) were now on remand awaiting Crown Court trial. Henry had thought that he would have been glad to get back to being a landlord because he really believed his policing days were well over and he hadn't enjoyed the 'consulting' experience too much.

He had been keen to get back to managing Th'Owl and being part of the community, but a few weeks down the line he was starting to think that maybe he was wrong.

Quite quickly, he had become sloth-like, struggled to find any motivation and had begun to think that, without Alison in his life, running Th'Owl had become meaningless and had lost its sheen.

In turn, these thoughts made him mull even more about losing Alison and, very quickly, the knock-on was to make him morose, snappy and unpleasant to be around.

This led to more drinking – which was far too easy living in a pub – and spending time on the wrong side of the bar, culminating in a boozy night with the regulars to celebrate, at last, the final extinguishing of the moorland fires. It was a night that included Maude Crichton and following her home across the village and ending up in bed with her.

Which had actually been nice.

But not what Henry wanted.

In fact, he wasn't sure what he wanted.

He certainly didn't want to hurt Maude, who was lovely and decent and did not deserve to be led on or given the wrong signs about a possible relationship.

In the shower, Henry applied shampoo and lathered up his close-cropped hair. He stood under the jets with his eyes closed, leaning with both hands on the wall, his head hanging between his arms.

Worryingly, he thought, just at this point and for some reason he could not fully understand, his life seemed a bit worthless.

The pub was a success in spite of the massive downturn in business during the wildfires, and it was picking up again to pre-fire levels as bookings poured in thick and fast. His relationship with Ginny was good, although she was beginning to get a bit testy with him when he forgot to do basic things such as pay suppliers on time.

Which was another thing that concerned him: his lack of concentration skills and his growing inability to remember stuff.

Not that he thought he was suffering from the early stages of dementia; it was just that – to put it bluntly – he was bored shitless.

Tom Noonan parked his Range Rover on the old logging track in Azers Wood. He and Henry Christie slung their equipment and supplies over their shoulders and began the climb up Haylot Fell, across black and burned grassland that, just a few short weeks after the fires, was already beginning to show signs of regeneration, green shoots appearing out of the blackened, sooty earth.

Henry was amazed at how quickly this rebirth had begun to happen and said so to Tom.

'Nature.' The older man smiled. 'Wonderful. Always comes good.'

Henry glanced at him. Noonan was a local man, just creeping into his eighties and one of Th'Owl's regular customers; he and his wife came in most weeks for lunch. Henry had got chatting to him one afternoon and somehow the conversation turned to fishing.

Henry revealed he once used to be a fairly keen fly fisher but probably hadn't picked up a rod in twenty years, although he knew he still had one because he'd packed it when he'd moved to live permanently at The Tawny Owl with Alison.

Tom Noonan was a retired aero engineer, whose story fascinated Henry; he had been involved in designing the TSR2, a fantastic supersonic fighter jet that was cancelled before completion in the 1960s, despite the many millions spent developing it. Henry remembered from his childhood that it looked just like a spaceship.

Tom was also a keen angler, regularly fishing the River Lune and its tributaries as well as the many reservoirs and lakes in the area. There had been one of those rarely followed-up conversations about how, one day, they must go fishing together. Usual male promises.

However, one recent lunch time, just after the wildfires on the moors had been finally, hopefully, extinguished, Tom and his wife were eating at Th'Owl. Tom mentioned to Henry his intention to check out the current state of a tiny lake, nothing more than the size of a small Lakeland tarn, on Haylot Fell. It had been stocked with a few brown trout earlier in the year; he expected the fires would have devastated it, but he needed to know and invited Henry along.

Henry had jumped at the chance and later that same day, after he'd burrowed in the store rooms and found his old fly rod, reel, line and box of flies, he spent a few hours practising casting on the rear lawn of the pub until he could do it without too much embarrassment and did not snag the hook in his backside at every attempt.

The walk up the fell now was quite arduous, and Henry was soon gasping for air, though the much older Tom wasn't even breathing heavily. He was built like a broom, no weight on him, and Henry took note of that.

'I'm not that hopeful,' Tom admitted over his shoulder.

'You never know,' Henry said.

'Too much crap from the fires is my guess, but it is in a fairly protected position, so you never know.'

'Fingers crossed,' Henry gasped, hoping the conversation was over.

Henry had Google-Earthed the position of Kendleton Syke, which was the name of the tiny lake, and also checked an Ordnance Survey map to see that the lake was situated under the lee of a high crag called Rushbed Crag, so it was possible this natural barrier could have prevented the ravages of the fires from taking their toll on the waters.

It took about half an hour to reach the lake, and as the two men looked across the surface, they could see it had a red, rusty colour to it. Tom told him this was not unusual as it mirrored the underlying rock and soil. They circumnavigated the lake and found a grassy outcrop from which they decided to cast their lines and see how it went.

Henry fumbled nervously as he assembled his rod and fitted the reel and threaded the line he'd bought from a field sports shop in Lancaster, and then tied on a leader before attaching the fly. Eventually, as he tested the strength of what he'd done, he was quite pleased with the end result.

Tom had put his own gear together like the expert he was and waited for Henry with a wry smile.

'Think I'm good to go.' Henry grinned back.

'I'll stroll along this way' – Tom indicated the direction he'd be taking along the bank – 'and you can start here if you like? Seems a good enough spot.'

Henry watched Tom retreat, then turned and looked across the water which was still and had no signs of fish rising. He laid his landing net out to one side – *as if*, he thought – stepped to the edge of the water and fed out some line from the spool prior to the first cast.

In spite of fully expecting to feel the hook imbed itself in his scalp, he impressed himself, and after half a dozen practice casts he got the hang of it and produced a good one which landed delicately across the surface of the water. He gave the leader a couple of seconds to sink below the surface, then started to draw the line back in, in the hope that if a fish was there it would be fooled into thinking it was a real fly and take it.

That was the theory.

He caught nothing with the first cast, but, with a sudden feeling of elation within him, began to focus his mind and cast again.

He glanced occasionally at Tom who was deep in his own world, casting smoothly.

Half an hour later, not having changed position or caught anything, Henry decided to move further around the lake for a different perspective. He made his way behind Tom who was convinced there had been some interest in his flies. Henry pointed to a precarious-looking rocky outcrop under the crag which jutted out into the water.

'Don't break an ankle,' Tom warned him. 'I'm too old to be carrying you back to the car.'

'Airlift me if necessary,' Henry suggested. He gave Tom a pat on the shoulder and walked on, keeping to the shore, then having to cut slightly in before reaching the rocks which were jagged and broken with fissures of varying sizes between them – some merely cracks, others wide and deep crevices which took long strides to negotiate.

Henry picked his spot, clambering across the rocks, glad he had taken Tom's advice to wear proper walking boots for protection. He stood on the edge of the rocks and scanned the water – and maybe saw a fish rise, or maybe he was kidding himself.

He did a few test casts, then finally allowed his line to sail long and rest on the surface without causing a ripple.

A good cast. He flushed with a tiny bit of pride.

He began to draw back the line, fully concentrating, focusing.

Then he felt it: a gentle tug on the line.

He gasped. His heart did a little flutter as a surge of excitement skittered through him.

There were definitely fish in there.

If he could just entice . . . the line suddenly went taut and he responded by bringing it up quickly, hoping to imbed the hook into the fish's mouth, then the surface of the water exploded as a lovely brown trout broke through, trying to jettison the hook.

Henry tried not to panic. That was the thing that would lose a fish.

Calm calculation was necessary to hook the beautiful little thing.

He drew his line in smoothly by hand, not too quickly, allowing it to spool down at his side while at the business end the trout dived and writhed and fought to free itself.

Henry worked it, followed it, loosed the line, tightened the line, all the while bringing it closer and closer to the net. He knew he was smiling, almost laughing with glee. What an incredible feeling.

But he also kept a lid on it. Kept control. The whooping and hollering could come later.

For now, concentrate – something he'd been unable to do for a while.

Reel the little beauty in.

Which he did – up to the point when he bent down to reach for the handle of his fishing net at his feet, while keeping an eye on the line and position of the fish which he had brought to the surface.

He felt for the net with his fingertips but did not look down.

Until he had to because he could not quite find it.

He glanced down to his right – and took his eyes off the water.

It was as if, somehow, the fish knew.

And just that microsecond of reduced drag gave the fish the chance it needed. The hook came out and it was gone.

With disbelief, Henry deflated visibly, sat back on his bottom on the cold rock and, with a wry smile on his face, drew in the remaining line, fishless. He looked across at Tom on the other side of the lake who gave him a gesture which said, 'Bad luck, mate.'

Henry chuckled, but the thrill stayed with him as he laid down his rod and reached for his rucksack to get his flask of coffee, at the same time glancing around at the scenery, across the water and craning his neck to look up the face of the crag, feeling excited and pretty happy to be out here in this awesome environment . . . up to the moment he saw the hand protruding out of one of the wider fissures at the foot of the rock face.

He stood up slowly and walked across to look down to see, jammed between the rocks, the body of a young woman who, on first glance, would seem to have fallen from the top, straight down into this wide gap.

Henry exhaled and swore.

THREE

'You reckon she fell from up there?' Jake Niven asked Henry. Jake was the person who, much earlier that day, had received a couple of choice words of abuse from Henry on his walk of shame from Maude's house. Jake's posting to Kendleton as the rural beat officer had been one of Henry's last acts as a detective superintendent: he had fixed it for Jake to move into the vacant post in the village, a move that had saved Jake's marriage and also given Kendleton a popular and effective bobby who was now very much part of the community. He had also become a good friend to Henry.

Jake peered up the crag, then down into the fissure where the body was wedged.

It was a sheer drop, a distance of about forty feet at most – no comparison with somewhere like Beachy Head – but to plummet off it, straight on to hard, jagged rock would mean severe injury at best, death at worst.

Henry followed the trajectory of Jake's gaze which was calculating the distance from top to bottom.

It was probably a no-brainer.

Looking down at the body, twisted and broken, the injuries Henry could see seemed consistent with a fall, but if Henry had still been an SIO and this death came his way, he would never have just assumed it. The old-time mantra 'Think murder, then work backwards' had rarely let him down.

The chances were that this girl's death could be just a tragic accident – very sad – but there were many other scenarios to consider. However, that wasn't his problem anymore.

He was now a member of the general public. He'd found a body, not messed with it, and called the police. That was as far as his involvement went, other than his duty to make a brief witness statement.

Henry answered, 'Probably' to Jake's simple hypothesis. Then almost enigmatically added, 'Except . . .'

Jake pounced on it. 'Except what?'

Inwardly Henry groaned. 'OK, yeah. I've no doubt she did fall from the top, but the thing I would be asking myself now is this . . . if I was investigating it, which I'm not because I'm not a cop anymore—'

'Henry, stop pissing about, will you?'

'All right.' He squatted down on his haunches at the edge of the fissure. Jake did likewise. 'First of all, she isn't exactly dressed for a walk on the moors, is she?'

'No, she's in her night things.'

'Correct.' He glanced at Jake. 'Have you got any missing persons reported in the area?'

Jake shook his head.

Henry went on, 'And something else on first glance – bearing in mind this is just based on what I can see without close examination – this is a small female body down a crack and we can't actually see very much of her. In fact, there is quite a lot of debris, leaves and soot from the fires that seems to have accumulated on her, so without moving her we won't really know anything for certain.' Henry took a breath. 'So, she's wedged sideways, her head is twisted down at an unusual angle, her neck maybe broken by the fall, maybe not, but her right arm, which is sticking up – what I saw – has a torn strip of tape on it, maybe duct tape or something similar.' Henry pointed at it, then pointed further down at her right ankle and said, 'As does that. Her limbs look as though they might have been taped together.'

Jake's eyes took in what Henry was saying, then the two men looked at each other. Jake said, 'Oh.'

'Something to ponder, maybe?' Henry gave him a thin smile. 'Any idea who's turning out to this, detective-wise?'

Before Jake could answer, his personal radio (PR) squawked up. 'PC Niven receiving?' a woman's voice inquired over the airwaves.

'Receiving,' Jake replied, glanced at Henry and mouthed silently, *Diane Daniels*, followed by a salacious wink.

Although Diane Daniels had been a cop for most of her adult life – she'd joined Lancashire Constabulary at the age of twenty-two, first as a response PC on the beat, later as a detective constable on Child Protection Units and then on to CID, and she'd dealt with many fraught and stressful situations in regard to child and other domestic abuse – she had never really attended many murder scenes in her career.

Like many cops, she harboured a vague ambition to be a murder squad detective but, when faced with the reality of violent death, she had baulked somewhat and found herself to be quite affected by it. Not that she was particularly squeamish, but she found it hard to come to terms with.

That hadn't prevented her from doing her job, but she had realized, maybe the hard way, that being on the Force Major Investigation Team (FMIT) and having to turn out to deal with fresh (or rotting) corpses on a daily basis was probably just a pipe dream and she should stick to what she was good at.

This had been hammered home to her about a month before when she had been obliged to attend two of the worst murder scenes imaginable.

She had started a week of evening cover duties in her role as a CID officer in Lancaster and had attended a gas explosion, caused deliberately by a man who had brutally murdered his ex-girlfriend and her young daughter; this was followed by having to attend the double murder of John and Isobel York whose bodies had been dismembered, their heads and limbs hacked off in a brutal execution.

The murder scene had been discovered by Henry Christie, who had then been 'coerced' (his word) into becoming a consultant on the subsequent murder investigation. In fact, bringing the offenders to justice had not taken long, and Henry had, seemingly, been more than happy to return to his role as pub landlord.

But what had been unearthed beyond the horrific deaths of the Yorks were two more dead bodies and a huge stash of money running into many millions of pounds sterling and other currencies. It seemed the Yorks had been involved in a money-laundering and body-disposal operation of staggering proportions.

Diane had fully expected – nay, wished – to be sidelined from this subsequent and huge investigation and return to her normal CID duties; from there she had hoped to wangle her way back to child protection work, which she was very comfortable with, knowing she could do an important job, and if that was what the second half of her police career was all about, then so be it.

However, that was not to be – as the summons to the office of the head of FMIT, Detective Superintendent Rik Dean, Henry Christie's successor, proved, just a couple of days after Henry had retreated back to his pub in the country.

The 'interview' began with one of those 'Do you know why I've called you in here?' questions that always terrified lower-ranking members of staff. The question that sends their minds into overdrive as they try to recall the transgression that had finally screwed them up but which they couldn't quite remember committing.

After a ten-second delay, Diane gave in and said, 'No, sir, what have I done wrong?'

Rik Dean had chuckled. 'Nothing – quite the opposite actually.' The superintendent looked relaxed now, completely different to the man who had been stressed out of his mind while trying to deal with a huge outbreak of violence in Lancaster that resulted in a drug-related murder, the killing of a cop and an escape from police custody of a suspected murderer – plus the deaths of the Yorks. All in one night. All connected in some way, however tenuously. He had been run ragged in his attempts to coordinate the police response.

In among all this, Diane had been dispatched to the murder scene at the Yorks' farmhouse, where she had linked up with Henry Christie.

'Thing is, Diane,' Rik said, 'I've been pretty impressed by the way you took on the double murder and the way it got resolved. I know there's still a lot of work to do with it, but what I'd like – and I've run this past the chief constable, which I hope is OK – is to get you transferred temporarily on to FMIT to begin with and also promote you temporarily to detective sergeant from tomorrow.'

Diane's mouth popped open.

'Er, you have passed the sergeants' exam, haven't you?' Rik asked worriedly.

'Yes, boss.' She had taken and passed it almost as soon as she came out of her probationary period, but had done nothing with it. She didn't really have any great ambition to rise through the ranks, but she'd thought that to have the exam behind her would be a good thing for when, if ever, the mood took her to try for promotion.

'Good. Thought so,' Dean said, relieved.

'To what end, though?'

'Well, clearly the investigation around the Yorks is much wider than just their deaths – regarding the money, firearms and two bodies – so I want you to take a leading role on that side of it. Identify the two young men found in the garage walls and look at where the money has come from and where it's going to. Obviously, you lucked into a huge money-laundering operation and we need to chase it and see what turns up. What do you reckon? Say a six-month secondment for starters with a view to a permanent transfer further down the line, though I can't guarantee a substantive promotion at the moment.'

'Do I have a choice?'

'No.'

'But why me?'

'Like I said, I've been impressed by you. I know a good jack when I see one.'

And this was why Diane had frequently returned to the Yorks' farmhouse over the following weeks: to immerse herself in the crime scene, to get to understand the Yorks (dead though they were) and because something was perpetually nagging away at her mind.

She had been on one of her many visits to Hawkshead Farm when she heard the call over the radio from the comms room at HQ asking Jake Niven to attend the discovery of a woman's body by a couple of anglers at a small lake in the moorland somewhere up behind the farmhouse. With a frown on her face, she had listened for updates from the scene of what was initially reported as a fatal accident.

She had completed yet another walk-through of the murder scene at the farmhouse because of that 'something' that was eating away at her, while waiting for an update from Jake which never seemed to come until, finally, annoyed by this, she radioed through to him.

'PC Niven receiving?' she asked.

'Receiving.'

'Any update on the body yet, Jake? DC Daniels here, by the way.' She was outside the farmhouse, now wandering slowly around the perimeter of the detached four-car garage in which the bodies, guns and money had been discovered in the wall space.

'Not so far. I'm at the scene and looking at the body at the moment. It looks as if a white female, maybe twenty-ish, has fallen from the top of a rocky crag into a crevice below the rock face, next to the lake where these two guys were fishing.'

'A walker, you reckon?'

'Not unless she was a sleepwalker.'

'What do you mean?' Diane asked irritably.

'She's dressed in her night things – pair of pyjama shorts and a short-sleeved top.'

'You're joking.'

'No – straight up, Diane. And there's something else, too.'

'Go on.'

'Looks like her wrists and ankles might have been bound by tape.'

Diane was silent for a moment as she took this in. Then: 'Just out of interest, where is this location you're at in relation to Hawkshead Farm, where the Yorks lived?'

'Essentially up over the hill behind the farm, maybe two miles away at most.'

'OK, I'm coming over to have a look – by car obviously. Can you give me directions?'

Henry had listened to the radio conversation between Jake and Diane and had been surprised to hear her voice at the other end of the ether.

Henry had first met her several years earlier when he'd been a detective super on FMIT. He had been off sick, recovering from a gunshot wound to the shoulder caused by a somewhat irate young woman who had taken a sudden dislike to him after he'd discovered her nefarious deeds.

Although he had been off sick, his then chief constable – Robert Fanshaw-Bayley – had asked him to 'pop' over to Yorkshire to offer his views and experience on two seemingly unconnected, unsolved murders, the investigations into which had stalled to the point of embarrassment.

FB, as the chief was known, had selected Diane to accompany him.

The two murders – and another – were discovered to be linked, and Henry and Diane had found themselves pitted against a wicked cabal of corrupt cops who had tried, obviously unsuccessfully, to murder the pair of nosey Lancashire detectives.

Following this, he and Diane had not crossed each other's paths until Rik Dean deployed her to cover the double murder of John and Isobel York that Henry had stumbled across during a welfare check.

When they parted company after arrests were made, Henry had assumed that Diane would have tried to get back to child protection and he had not expected to see her again, ever. He realized that, in spite of her skills as a detective, she wasn't comfortable investigating murders.

Henry knew it wasn't for everyone: the reality was tough, even for those who were cut out for it. But sometimes it was those who didn't know how good they were who should be investigating murder, and she was one of them. She might not like dead bodies, but she knew how to deal with them.

He waited eagerly to find out why she was still turning out to suspicious deaths.

Henry watched Diane trudge up through the fields with a grin quivering on his lips.

She spotted him from afar and felt quite self-conscious under his scrutiny, slightly embarrassed even, yet very happy at the same time, a mix of feelings she could not quite comprehend.

By the time she reached him, she was breathless but smiling widely. 'I'll take a wild guess: you're one of the anglers who found the body,' she said.

'Yep.' He jerked his head for her to follow him. She caught up and he led her across to the tiny lake underneath the crag. 'Out to check whether the wildfires have had a detrimental effect on the waters, cast a line in, see if anything rises to the fly.' He pointed across the lake to Tom Noonan, who was still fishing as though nothing was going on. Jake Niven was chatting to him and noted Diane's arrival with a quick wave. 'Catch anything?'

'Absolutely. The water was murky, but I still caught one.' Henry held out the palms of his hands two feet apart to indicate the size of the fish.

'Yeah, right.'

At the water's edge, Henry pointed out the crag and the fractured rocks at its base, explaining that it looked as though the young woman had fallen from the top into one of the cracks below.

'Have you touched the body? Moved it? Kicked it?' Diane asked.

For some reason – as though the questions were an affront to his previous professionalism, as opposed to basic questions any detective would ask – Henry considered giving an aggressive answer or a facetious one. Instead, he bit his tongue and said, 'Nah.'

There was a pause, a hesitation between them as they eyed each other.

'I'll leave you to it, then,' Henry said.

Diane's lips parted in disbelief. 'Are you not going to show me?'

'I've already trampled around it enough,' he said as Jake arrived back from chatting with Tom Noonan. 'I'll leave it in your capable hands.'

'You're going?' Jake asked Henry, who then looked at Diane; both cops had puzzled expressions.

'My work here is done. Plus finding a body has put the kibosh on the fishing experience.' He found it uncomfortable that both of them seemed to be expecting him to take the reins. At least that's the impression he got. 'Of course, I'll give you a witness statement if either of you wants to pop by the pub. You know where to find me.'

He patted Jake on the shoulder, gave Diane a nod, then walked over to Tom Noonan who was now packing away his fishing gear.

He didn't look back.

Henry spent most of the rest of the day in the cellar, which he called the 'heartbeat' of the pub. Someone on one of the licensees' courses he'd once attended told him, 'Shitty cellar, shitty pub.' He was a house-proud landlord, and he had ensured that below ground in The Tawny Owl was always immaculate.

He emerged after three hours' toil, blinking in the real daylight like a salamander emerging from a cave, and gravitated to the bar where he checked out the pumps and did a general clear-out before the evening trade began to filter in.

Although local business had remained fairly constant during the moorland wildfires, the hotel side had plummeted – not least because Henry himself had actually discouraged customers from staying because the smoke-filled atmosphere was so unpleasant.

However, there had been an unstoppable upwards surge since the fires had been extinguished, and as he checked through the computer system, he saw the bedrooms were nearly all occupied – just one available – and the restaurant was fully booked.

There would be no room to move tonight, which was obviously excellent for the business; it was also good for Henry who would be too busy to get maudlin and reflect on his personal life.

It would be one a.m. at the earliest before he would clamber into his own bed and then, he hoped, sleep through until six and the start of another long day.

He had his first drink at eleven p.m.

Up to that point, he had worked hard at front of house, chatting to the diners and drinkers, serving and enjoying his role as mine host. He was basically a shy man, usually happy in his own company, but always flexible enough to change hats and characters depending on what situation he was in: outgoing, authoritative, when he was a cop; loving as a husband (although that halo had slipped on too many occasions); and having the required bonhomie as a publican, although he could never have guessed just how hard and complex the job actually was.

Dining finished more or less at nine thirty and by eleven most of the residents had eaten/drunk their fill and retired to comfortable bedrooms, leaving a few hardy locals in the main bar. Often the same few stayed on boozing steadily until midnight, and that night Henry was in no mood to turf them out before then.

Over the last few weeks, this had been Henry's vulnerable time: when the hard work of the day was done and he could take a breather by sliding around to the opposite side of the bar and joining them.

He had noticed something, though.

Sometimes he could join these people, whom he classed as his friends now, have a couple, go to bed.

But there were an increasing number of occasions when it all went too far and he couldn't stop himself. He had the one or two obligatory drinks and saw the customers out, locked the doors and then found himself a comfy seat in the bow window with a bottle of whisky snaffled from behind the bar. He would stare blankly out of the windows at the village green beyond and take a sip, keep it swilling around his mouth, then swallow it with a gasp as the neat spirits burned his throat.

He would immediately begin to think bleak thoughts.

How what he was doing was now pointless.

Without Kate – his first wife who had died from a very aggressive form of cancer.

Now without Alison, cruelly murdered by her deranged (not a word Henry used lightly) ex-husband.

He felt as if he was peering down an increasingly narrow, darkening hole.

So he took another drink.

And then the bottle seemed to consume and overpower him, and somehow he would wake up hours later, feeling terrible, but at least having found his way to bed.

And – the previous night – Maude Crichton's very large bed.

Which didn't make him feel great either.

That night, on the day he had been fishing and found a body, all the signs were there that he would crawl his way into a bottle again as he ushered out, in a friendly way, the last of his customers and closed the door.

For the last hour he had been thinking of nothing but the half bottle of Jura left at the back of the bar, and he had claimed it as his own before settling down at the window again, putting his feet up on another chair, knowing he was going to get very drunk.

The figure leaning on the jamb of the bar door made him jump.

'Jeepers! I thought I'd locked the front door.'

'Obviously not,' Maude Crichton said. Dangling from the tip of her finger was the key ring on which swung the key to the front door of Th'Owl. 'Anybody could have waltzed in.'

Despite himself, Henry raised the half-empty bottle of Jura towards her. 'Join me for a nightcap?'

Already he could feel his determination to respect Maude waning while the feeling in his lower belly waxed.

The Tawny Owl opened officially for business at seven a.m., providing breakfasts for the residents and also to catch any passing trade. Often the place was busy with gamekeepers, farmers and others involved in the life of the countryside.

'He's usually up and about by now,' Jake Niven said to Diane Daniels.

They had met on the car park, Diane having driven across from her flat in Lancaster in a converted warehouse on the old wharf by the River Lune where it looped through the city. She was now driving a neat eight-year-old Mercedes SLK which had replaced her ancient Peugeot 406.

'Have you seen him since yesterday?' Diane asked. 'He was very brusque with me.'

Jake shook his head. 'He's been a bit off for a few weeks. Not sure what's eating him.'

Diane shrugged.

They walked into Th'Owl together, entering as Ginny shouldered her way from the kitchens, bearing two plates of full English breakfast for a couple in the dining room. 'Be with you in a second,' she called.

She slid past the two cops, delivered the food and came back, wiping her hands on her apron.

'Hi, Ginny,' Jake said. 'We've come to see Henry. Is he about?'

Ginny's mouth went tight and she rolled her eyes. 'Not managed to get out of his pit so far,' she said, holding back the tut.

'Is he OK?' Diane asked.

Ginny inhaled and exhaled a deep long sigh. 'I don't think he is,' she admitted. 'He hasn't said anything. He wouldn't. But I get the feeling mum's death is only now really starting to hit him. Bit of a delayed reaction, but grief can be like that. I think he's become a lost soul,' she said insightfully. A tear formed on her lower eyelid. She rubbed it away with the heel of her hand.

Diane touched her shoulder. 'Hey,' she said tenderly.

Ginny's bottom lip wobbled. 'Worried about him.'

'I get it.'

'Anyway,' Ginny said, taking a deep breath, trying to shake the feeling. 'Work to do, people to feed. I've knocked on his door twice, but you're welcome to try and rouse him if you want.' She paused. 'He's been drinking. A lot.'

She let the officers through to the owner's accommodation. 'Be my guest.'

They went through. Straight ahead was the hallway with bedroom doors on one side, doors to the lounge and kitchen on the other. Diane knew which was Henry's room; she had spent a couple of nights in the spare bedroom when she and Henry had worked on the Yorks' murders and it had been convenient for her to crash at Th'Owl because of its proximity to Hawkshead Farm.

Diane tapped on the door, then put her mouth close to it. 'Henry, it's Diane Daniels.'

There was no response.

She tapped louder. Then it became a proper knock.

'Henry?' She raised her voice.

Finally, after more knocking and calling she tried the door handle which turned and the door opened with a creak of its hinges.

'Henry? We're coming in,' she said.

Henry's bed had not been slept in, but then a voice from behind made her and Jake spin.

'What the hell are you doing in my bedroom?'

FOUR

Even though he'd had a long shower, a shave, a change of clothes, a hearty breakfast and two large Americanos, Diane Daniels looked across the dining table at Henry in the restaurant area of The Tawny Owl and could not help thinking he looked like one of those dogs with skin that was four sizes too big for him.

He looked a sullen mess.

Other than seeing him the previous day at the fishing lake, she had last seen Henry about a month before when he had sailed off into the sunset, leading a mob of villagers up to the moors to dig out a firebreak in order to hold back the spreading wildfires that were closing dangerously in on Kendleton itself. Since then she had neither seen nor heard from him.

Even though she'd been full-time busy with the murder investigation and its many strands, for some unaccountable reason she felt miffed that Henry had not been in contact with her at all, not even a voicemail or text. She had wondered why she felt aggrieved by this lack of contact and was annoyed with herself for even feeling this way.

She hoped it was a 'friend' thing rather than anything else.

And looking at him now, his face like a crumpled pillow, she was pretty sure it couldn't have been anything else – not least because of the age difference between them.

She allowed her lips to purse and twist.

Then, after a few brief words of foreplay, 'I'm saying this because I consider us to be friends.' She laid into him good and proper and said, 'You literally do look like a bag of shit, Henry. You look like a cat's slept on your face.'

He was sipping his second coffee and raised his eyes over the rim of the mug, took a gulp then put the mug on the table.

'Thanks for that.'

'That said, how are you?'

'I'm OK. Thanks for asking.'

Diane tilted her head and scrutinized him critically.

Henry said, 'What?' with a sneer.

She shook her head in exasperation. 'Never mind.'

'So what can I do for you? What's so all-fired important you came raiding my bedroom en masse?'

'I need to get a statement from you about yesterday.'

'Jake could have done that.' He turned and saw said Jake emerging from the kitchen with a fat breakfast sandwich in his mitts. 'I hope you've paid for that,' Henry called, stopping the PC in his tracks.

'Uh, I can do,' Jake said guiltily.

'Forget it,' Henry said and turned back to Diane. 'So?'

'Yes, he could have done,' she said, giving her shoulders a little shrug. 'But I wanted to see you, catch up with you, have a friendly chat and all that.'

'OK,' he said, unimpressed and wary. 'I found a body, phoned it in, handed it over. Pretty short statement. I could've texted it in.'

'Henry!' She leaned across and whispered, 'What the hell is up with you?'

'I don't know,' he said brusquely, then stood up and left the room, shouldering his way past Jake without even looking at him.

Diane watched Henry turn towards the front door of the pub. She spun in her chair and a moment later saw him walk out of the door, across the paved area and sit on the low front wall.

She glanced at Jake who had come over to her, wiping his mouth with a napkin.

'What's eating him?' Jake asked. 'Moody sod.'

'I don't know.'

'Wouldn't mind,' Jake said, adopting a knowing, mock-confidential tone, 'but he's succumbed to Maude Crichton's charms – and money, if he has any sense.'

'Really? The millionairess?' Diane's surprise wasn't feigned. She'd encountered Maude when working on the Yorks' murders, had been aware of Henry's discomfort at Maude's obvious interest in him.

'Clocked him coming out of her house yesterday morning. Wouldn't surprise me if he was there last night, too. If he plays his cards right, this place could get a mega facelift.'

'Maybe that's his problem.'

'All I know is that if he's expecting me to pay for a bacon bap, he really does have a problem.'

Diane went outside and sat next to Henry.

'Don't,' he warned her instantly. He didn't even look at her.

She held up the palms of her hands. 'I won't.'

'So – what, then?'

She sidled right up alongside him, hip to hip, leaned in front of him and drew his face around with the tips of her fingers so their eyes were only inches apart and the only way he could avoid looking at her was to close his own eyes.

'Henry,' she said softly. 'Yes, you do look a mess; yes, you're probably going through something I don't understand; and, yes, because I consider us to be friends, I am concerned about you. But I'm not going to pry and I'm not going to make you say anything you don't want to, OK?'

He swallowed visibly and audibly. 'OK.'

'That said, it doesn't mean I'm going to give you any space to avoid me. I'm here to take a statement, that's true enough – but there is something else.' She stopped, seemed to prepare herself to say something. Then: 'As a friend and former colleague, although you mightily outranked me . . . and to paraphrase some dialogue in a slushy film . . . I'm just a detective standing – well, sitting – next to a former detective who used to be, probably, the best detective in Lancashire, asking that former detective to help me track down a killer.' She paused. 'What do you say?'

Henry was about to respond when his mobile phone rang.

Detective Superintendent Rik Dean said, 'Well?'

Henry held the phone slightly away from his head and scowled at it, then put it back to his ear and said, 'Well, what?'

'Well, have you said yes?'

'Have I said yes to what?'

'To what the soon-to-be DS Daniels has asked you . . . She *has* asked you, hasn't she?'

Henry eyed Diane suspiciously and spoke while looking at her. 'It might be on the tip of her tongue.'

He thumbed the end-call button and now faced her squarely.

'He told me to tell you there's still seventeen grand left in the pot allocated to paying you as a consultant. He said I should offer it to you to come back for a month.' Her explanation was cautious.

'Why would I want to do that?'

'You know something, Henry – up until me seeing you yesterday and now today, I would have asked the same question.

'And now?'

Henry and Diane were walking across the village green towards the stream. Not many weeks before, the air would have been clogged with the smoke from the wildfires, but now it was clear and pleasant, more or less back to normal. Even the smell of the flowing, fresh water of the stream could be inhaled.

'The timing's right. You need it. I need it too, don't get me wrong, but you definitely need it.'

'So have you become a psychologist?'

'You need it because it's what you do best; I need it because I want to pick your brains. I want you to guide me through this maze of an investigation that seems to have so many threads but doesn't seem to be getting anywhere.'

'Like a thousand-pound-a-day mentor?'

'If you want to put it that way.'

Henry walked to the edge of the stream, picked up a small stone from the bank and lobbed it downstream where it disappeared with a plop.

Inside he was fighting this. He'd helped the police over the deaths of the Yorks, having demanded an outrageous fee for his services (and getting it, much to his surprise), but he had quit as soon as the arrests had been made, desperate to get back to The Tawny Owl because he wanted that to be everything for him – his life, his whole raison d'être. But it wasn't playing ball with him.

He knew if Alison had been there, all would be great.

But she wasn't.

He turned back to Diane who was standing a few feet behind him with her arms folded. '*DS* Daniels? Did I hear right? Soon to be detective sergeant?'

'Temporary. My inducement to continue on FMIT for a few months and look into various aspects of the York murders. Sergeant's pay helps towards the car and mortgage,' she admitted, 'though I'm still flat broke.' Henry knew she had been on her knees financially since the break-up of her marriage and the purchase of her flat in Lancaster.

'Rik does have a tendency to dangle money in front of people's noses to get what he wants,' Henry observed.

'So why not be quids in for a couple of weeks?'

'I'll need to speak to Ginny. She'll have to be fine with this . . . not least because I've hardly been pulling my weight around here for the last few weeks.'

'She'll be fine with it. She loves you,' Diane said. Henry frowned. 'Don't ask – I just know these things. Look, Henry' – her voice went to persuasive and she angled her head as she spoke – 'this investigation – it's massive, as you probably guessed. It's not just about the murders of the Yorks; it's about even more murders, about money laundering on a pretty huge scale . . . it'll be about gangsters and organized crime, and a couple who maybe got in too deep. Those kind of things you love. And not just that – the body you found yesterday . . .' Henry waited. Diane sighed. 'We didn't realize it at the time, but it became apparent to me there was someone else in the farmhouse at the time of the murders, and I think the person you found up by the lake was the one. We've been trying to trace the Yorks' daughter, Bethany, since the murders and now I'm certain we've found her.'

Henry was nodding along to this.

'It seems she managed to escape from the scene, but finding her body has thrown up even more questions,' Diane said.

'Like why did she have tape on her wrists and ankles?' Henry ventured.

'You noticed, I know. But that's not all. I managed to arrange a post-mortem late last night. Thing is, her injuries are consistent with a fall, but what pushed her off the edge of Rushbed Crag were the two bullets in her back. You wouldn't have been able to see that from the position she was in down the split in the rocks. She was shot, yet the whole thing doesn't tie in with what went on at the farmhouse in relation to her parents – seems a whole separate thing.'

Diane paused and let Henry process this information.

Then she said, 'So there you are . . . meaty, complex stuff.'

'OK.' Henry looked her in the eye. 'I'm just a knackered old ex-detective standing in front of a younger, talented detective who doesn't yet know how good she is and probably doesn't need my help at all . . . where was I? Oh, yeah, so this knackered old ex-jack knows that acceding to this request might just be the tonic he needs to get a wayward life back on track.'

Diane was standing tensely as Henry made his little speech, and her shoulders fell in relief.

'But,' Henry warned, 'I'm not doing it just for the Queen's shilling, I'm doing it because it suits me, OK?'

Diane could not resist grabbing and hugging him tight, but while she was in the middle of this display of affection and relief, Henry's phone rang again.

Rik Dean.

Henry answered it. 'I've said yes, OK?' Then he hung up abruptly.

Henry felt as if he needed another shower, as if he needed to start his day again, but he held back. The fact was he did have a glug of excitement in his belly as he walked with Diane to the rear of her snazzy new sports car and opened the boot to reveal two sturdy supermarket carrier bags in which she had brought a selection of documents relating to the investigation into the other two bodies found by her and Henry at the farm a month ago – the two young men in the garage wall space – plus the enormous amounts of money and the weapons also found secreted there.

Henry looked over her shoulder into the boot.

'I'm not supposed to have done this,' she admitted. 'But needs must.'

'Bait?' Henry guessed.

'Just like fishing.'

Henry put a hand on her shoulder. 'Tell you what, leave that stuff in there for the time being. We'll come back to it later. I know I need to read it thoroughly, but it will take some time.'

She stood up. 'What then?'

'Crime scene – and you can feed me some snippets along the way.'

He slid into the passenger seat alongside her and she fired up the car. He was impressed by it, but being so low-slung it wasn't a car he would have chosen for himself. He already knew he would have to haul himself out by grabbing the door frame.

He complimented her, though. 'Nice: a bit different from the old Peugeot.'

'It wouldn't have been financially viable to get it repaired,' she said sadly. She had inherited the Peugeot from her late father, and although it was ancient, she had been reluctant to part with it, but when it had been smashed up in a frenzied attack on her and Henry on a Blackpool housing estate, its days were numbered. 'I get some car allowance for this from FMIT, so I can just about manage it.'

She spun the wheels for Henry's benefit as she drove off The Tawny Owl car park and then out of Kendleton, travelling up on to the moors on tight, sometimes single-track roads, until she turned into the long driveway leading up to Hawkshead Farm.

It looked a sad place now. The tarmac at the front was still charred black in five distinct areas where the classic cars belonging to the Yorks had been set alight, along with Henry's own restored Land Rover. All the windows were boarded up, and the side door, which was used as the main entrance, had been covered by a lockable steel over-door, for which Diane had the key.

The whole property was still an ongoing crime scene, although she told him its eventual disposal was now in the hands of solicitors.

Although the memory of the murder scene was still vivid for Henry – one of the worst he'd ever visited – he wanted to reacquaint himself with it, so he did a slow walk-through again, listening to

Diane's up-to-date commentary as she led him around the house and up on to the first floor where he had initially discovered Isobel York's butchered body in the bath; then, one floor up in the attic, where he'd found John York, similarly hacked to pieces, although his head and limbs had been left out for display on the full-size snooker table there.

He stood there, remembering it all.

'It looks like the Yorks may have been going to do a runner,' Diane told him. 'I think they might have been coppering up, if you will – getting the money they had ready to run with it. We found ferry tickets when we searched the place, plus a series of overnight Airbnb bookings right across Europe – France to Italy and down into Greece. I think they realized they were in too deep – but that's only a theory. Whatever' – she shrugged – 'we'll never know for certain.'

She took him back downstairs to the first floor, explaining as she went, 'Obviously this place has an agricultural history, and what we didn't spot at the time but discovered in a subsequent and more detailed search of the property was this . . .'

By the time she'd said this, she had moved along the hallway and was pointing up to a loft door. It was inset in a wooden frame, but the whole thing was flush with the ceiling and painted the same colour, white, so was relatively well camouflaged. 'It could once have been a hayloft, but it's actually another bedroom, and I'm pretty certain the daughter, full name Bethany Jane York, was in it when her parents were being murdered by our two travelling friends working on behalf of the lovely Costain family in order to give some London gangster we don't even know yet a very bloody nose.'

She was referring to the perpetrators, one of whom was on remand, the other dead.

They opened the drop-down hatch using the button on the wall and clambered up the extending ladder that formed the stairway into the bedroom above.

There wasn't much headroom for a tall person, so both Henry and Diane had to dip their heads: he was six foot two and she wasn't much less. The bedroom was quite large, though: an ideal space for a growing youngster.

Diane said, 'There was an empty bottle of vodka down by the

side of the bed which suggests Beth could possibly have been drunk and asleep when the killers came in and they simply didn't know she was here. A blood sample from her body will tell us if she had alcohol in her.'

'So, at some point in the evening she wakes up and flees into the field, terrified, panicking at what she's seen . . . found,' Henry mused out loud. 'In terms of identifying the body, have we found any fingerprints to make a comparison?'

'We're comparing prints from the vodka bottle with prints we managed to take from the body and also prints from her flat in Manchester, where she went to uni. Those results should be with me later today and we'll know for certain if the body you found is Beth – but I'm one hundred per cent it is, even now.'

Henry listened, looking around as Diane spoke. When she finished, he said, 'So when she fled, which is a good hypothesis, how she got shot remains a mystery – unless her parents chased and shot her before their own deaths.'

Henry screwed up his face at that, as did Diane. Unlikely.

'Obviously, we haven't had time to make any ballistic comparisons yet, but I spoke to a guy on firearms this morning who had a quick look for me – nothing official – and he said the slugs taken out of her did not match any of the weapons we took from her parents' killers.'

'And there is that tape on her wrists and ankles, too,' Henry said.

'Which is a puzzle.'

'So, she's run away, ended up with two bullets in her back and tape around her limbs?' Henry had stooped around the bedroom as he talked and picked up a photograph of John and Isobel York standing, grinning, on either side of an attractive teenage girl. The daughter, Bethany. A nice family photograph. He looked at it for a while. Just a normal-looking family – whatever 'normal' was these days – happy and proud. It was the kind of picture that had often inspired Henry as a murder squad detective.

And he got that same old feeling again. The stirring in his chest, the tightness in his throat . . . the anger in his veins.

And he knew that whatever the background to this whole affair, whatever circumstances had brought brutal killers to the Yorks' doorstep and whatever the reason that Beth York had had her whole future taken away from her, he would ruthlessly hunt down her killer.

He showed the photo to Diane, who said, 'I'm sure it's her in the mortuary.'

'Where are you up to with this? What was your next move going to be?' he asked her.

'To follow the money,' she said. 'Kinda.'

It was something she had already started to do. Kinda.

One of the obvious threads of the investigation, a good starting point, was to dig into the background of the Yorks' business dealings. To begin with, there was nothing very spectacular or interesting, and it was quite tedious to investigate.

John York had been a qualified accountant who had diversified into financial management. It was a small enterprise with just himself and a secretary, and it seemed to generate a decent enough income for a good lifestyle. He looked after the business accounts for a number of small and medium-sized businesses in North Yorkshire, in the Kirkby Lonsdale area, and also in Lancashire around Lancaster and Morecambe. This had been his basic business until he moved into investing money for individuals – mainly older, retired folk.

But that changed about four years ago when the secretary he had employed for ten years was suddenly let go and his wife, Isobel, stepped into her shoes. At the same time, the contracts with the businesses for which he had done the accounts for many years were also terminated, with the exception of a few individual clients.

Diane was explaining these findings as she drove Henry back through the countryside in the direction of Kendleton and then through the village towards Lancaster.

'So the nature of the business changed,' he summed up.

'Would seem so. A lot of long-standing clients were dumped, but some individuals kept on. I've spoken to a few of the companies he threw over, and none understood why; he gave them no reasons, yet all of them say their relationship with him was good, no money owed in either direction. I've spoken to a few of the individuals he did keep on, but none report any issues and none knew anything about him ditching the other businesses. None cared, to be honest.'

'You wouldn't, would you?'

'Suppose not. Anyway, our financial people have had a quick sift through John York's accounts – the ones we've managed to uncover – and they tell me the volume of business he was generating wasn't commensurate with the lifestyle he and Isobel were leading. The fancy cars, the fancy home, multiple trips abroad. We haven't managed to find many bank accounts yet, though, and the ones we have don't have much cash in them, TBH.'

'TBH?'

'To be honest.' Diane scowled at him. 'Modern speak. Keep up, Mister Dinosaur.'

Henry shrugged. He was happy to be a dinosaur. 'So where are we going now?' he asked.

'I've tracked down the secretary he got rid of, and there is one client still on his books who was a business client first and then an individual client. I've been after speaking to him for a while about this, but he's been uncontactable. I thought we'd knock on his door on spec.'

'Name?'

'Jack Carter.'

'Oooh,' Henry said, 'the gangster?'

'What?'

'Nothing . . . I didn't expect you to understand a cultural reference from the early seventies, TBH.'

Henry sat back, and even though he felt as if his backside was skimming the road in the low-slung car, he enjoyed the ride. Diane drove to the M6 at junction thirty-four, then looped around on to the new link road from the motorway which sliced across through Morecambe to the port of Heysham, from which ferries crossed the Irish Sea.

But before reaching Heysham, she came off at the Morecambe exit, drove into the resort, down to the seafront, and parked on the promenade in an area called Bare, opposite a pleasant-looking café on the corner of a side road.

'She works here,' Diane said, pointing to the café named Fell View in celebration of the magnificent panorama across Morecambe Bay towards the mountains of the Lake District.

In fact, Jenny Peel, a smart lady in her mid-fifties, owned the establishment, and a few minutes after introducing themselves,

Diane and Henry were sitting with her in the large bow window of the café, sipping good Americanos.

Henry listened in as Diane did the probing.

'Yes, it was a shock,' Jenny answered. 'I'd been his secretary for ten years, did a good job; relations were good, too . . .' She paused, then added, 'I think.'

'So what happened?'

Jenny shrugged. 'Not sure. I remember lots of closed-door discussions and hushed conversations between John and Isobel. Maybe the business was going down the pan. I never officially had access to the accounts.'

Diane picked up on the crucial word and asked, 'Officially?'

Jenny squirmed slightly uncomfortably. 'I could access John's computer. It was part of my admin role, although going into the accounts wasn't; those files were password-protected but it was easy enough to get into them if I wanted to.'

'Did you?'

Jenny gave a quirky smile. 'Up to the point of those hushed discussions I just mentioned, which is the point where things changed and the whole feel of the place altered – the short-notice trips to the Canary Islands, Cyprus – I never even thought of looking.'

'Hey, it's OK,' Diane reassured her. 'We just want to know anything that could help us with this very serious investigation . . .'

Jenny Peel shuddered at that thought. She looked at them, her eyes hovering on Henry a moment or two too long, then she looked pensively out of the window across the bay. The mountains were clearly defined. She turned back to the detectives.

'I mean, I can't complain really,' she said. 'He did dump me and it was a shock, but I got almost thirty grand from him in severance pay, which he didn't have to do, and it went on the deposit for this place.' She waved her hand at the café. 'It's a bit oldie-worldie, but it makes money all year round and the coffee's good. I guess he felt guilty . . . Anyway, the point where things changed came first with the sale of one client's business and then John being asked to invest the money from that sale on the QT, out of the way of the taxman. That's when the trips abroad started happening, which were, I think, to stash the money in property.'

'Who was the client?'

'A haulier called Jack Carter.'

Diane pursed her lips and looked at Henry, arching her eyebrows.

'How much are we talking about?' Henry asked Jenny.

'One and a half, maybe two million.'

Henry was impressed. 'And neither John nor Isobel talked to you about this?'

Jenny shook her head.

Diane said, 'So when they started doing this work for Mr Carter, that was when they let you go?'

'Well, not quite then . . . it was a bit later, actually . . . not long after Mr Carter introduced them to a new client – a woman. God, she was dripping gold and diamonds, she was. Came up in a fancy Rolls-Royce, one of the sporty ones with a convertible roof, y'know? And she had a driver who, if you don't mind me saying, was a bit phwoar!'

Diane chuckled.

Henry blinked.

'Anyhow,' Jenny continued after a brief pause for reflection, 'John treated this woman like royalty, got me scurrying around making brews and getting fairy cakes. Upshot was more closed-door meetings, with Jack Carter in and out all the bleeding time – and then I got the brown envelope, and I was gone and bought this place which, to be fair, was always on my to-do list.'

'What was this woman's name?' Diane asked.

'I don't know. Far as I can tell, her name never got written down anywhere.'

'And how long ago would this be?'

'Four years,' Jenny guessed. 'If you gave me some time, I'd probably be able to be more precise. As for her name, I actually vaguely remember writing it down in an appointments diary, now I think about it. Not sure, but I might possibly have it somewhere.'

'Well, if you could find it, that would be great. If not, no problem. You've been a big help, so thanks.'

Henry said, 'Could I just have your mobile number in case we need to contact you again?'

'Sure.' She told him and he entered it into his phone. 'I take it you think John and Isobel were in something they couldn't control?'

'You might have hit the nail on the head,' Diane said, 'but it's still early days in what looks like being a complex investigation.'

They took their leave, strolled across the promenade to Diane's car, but walked past it up to the sea wall and leaned against the railings to look across the bay which, with the sea so far out and the sun up, was the colour of silver and gold.

'Jack Carter next?' Henry asked.

'Jack Carter,' Diane confirmed.

FIVE

Four years earlier, Marcie Quant's husband, Brendan Quant, thirty-nine years old, had died in a hail of bullets. His torso was shredded by a line of slugs from a machine pistol fired by a screaming young buck balanced on the back seat of a scrambler motorbike as it swerved past.

Brendan had been unfortunate enough to have been negotiating a deal on behalf of Dunster Cosmo in the melting pot of inter-gang violence in Liverpool.

Even though Brendan had not been the target – he was more collateral damage than anything – it didn't make the pill of his death any easier for Marcie to swallow. She grieved badly, on and off, for a long time. She and Brendan had been childhood sweethearts, married at eighteen, and although their idea of fidelity was fairly loose, they stayed together and built up a thriving criminal enterprise based mostly on investing and looking after the funds of people like Dunster Cosmo, one of London's wealthiest and most brutal mobsters whose own business incorporating drug and people trafficking generated millions each year, most of which he had, somehow, managed to hide by using the services of folk like Brendan and Marcie.

But the problem was – and this is something that Marcie regretted most on Brendan's passing, the thing that caused her most grief – Brendan had been the brains of their little outfit, and although she was very much an equal partner, Marcie was content to wallow in the more glamorous side of their lifestyle as opposed to having to do the work to place the funds that came their way for safekeeping from the likes of Cosmo.

The other facet to that problem was that people like Cosmo believed that because Marcie and Brendan were equal partners, each would know as much as the other about the ins and outs of how the business ran.

Which wasn't quite true.

Throughout their marriage, Marcie had given that impression – but it was all complete bullshit. She was no dizzy blonde, but she knew nothing. Although she was quite happy to perpetuate the illusion to others that she was fully conversant, in reality it did not interest her one jot.

Brendan hadn't minded. He was besotted by her, she with him, even though both of them had occasional affairs or one-night stands (to keep the marriage alive, they claimed), and the relationship was tempestuous with frequent outrageous arguments that usually ended up in bed and fucking. The thing was that, jointly, they never wavered in their aim to live well, spend hard, avoid the bullets and die happy.

The reality and fragility of her situation hit her hard at and after Brendan's funeral.

Deeply rooted in the criminal fraternity of north London, it was one of those gatherings the police were reluctant to show their faces at; they kept well out of the way, other than to intrude with very long lenses. This reticence by the cops was due to the fact that in order to honour Brendan, who had been such a likeable rogue, all rivalries between warring factions were suspended for the day (or until the first few pints were sunk), so that Marcie could at least have her husband cremated in peace; if the cops stepped in, there would have been mayhem and a lot of bloodshed. Probably.

It had gone well. The underworld had done him proud.

Brendan's body, encased in a cushion-lined casket at the chapel of rest, had been transferred on to a carriage pulled by two magnificent shire horses courtesy of a local brewery (part-owned by Dunster Cosmo) which set off for the crematorium some five miles distant, the cortège led by two bowler-hatted undertakers who walked solemnly in front of the horses all the way.

Without any police interference, four cars and two motorcyclists, also provided by Cosmo, formed the equivalent of a security escort, moving ahead and leapfrogging the procession to block junctions to allow unhindered passage for the horses, with Marcie sitting regally and alone in a long black limousine behind, a dark veil pulled dramatically over her face, the epitome of a grieving widow.

The streets were lined with people, mostly curious about what was going on, and their appearance made it seem as if Brendan had been a cherished member of the community (he wasn't – he was feared by many) and would be missed (he wouldn't).

Eventually, after many traffic hold-ups, the cortège drew into the crematorium grounds, which were huge and wooded, with many acres of headstones, and although Brendan would have an intricately carved headstone among all these, his ashes would be scattered elsewhere, according to his wishes.

Once the coffin had been slid off the carriage, it was borne into the crematorium by six of his mates acting as pallbearers who made their way through a throng of besuited shitbags and a haze of cannabis smoke, with several spliffs being reverentially flicked on to the coffin as it passed on the last section of its journey. The service inside the packed crematorium was presided over by a humanist preacher, and the curtains finally closed on the coffin to the strains of Robbie Williams' 'Angels'.

The post-crematorium bash was held at a nearby pub – one of Cosmo's – which did Marcie proud with a lavish buffet, free drinks for all and even a melancholy violinist who played soft dirges in the background until some drunk snapped her instrument.

There was even a private room with a bar set aside for Marcie and a few of her closest friends and relatives.

These people obviously included Cosmo. Although he was generous and gracious on the surface, Marcie could see that this was a veneer masking his eagerness to ask her some very direct questions.

About money.

Marcie was dreading the moment, so she put it off for as long as possible with floods of tears and by mingling with other guests and generally avoiding Cosmo.

Until the moment came when, clearly irritated, Cosmo took her firmly by the elbow, gripping the soft skin at this joint between his finger and thumb, and led her firmly away into the private bar, which suddenly became extra-private when two of his heavies cleared the room and took up positions by the door.

Cosmo sat her down at a zinc-topped table.

Her veil was still down, but Cosmo raised it and pushed it back over her head, smiling sadly at her.

'Sweetheart,' he began.

Her stomach tightened.

'You know how very, very sorry I am about Brendan's demise. So tragic, but the luck of the draw. He was a good guy and did a lot of good things for this community. And me.'

'Thank you, Dunster,' she croaked, trying to force out another flood of tears, but she seemed to have dried up. 'He always liked you, as I did – do.'

Cosmo held her gaze, and she did her best not to avert her eyes, which was hard because this bastard, in spite of the fact he was in his mid-sixties, was still intimidating. She knew she could not waver.

'But Brendan's been dead a month now,' Cosmo said. It had taken this length of time to get the post-mortem done and for the coroner in Merseyside to release the bullet-ridden body back to Marcie. 'Things have to move on. So, please don't think I'm being sexist here, sweetheart, because you know I'm not, but I have to ask: do you know what you're doing?'

'What do you mean?'

'In business is what I mean. Our business. I'd hate to think that you were a hanger-on floozy, living off Brendan's scraps.'

'Dunster Cosmo!'

'Like I said' – he held up his hands to pacify her – 'I'd hate to think it.'

'Well, you don't have to think it because me and Brendan worked as a team. I know all the ins and outs, so you don't have to worry about a thing,' Marcie assured him.

'That's good, Marcie.'

'Not a problem, Dunster.'

'Good, because I want to continue investing. I got cash coming out of my ears.'

'Not a problem, Dunster.' Then Marcie asked coyly, 'So what does that mean?'

'At the moment, I've got about four mill stashed, burning a hole in my pocket, and I need it putting away for a rainy day, my love.'

One thing was for certain: Marcie Quant had needed the release provided by the three outstanding orgasms delivered to her by Darren McCabe, two from Darren himself up to the point of his first pile-driving climax and the third from Darren's tongue as Marcie lay back and allowed him to do what he had to do to bring her to another earth-shuddering moment.

Later that evening, when everything inside her had subsided, and she was lying alongside McCabe in the gigantic bed she had previously shared exclusively with the month-long-gone Brendan, smoking, blowing lazy rings up towards the ceiling where they burst like wisps of cloud, and with a large glass of good whisky balanced on her breastbone between her boobs, Marcie said, 'I'm fucked.'

McCabe – he too was lying on his back, sipping whisky but not smoking – said, 'I know,' with a smirk.

'Not in that sense.' She blew out smoke down her nostrils. 'In the sense that I don't know the first thing about business. I'll admit it.' She made a perfect circle with her lips and popped out another smoke ring which rose listlessly above her like a hazy halo before it evaporated. 'I just let Brendan get on with it and enjoyed the cash, the Botox, a tit lift, the fanny tightener—'

'And me,' McCabe interjected.

'Yeah, yeah, and you on the side, but not seriously.' She poked the tip of her tongue out at him. He was just a piece on the side, an occasional fuck, but McCabe had worked for Brendan as an enforcer, and anything more while Brendan was alive would have been ludicrously dangerous, although she'd always liked McCabe. 'As I was saying . . . this is all very well, but Dunster Cosmo is – was – Bren's main client, if you will, and since he died, I've been through everything. His desk, his computer, his bank statements – everything I can lay my hands on – and I can find no inkling as to what he did with Dunster's money. Again, fine' – she swallowed nervously – 'but when Dunster comes a-knocking and asks for his money, asks where it's invested or, God forbid, just says, "Give me my money", I just don't know where the fuck it is. And then I'll be a dead widow.'

'So Brendan's been stealing it?' McCabe asked incredulously.

'I don't know, I just don't know. I have no idea who he's been dealing with, I don't know his contacts. Essentially – and you'll get the drift here – I know fuck all . . . and now Dunster wants me to keep investing for him!' She paused. 'I'd run, but I haven't got any money to do that with. I've maxed out all six of my credit cards since Bren got shot, so I'd get as far as Dover ferry terminal. Might make it to Calais at a pinch.'

She went silent, staring at her reflection in the mirror on the ceiling.

'Cosmo was right, even though he doesn't know it yet. I *am* a hanger-on floozy.'

'He's got four million in cash – euros and sterling – that he wants me to take care of,' Marcie said to McCabe. They had made love in the shower, a continuation of her night of ecstasy, and now they were sitting on opposite sides of the bed. It was the morning after. She had a bath towel wrapped around her. McCabe was naked, just starting to get dressed.

'Run with it,' he suggested. 'Take it. Disappear.'

She snorted a laugh of derision before firing up her hairdryer.

McCabe eased himself into his boxer shorts as he thought about Marcie's predicament.

'How often does Dunster ask for any money?'

'As far as I know, not often, but don't quote me. I think he gets a chunk back every year in interest, but I'm not certain. All I do know is that the money he gave Brendan to invest was only a small proportion of what he actually makes, so he makes tons. He lives off cash, mostly, and what he gave to Brendan was old-age money – his pension pot.'

McCabe arched his eyebrows as he considered the sums involved, then said, 'And you have no idea what Brendan has done with the money, where it is and who it's invested with?'

'Nope. As long as I got a diamond necklace now and again, got swished around in that Roller that's parked on the driveway, I didn't give a flying fuck. I can't believe I'm even saying that now. If I was a bloke, I'd be a dickhead.'

'Hey!' McCabe walked around the bed and stood in front of

her, pulling on his shirt. She switched off the hairdryer. 'Brendan looked after you. That's what matters.'

She screwed up her face. 'Yeah, right. I am so fucking annoyed with myself.'

'How much do you think there was? How much did Brendan actually invest?'

Marcie shook her head. 'Untold millions.' Off McCabe's look of disbelief, she said, 'No, honestly. Lots and lots and lots and lots and . . .'

'I get the picture.' McCabe knelt down in front of her, pulling the towel away. 'What about . . . what if Dunster didn't know you didn't know . . . what if he thought you were just continuing the business as normal?'

Marcie gave him a blank look. 'You'll have to run that one past me.'

McCabe narrowed his eyes. 'I might know someone who could help us out.' He pushed her gently backwards on to the bed and lowered his head between her legs.

It worked – until it didn't work.

Which is why, some four years later, Darren McCabe was sitting, waiting for Jack Carter to put in an appearance.

Looking back, McCabe half wished he had done a runner when he'd had the chance – that is, after he'd fucked Marcie Quant a few times and then learned she had no business acumen whatsoever. He could have found gainful employment anywhere – he was good at breaking fingers and, if necessary, pulling triggers.

But this was only half a wish because of several factors that ambushed and surprised him.

First one was that he was basically an animal, and Marcie Quant, he discovered, was phenomenal in bed and exhausted him like no other woman ever had; second one was that he fell in love with her, and the third one was a child.

The latter was the thing that completely screwed up his whole world, and Marcie's too if she was honest.

A baby boy called Arthur.

Arthur McCabe. Had a great ring to it.

And despite himself, McCabe loved what he had accidentally

created, which was one thing he had never really had before – a family.

And now he was acting to protect that entity, because life had become very complex and dangerous indeed.

To begin with, the idea – though fraught with danger – had been simple: fool Dunster Cosmo into thinking that all was well with the world of high finance, his money was safe and secure, earning just enough interest to keep him happy, and keep up this pretence until Marcie and McCabe and, subsequently, little Arthur were in a position to back out and flee.

Which is where Jack Carter came in.

The idea was mooted by McCabe at his and Marcie's first breakfast together after her husband's funeral four years ago, at a fast-food place in Tottenham, where they'd feasted ravenously on sausage and eggs after their night of passion. It was the only food that seemed just right after a cremation, alcohol, sex and the realization that if things went wrong, the biggest, meanest gangster in north London would be after spilling your blood.

McCabe said, 'You know I once worked as muscle for a haulier up in Lancashire?'

Marcie nodded. She recalled, 'After you came out of the army. You told Brendan once.'

McCabe said, 'Dishonourably discharged . . . but I'll never regret putting that drill sergeant's fingers down the toaster.' He chuckled at the memory. 'Lucky not to get clink. Anyway, I did a lot of labouring jobs all over the place and, just by luck, I met this guy who was having some problems with contractors at the building site I worked on.'

'What sorta problems?' Marcie bit into a hash brown which tasted much, much better than it should have done.

'Intimidation stuff, threats – nasty ones – damage, that kind of thing.'

'Did you put fingers into toasters?'

He smirked. 'I put people into crushers . . . in fact, I'm pretty sure there's one body in the hardcore underneath the Broughton bypass,' he said. Marcie scowled. He explained, 'It's a new road just north of Preston.'

She had no idea where Preston was and said, 'Um.'

Nor was she concerned by the revelation, which suited McCabe, and he wasn't even sure of his claim either, but he definitely had fed a guy into a stone-crushing machine and he did end up as hardcore, but he wasn't completely certain which road he was supporting.

They drank their coffee, then McCabe said, 'We need to travel north.'

He made a call and not long after the pair were cruising north in the Rolls-Royce with McCabe driving. A smooth, fast journey, one stop for a piss and a brew on the way at some services near Birmingham, then back on to the M6, leaving that motorway at junction thirty-five and driving towards the picturesque, affluent area around Warton, then to Jack Carter's house in a village called Silverdale.

It was set in its own grounds, stone built, huge and with a curving driveway. McCabe parked the Rolls outside the front door.

'Nice pad,' Marcie commented. She'd slept most of the way, reclining as far back as the passenger seat would allow, and McCabe had constantly eyed her, liking more and more of what he saw.

The front door opened, and Jack Carter stepped out to greet them.

He was a small, slightly rotund man, blond, ruffled hair, who looked affable with a broad smile but suspicious eyes.

A few minutes later they were in the lounge, drinking coffee.

'Yeah, well, nice to see you, McCabe, but what do you want of me?' Carter asked directly.

'Heard you sold up, lock, stock.'

'Pretty much. Business was losing money hand over fist and had to get out. Plus the whole shebang's full of scammers and non-payers which drags you down, you know? Took a rotten loss on the sale,' he said.

'Not what I heard,' McCabe said.

Carter's affable veneer tightened up. 'What did you hear?'

'That you sold up for a good profit . . .'

'Who told you that?' Carter demanded.

'Grapevine.'

'It's not right,' Carter snapped. 'Anyway, how's it your business? You traipsed all the way up here for this?'

McCabe and Marcie exchanged glances, then Marcie, who had hardly spoken up to this point, said, 'Mr Carter, it doesn't matter to us what you did with your money. We wish you the best, and you're right, it ain't our business, but the fact is we're in a bit of a predicament and we need some help—'

'I'm not in the lending business,' Carter interrupted sharply.

'We don't want to borrow money,' she said.

'What do you want, then?'

'Darren has it on good authority that you invested the money you made from the sale of your business,' she said, then paused.

Carter said cagily, 'Go on.'

'We want to know who you invested with, which company dealt with it, because Darren also has it on good authority that your money got invested without recourse to the taxman.'

'Are you threatening me?'

'No, but we have money to move and we need someone to move it for us,' McCabe said impatiently.

'Oh, I don't know . . .'

'Please, Mr Carter, we're not here to cause you problems. We just want to know of someone trustworthy who will invest some money that has . . . er . . . come my way,' Marcie said.

'How much are you talking?'

'Initially, four million.'

This caused Carter to put down his mug. 'Initially, you say?'

Marcie nodded. McCabe nodded.

'With the prospect of much, much more,' Marcie added.

'I want an introduction fee,' Carter said immediately.

John York had been handling the legitimate side of Jack Carter's business accounts for many years, as well as the shadier aspects. There had to be a legitimate front to Carter's haulage company because it was too risky to run trucks on UK roads without all the necessary documentation and licences. If the authorities – specifically VOSA, the Vehicle and Operator Service Agency – got their teeth into you, they were like a Jack Russell terrier with a rat and rarely let go. So Carter's dozen or so vehicles were duly licensed and he worked hard above the radar and twice as hard under it, filling his trucks with illegal loads and dumping them in places where they shouldn't have been dumped.

But his legitimate contracts were good and formed the basis of his company's sale which grossed him close to two million as a going concern when he eventually sold up. What bothered him was that if he legitimately took this money and declared it to the tax authorities, he would probably have to share, even with expenses, far too much with the government.

Carter wasn't prepared to do that.

So he asked John York if there was any way this sort of generosity could be avoided.

York said yes.

He handled the sale of the business, hid the cost, falsified accounts, and by declaring the business had netted (not grossed) £150,000 (instead of the two million), he kept Carter's tax bill down to less than a third of that, leaving him with about £1.9 million, which York then – literally – took abroad. Through a Russian company based in Cyprus, he invested in new-build housing around the Paphos and Coral Bay area of the island, which soon doubled the investment, thank you very much.

To Marcie and McCabe, Carter said, 'For fifty K I'll put you in touch with the man who looked after me.'

Marcie didn't flinch. Instead, she nodded.

And the first four million belonging to Dunster Cosmo was handed over to John York in a suitcase to be invested wisely.

Over the next four years a further nine million went in the same direction . . . plus a couple of bodies for onward disposal.

The request – nay, demand – came out of the blue.

It had all been going well. John York had – certainly on the face of it – delivered on his promises. He had taken Cosmo's money and supposedly invested it through Russian and Chinese companies in Cyprus and the Canary Islands, providing a healthy income for the London gangster. That income was paid into offshore accounts in the Cayman Islands and the Channel Islands, from which fat fees were extracted by Marcie as she and McCabe began to build a sort of life together, at first just themselves and then with little Arthur McCabe, a very fast-growing baby.

Cosmo seemed content to take the benefits of the interest payments coming his way without too much direct interest in the Yorks. He did meet them once, visiting their renovated farmhouse in Lancashire, which terrified the couple, particularly when Cosmo informed them, with one of his nice smiles, that if they ever cheated on him in any way, they would end up dead.

They promised everlasting loyalty as they showed Cosmo around. During the course of the tour of their house, they pointed out the large field at the rear of the farmhouse which belonged to them. Cosmo had regarded this area thoughtfully but said nothing.

A couple of days later Cosmo turned up at Marcie Quant's flat in Greenwich, accompanied by two of his heavies.

She was still in bed, revelling in an hour of 'me' time while McCabe took Arthur up to Greenwich Park in the pram, and the knocking on the front door made her jump from her light snooze and swear heavily as she rolled out of bed, grabbing a soft dressing gown and sliding her feet into slippers with floppy bunny ears.

'I'm coming, for God's sake,' she bellowed, staggering into the living room. She and McCabe now lived in a ground-floor flat, which was a very big comedown from her days with Brendan, but needs must. It was spacious, had a bit of a front garden and rear yard, and was worth almost half a million. She peeked through the drawn curtains and saw, parked on the road, a scruffy van that she did not recognize.

The knocking continued, and Marcie went into the hallway and put an eye to the peephole. What she saw through the fish-eye lens was a grossly distorted image of Dunster Cosmo's face and extra-large nose as he peered into the lens from the opposite side. He now pounded on the door.

As he stood back, Marcie could see he was accompanied by two of his heavies, and she didn't like the fact that, somehow, they had managed to get into the foyer through the front door, which meant that one of the other tenants in the block must have buzzed them in. Cunts.

'Marcie, Marcie, open the fuck up, bitch! I know you're in there, so come on.'

'Wait a second,' she called through the door.

She had no idea why he was here, especially with the two goons, but she didn't want to take any chances by being only in her night things. She wanted to be fully dressed and ready to run, because she didn't trust him not to try anything dirty with her. She ran back to the bedroom and quickly pulled on jeans and a hoodie, and put her mini-Taser, which looked like a mobile phone, into a pocket. Just in case.

An unexpected visit from Dunster Cosmo could never bode well.

Pushing her hair into place, she opened the door and three jumpy men swarmed in.

In fact, she had never seen Cosmo look so worried – shitting himself, she thought.

He launched into the reason for the visit immediately. 'You an' McCabe, I want you to do something for me. Where is he?'

'He's out . . . and . . . OK, what?'

'I mean, you've basically scavenged off me these last few years,' he said. He was red-faced and out of breath, wearing a zip-up jacket which made Marcie swallow when she saw what she thought was blood splattered up the right-hand side of it.

'I think you'll find it's called commission, not scavenging.'

'OK, parasite, then . . . anyway, whatever . . . I call it living off my money.'

'It's business,' she insisted.

'Whatever, whatever . . . anyway, you're going to earn it now. I need you to do something for me.'

'Fuck would that be, then?'

'Here, come here.'

Cosmo led her outside, his two men following, one of them eyeing her with undisguised lust. She sneered at him, tempted to zap him.

Cosmo hustled towards the parked van on the road outside and he went to the back doors. Marcie followed. He stopped, turned sharply and said, 'Van's clean, but you're gonna have to torch it after.'

'After what?'

'Stand back,' he said dramatically, and opened the van doors with both hands.

'I can't believe I'm taking a baby with us to dispose of two bodies and some guns.'

They were on the M6, heading north.

McCabe was at the wheel of the van, his jaw rotating furiously, just as it had done for the past twelve hours. He was keeping the speed to sixty miles per hour, to comply with the sticker on the back, which said the vehicle wasn't permitted to travel above that speed.

It was hard but necessary; the last thing they needed was to get pulled over by the cops even though the bodies in the back had been hidden under tarpaulin and a few sacks of horse carrots.

Marcie glanced over her shoulder into the rear.

In fact, the bodies were not that well concealed, and a half-blind copper could have found them, so she hoped the van was as clean as Cosmo claimed, because if they activated an ANPR checkpoint on the way, they were doomed, even if McCabe was armed with a handgun.

She looked forward again, resting her right hand on the rear-facing baby seat they'd had to quickly install in the middle of the bench seat so that Arthur was secured between them. At the moment the little lad was sleeping soundly to the rhythm of the engine, but that state of affairs wouldn't last for much longer, and when those beautiful brown eyes flickered open, he would demand to be fed. That meant a pit stop because Marcie didn't want to chance breastfeeding in a van on the motorway with dead people in the back.

'Why us, why us?' McCabe had chuntered remorselessly.

Marcie was a bit more philosophical now, even though she did not like the situation one little bit. 'It's academic now. It is us, and he wants to get rid of the two lads he's shot in the face as far away from London as possible. Which is why we're off to see Mr and Mrs York who, Dunster noted on his visit to see them, have lots and lots of land where these two unlucky sods can get buried and become actual sods.'

'Why did he kill them in the first place?'

'Because he's at war with a bunch of uppity gyppos trying to muscle in on his county lines business, is what I'm hearing . . . the name Costain rings a bell. Big, big fallout.'

'Fuckin' big fallout,' McCabe muttered. 'Two dead guys.'

'Probably best we don't know – that way we can claim innocence.'

At least that made them chuckle – the thought of them being innocent – and they were still chuckling when they came off the motorway on to a service area north of Birmingham, where Marcie scooped up Arthur who had just woken and said, 'Time to eat and change that shitty nappy.'

They left the van locked and went to eat.

* * *

John York's meltdown was almost catastrophic as he watched McCabe heave out the bags of vegetables and drag the tarpaulin sheet off the two bodies that had begun to reek as they decomposed.

John backed away, terrified, pinching his nose from the disgusting stench. 'No, no, no, no, no,' he gabbled. 'This is not going to happen. You need to go, get away now. I won't say a word but we – I – can't be involved in this level of criminality.'

Marcie had Arthur cradled in a baby sling to her bosom. He was sleeping contentedly again.

McCabe grabbed York by his shirt front and slammed him hard up against the side of the van, making one of the panels bow inwards. He slapped him hard and growled menacingly into his face. 'Oh yes, you can, you spineless piece of shit.'

York whimpered but tore himself free from McCabe's grip, gasping, 'You're asking me to hide or dispose of two dead bodies and some guns! Yes – I'm fucking spineless . . .'

'Not asking – telling,' McCabe corrected him.

'Hey, keep it quiet, you'll wake the baby,' Marcie said.

John York's head snapped towards her in disbelief. 'You've brought a fucking baby with you? What sort of people are you?'

'Hey, if you didn't already know, John,' Marcie said, 'we're people just like you. People who are in with the big boys.'

They dragged the two bodies out of the van and laid them side by side on the tarpaulin with the weapons. McCabe helped John York to pull the bodies up the side of the farmhouse and across to one of the doors of the four-car garage where he stood back and said, 'Leave 'em with you.'

'You've got to be shitting me,' York panted. He looked desperately at Isobel, who had watched the whole thing in a catatonic state.

'Nope.' McCabe looked around and saw a hose pipe on a reel connected to an outside tap. He drew the hose to the back of the van and swilled out the floor pan. A few minutes later, he and Marcie and Arthur were driving away, leaving the stunned couple and their Great Dane standing over two dead bodies and wondering what the hell they were going to do with them.

The next couple of days were relatively chilled.

Marcie and McCabe were ensconced in their pleasant but dreary domesticity in Greenwich, although McCabe did have to leave the flat one morning to do a job from which he later returned with £5,000 stuffed in an envelope and a few bags of good-quality weed.

Marcie asked no questions but kept an eye on local news coverage on TV and tried not to sit forward when an item came on about a shooting in central London where the body of a man with 'underworld connections' had been found, shot twice in the back of the head in what the police called 'a targeted attack'.

She was sitting on the sofa at the time, curled up with McCabe, who had not even reacted to the news. Her smartphone beeped and she answered a call from an unknown number. It was Dunster Cosmo, probably calling from one of his pay-as-you-go disposable phones.

'Is it done?'

'Yes.'

There was a pause. Marcie wanted to hang up but didn't. She mouthed, 'It's Cosmo,' to McCabe.

'I need some money,' Cosmo told her.

'OK.' Marcie closed her eyes.

'Ten million. Cash.'

Another pause as it sank in. Then Marcie said, 'What the fuck?'

'Liquidate some of my assets. One week.'

The phone call ended.

Marcie looked at McCabe. She grabbed the spliff he'd just lit and took a long, deep drag of it into her lungs, blowing the smoke out, feeling light-headed and instantly under pressure.

There is a huge element of human nature which often tells people that by ignoring a problem it might go away. The head-in-the-sand mentality.

It is rarely true.

Marcie had allowed herself to believe that having invested Dunster Cosmo's most recent money through John York's overseas contacts, it was possible that if interest from that money kept rolling in, then Cosmo would be a happy teddy and would never get to know that he would never ever again see the hard-earned cash that Brendan – her dead husband – had supposedly invested for him before his untimely death on Merseyside.

But at least she knew where the money Cosmo had continued to entrust to her had gone over the last four years.

'He needs the money as soon as possible,' Marcie told John York over the phone. 'Ten million in his hand.'

'He can't have it.' York sounded as if he was trying to be forceful, but his voice was still wavy from having had to deal with two dead bodies dumped on his doorstep. 'It's not like it's in a cupboard in the kitchen, is it? It's invested.'

'And your point is?'

'The money is abroad. It's with financial institutions. It's with building companies. It's in land purchases. You've seen the paperwork. I always send you the paperwork. You can't just go to a cash machine and ask for it back. It doesn't work that way. These are long-term investments. It takes years for these things to mature. He needs to understand that, so you can tell him he's not having it.'

That phone call left Marcie Quant with several issues.

First, you didn't make Dunster Cosmo understand something if he didn't want to understand something, and it was unlikely he would want to understand the basics of investment: he wanted his money and he wanted it now. And he wanted more money back than he had given Marcie to invest since Brendan's demise (he was now becoming 'that fucking Brendan') because Cosmo was still under the impression that she knew exactly where Brendan had put Cosmo's money, which of course she didn't.

Second, there had been something in John York's voice that she did not like, more than just the words he had used.

When the phone call was over, she went for a shower, then drank two mugs of black coffee to clear her head and give her a controlled energy boost, before kneeling down at a floor-level cupboard in the kitchen, at the back of which was the fuse box for the flat. In the gap behind this she kept the slim file containing all the paperwork from John York relating to the investments he'd made for Cosmo in the last four years.

She sat at the kitchen table, opened her laptop and then smoothed out the documents.

To be honest, she wasn't expecting much.

She found even less.

She searched the names of the companies referred to in the documents on the internet.

There were no matches.

Not that she necessarily expected to find much, but some references would have made her feel better because even bent companies often had websites or mentions in police bulletins.

She searched for two hours with breaks for feeding Arthur and rocking him back to sleep.

Finally, she closed the laptop and sighed. 'Bollocks . . . I've been had again.' She smacked her head into her hands and kept it hanging there until something dawned on her.

'It's the only way out of this,' Marcie said, swaying from side to side to get Arthur back to sleep after a very greedy session at her breasts, both of which were now exceedingly tender. Breastfeeding might be good for the kid, but it took its toll on her, and she knew she'd have to have another boob job once he'd stopped sucking on her. She was moving gently around the lounge as Arthur's eyes closed. 'It makes perfect sense and there'll be no comebacks if we do it right.'

'You'll have to run that past me again.' McCabe frowned at her.

'Kill John and Isobel York. It's what you do, innit?'

'And how will that work exactly?'

'Make it look like a burglary gone wrong,' Marcie said, getting quite excited by the prospect. 'Uh, somehow . . . that would be your job. Kill them and then we can lie to Dunster because he won't know any different. He thinks that Brendan put his money through the Yorks, so if they're dead, there's a bloody good excuse for not being able to get the money! Simple.'

McCabe said, 'It's a shit plan.'

'It's better than nothing, because it looks to me like John York has been taking all the money channelled into him and has been lying about where it's been invested. He's provided bank and interest details, and he's actually paid interest, but I can't find any of the banks he's supposedly used mentioned anywhere on the internet, even on the dark web. They don't fucking exist, Mac.'

'But, like you say, he's been paying interest.'

'Yeah, on the face of it.'

'What does that mean?'

'OK, OK . . . he might have invested the money but lied to me about where, and maybe there is real interest being accrued . . . but you know what I think?'

'Go on.'

'He hasn't invested a penny of it.'

'But the interest? Where has that come from?'

'Out of the capital.'

'What do you mean?' He was struggling to get his head around the concept.

'I think – and I might be wrong – he's pretending to pay interest but it's coming out of the capital. Or he has invested the money just for himself . . . whatever, he certainly isn't willing to pay back the capital . . . and he sounded like he was lying and scared on the phone, and when I checked, there was no trace of any of the companies he's supposed to have invested in. So, whatever, we're in a shitty situation and a way forward is to kill John York and tell Cosmo we can try and get his cash, but it's doubtful because the guy's dead . . . You can make it look like a gangland hit or something, can't you?'

'He ain't gonna like it.'

'I don't fucking *like* it, but the day has fucking come round and we've got to deal with it.'

'How about I torture him? We'd get to know that way,' McCabe suggested.

'OK, do that, see what he says – but that still won't change the fact that Brendan had been pulling a fast one, and we don't know where Cosmo's money went, and now I think John York is doing the same thing. All right, it's fucking potty – I know, I get it – but it's a way of dealing with a shitty situation, yeah?'

'Right, right.'

'So will you do it?'

'I'd do anything for you, you know that.'

'Aww . . .'

'And I'm thinking it might be worthwhile taking Jack Carter out of the picture, too.'

'Why?'

'Because the cops will start rooting, and Carter is the only living link between us and the Yorks. It's just common sense.'

Marcie understood the logic. It was like an evidence chain that needed to be broken.

'Scope it out and do it.'

He did scope it out, but plans usually go awry, and the first part to do so was when McCabe climbed the hill behind Hawkshead Farm and John York's fleeing daughter ran into him as he came over the crest.

And now, as McCabe sat waiting patiently for Jack Carter to arrive home – and McCabe wondered if Carter's absence was significant or just a coincidence – he felt it was a bit of a shame he'd had to kill Beth York.

A bonny lass, running in fear. Probably had nothing to do with anything her dad was involved in. But she had been hysterical, and McCabe couldn't take the chance of letting her go. He'd trussed her up quickly so he could come back to her after he'd been down to the farm to check out what was going on. He'd used the duct tape he'd brought along for his intended interrogation of the Yorks, and he'd thought he'd done a decent job of it – but clearly not, because she had managed to break free and leg it up the hill.

He had gone hunting and eventually found her running blindly ahead of him, falling, crawling and not responding to his calls to stop. She was still fleeing for her life and would not willingly be caught by him again.

Suddenly, ahead of him, she had stopped and seemed to be teetering, trying to balance, her arms windmilling.

McCabe drew his Browning and double-tapped her in the back and immediately saw her disappear; he then realized that she had stopped suddenly because she'd reached a perpendicular drop over the edge of a cliff face.

He had approached carefully, obviously not wanting to topple over himself. Even with the NVGs on, he could not see where she had fallen, but he knew she was dead.

Having pursued her up and across the moor, he had become slightly disorientated in spite of the goggles, but he did find his way back to his parked car, and it was then that he realized the water bottle he'd used had fallen out of the side webbing of his rucksack. He knew he'd have to take the chance of leaving it, that it would be too risky to go back and try to find it.

And he had something else to do, which was to go and see Jack Carter and kill him.

But Carter hadn't been at home. He did not answer any calls to his mobile number or landline and seemed to have gone to ground. A month later he still had not surfaced, and Marcie and McCabe were highly suspicious, making it all the more imperative, in their eyes, that he was dealt with.

However, one good thing for Marcie and McCabe following the murders of John and Isobel York (an unexpected blessing they could not believe: someone had done their dirty work for them!) was that Dunster Cosmo went off the radar and made no more demands for his money to be repaid, as though he knew something about their deaths which he was not admitting.

McCabe adjusted the seating position in his car.

He was parked on the narrow country road close to the junction that led to Jack Carter's house in Silverdale, as he had been on and off for the last month since his visit to the farmhouse. Travelling up from the south was a pain, but the job was necessary, and occasionally Marcie and Arthur would accompany him and stay in bed-and-breakfast accommodation.

But for the last few days, and for a few days to come, McCabe was alone. He slithered low into his seat and let his mind wander about the possibility of some sort of future with Marcie. He was amazed he had come this far with her. He pulled the peak of his baseball cap down over his eyes, but then a car coming down the lane from behind caught his attention in the door mirror.

He slid further down.

The car drove past.

Jack Carter was at the wheel.

SIX

Henry and Diane talked money as they drove north out of Morecambe following the meeting with Jenny Peel, picking up the A6 towards Carnforth, then forking left and aiming for Warton and Silverdale.

'How much was there in the end?' he asked. He was referring to the cash found in the garage walls at the Yorks' farmhouse, and even more later, when Henry led the police raid on a travellers' site near Blackpool, where the money stolen from Hawkshead Farm was discovered. All the money had obviously been seized by the police, but Henry hadn't stayed on to count it. By the time that happened, he'd returned to The Tawny Owl to resume his life as a landlord and part-time fireman.

Diane uttered a contemptuous, 'Ugh, money!'

Henry grinned. He knew that cash coming into police possession was a nightmare to deal with and best avoided if at all possible. It depended on the circumstances, obviously. If the money was drug-related, it might need to be examined for traces of controlled drugs such as cocaine, and if the percentage was higher than the normal traces found in general circulation – most notes out there have drugs on them – then it was good evidence to show it was money from drug dealing. There was also the possibility of needing to examine it for fingerprints, or it might just need to be retained as found cash.

However, regardless of the circumstances, it was always necessary to count it and record the serial numbers, and then it had to be sealed and kept in a secure exhibits store. If it was simply 'found' money, it could be paid into a police bank account, but then there were problems with accrued interest and what to do with it.

The money coming in from the Yorks definitely had to be unpacked and recounted, the serial numbers noted and checked for drug traces.

'I would never have guessed just how tedious money could be – especially when I wasn't allowed to throw it on my bed and roll naked in it and light my cigar with it,' Diane said, implanting an image into Henry's mind that was hard to extinguish. 'Anyway, there was too much to count manually, so Rik Dean said we could use counting machines. We had to count it twice under strict supervision and record all the serial numbers too, though the counting machines did that for us, thankfully. We took dip samples to check for drugs and fingerprints – no results yet from the fingerprints.'

'So, how much?'

'All the money we recovered – the money found in the walls at the farm and the money found at the travellers' site comes to nine million, three hundred thousand in sterling, give or take – can't remember the exact amount. And two million, one hundred thousand euros and just short of a quarter of a million dollars. All seemed to be laced with cocaine and fingerprints . . . lots of fingerprints.'

Henry whistled with wonder. 'And the two bodies? Where are you with them?' He was now referring to the two murdered young men whose bodies he and Diane had discovered in the wall cavity in the quadruple garage at the farm alongside the money.

'Not doing terribly well. No fingerprints or DNA back as yet.'

'Surprising,' Henry said.

'Well, you would've thought so,' she agreed. 'The weapons we found with them, though, are the ones used to murder them, but we haven't found any other instances of them being used.'

'You think the Yorks killed 'em?'

Diane shook her head. 'Nah. Doesn't quite fit with what we know about them.'

'So, disposing of them for someone else?'

'And maybe that is why they were about to run,' Diane suggested.

'Have you done photos to press, social media and all that?' he asked, thinking he should probably have known the answer to that, but he hadn't been keeping abreast of the investigation.

'We have. No bites as yet.'

'Have you tried talking to the travelling community?'

'No, why?'

'Just a thought, really,' Henry mused. 'After all, the people in custody for murdering the Yorks are travellers – part of an organized crime group within that community, I know, but still travellers. Perhaps there's a connection.' He shrugged. 'And identifying travellers can be a problem . . . could be worth a punt.'

Diane considered this. 'Yeah, definitely.'

'They're going to be someone's sons or boyfriends, you'd think. Someone's going to be missing them, but it's not the natural inclination of travellers to come to the police, so perhaps we should go to them.'

Diane took the fork off the A6 at Carnforth and drove towards Warton, dipping under the bridge over which the West Coast railway line passed. Just before Warton itself she did a sharp left and took the road to Silverdale, the pretty, leafy village nestling between Warton and Arnside in beautiful countryside undiscovered by many. It was an area Henry knew well, had visited often over the years, although it had been a while since he was last there.

He moved the conversation on to Jack Carter and asked if Diane had any background on him.

'A bit. No criminal convictions other than a caution in his teens for stealing a trailer, which I suppose points to how he became a haulier. His name came up on several of those websites where you can find details of businesses and directorships. Over the years he's run a lot of companies and most seem to have gone bankrupt.'

'Sounds a bit of a chancer,' Henry said, then frowned. 'So if this Jack Carter introduced this woman in a Roller to John York, who then invests money for her on the QT, and then York gets a reputation for handling dirty money, which can be a lucrative trade, perhaps this is why he unceremoniously dumped all his clients and starts laundering dosh for crims. Easy money on the face of it.'

'Except that laundering money for criminals is never easy in the long run,' Diane said.

'Because it's rife with temptation,' Henry said, recalling the sight of the huge amounts of money he had come across when he'd initially entered the Yorks' kitchen. 'Bags of it turn up, often uncounted, and the temptation to skim can be hard to resist . . . I mean, why was there so much in the garage wall? Why hadn't it been laundered?'

'Plus two pretty fresh bodies,' Diane added. 'The pathologist said they'd only been dead for three or four days at most.'

'And guns and ammo.'

'It's a complex web, Henry.'

'Certainly is . . . but in my experience—' he began.

He was cut short when Diane interrupted and said with a smirk, 'Oh, hang on – do I detect a bit of mansplaining about to be unleashed on me?'

Henry ignored her. 'In my experience,' he restarted, 'and you'll like this analogy being a woman, as women do a lot of knitting when they're waiting for their men-folk to return home with the bacon . . . as complex as it all is, once you start pulling a loose thread, it all unravels very quickly.'

Even though she was driving, Diane managed to punch him very hard on the upper arm. 'I've never picked up a pair of knitting needles in my life.'

Henry rubbed his arm. 'I have.'

McCabe adjusted the ski mask on his head to look like a bob cap, slid out of his car and began a slow jog along the road, keeping low, using parked cars to hide himself so that when Jack Carter turned into the driveway leading up to his house, McCabe was sure he hadn't been spotted.

The drive was a leafy curve, and by the time McCabe's trainers hit the gravel, Carter's car had disappeared out of sight. McCabe began to move just a touch faster because he wanted to time his surprise appearance just right – to catch Carter somewhere between his car and the front of the house.

As McCabe came within view of the house, still keeping low behind some bushes, Carter was getting out of his car.

McCabe stopped abruptly and dived behind a tree.

There was about fifty yards between him and Carter, and McCabe knew if he sprinted too early, there was a chance that Carter could scramble back into his car and make a getaway; if too late, Carter might be able to lock himself in his house.

Not that he would have got away in either scenario, but it would alter the way in which McCabe wanted this to play out. He wanted easy, not messy.

Because what he wanted was Carter firmly planted on a dining-room chair, cable-tied, gagged, unable to move, with McCabe's Browning shoved up into the soft cleft of flesh under his chin.

It worked like a dream.

He picked up pace, drawing the Browning from his belt at the small of his back, and intercepted Carter two-thirds of the way between car and front door, even though Carter seemed to have his wits about him.

He screwed the gun into Carter's ribcage and bundled him up the front steps before he could even comprehend what was happening.

McCabe rammed him up against the door frame, growling simple, specific instructions into Carter's ear and twisting the gun in so hard he could not mistake it. After a short finger-and-thumbs fumble with the keys, they were through into the hallway, and McCabe continued the roughhouse journey, half dragging, kicking, prodding Carter into the dining room. He pushed him down on to one of the chairs, not giving him time to speak or protest, just dominating, always keeping up the fear aspect, never giving him a second, then forced him to cable-tie his own left wrist to the chair arm, before binding his right to the opposite one. He stepped back a few paces and smiled.

A torrent of swearing burst from Carter's foul mouth as he writhed and the chair jumped and almost toppled over. McCabe wordlessly clouted the side of the Browning into Carter's temple, splitting the skin in a jagged wound and both silencing and stopping Carter. For a moment nothing happened, then his head bled.

'What's going on, Mac, what the hell?'

'You've been noticeable by your absence.'

'Holiday. Been on holiday.'

'Without your phone?'

Carter had zero reply to that one, but he was still shocked – and now hurt – and desperately wondering what was happening.

Even though he knew.

McCabe stepped to one side of him, avoiding the possibility of Carter kicking out as his feet weren't tied to the chair legs. He slipped his hand into Carter's jacket and extracted the smartphone from the inside pocket.

McCabe arched his eyebrows. 'Or are you just lying to me?'

The blood from the cut on the side of Carter's head now drenched his face, neck and shoulder, soaking his shirt.

'What do you want, mate?'

'Some answers.'

'Why this, then? Why not just ask me over a brew or summat?'

''Cos I don't fire guns in cafés.' He pointed the Browning directly into Carter's face, making the man wince.

'Just ask, mate,' Carter gasped.

'What do you know about John York?'

'Eh? What d'you mean? I know just what you know. I introduced you to the guy, remember?'

'I said, what do you know about John York?'

'He's dead, for one thing.'

'What did you know about him before he died?'

'Fuck – nothing. He was just my accountant and financial adviser. He put money away for me when I sold up . . . you know all this.'

'You set us up, didn't you?'

'What d'you mean? No way.'

Slowly, McCabe began to circle Carter, causing the man's head to twist and turn to keep him in his sight. 'You saw a chance and conned Marcie out of the money, didn't you?'

'You are jestin'. I knew she was investing money for other people – bad people – so why would I? I'm not stupid. Look, you came to me, Mac. I didn't go looking for you. Yeah, I took my fee – I did, I know it. But that's all . . . and now I've lost all the money I gave to John, because he's dead and I've no way to follow it up.'

'You scammed Marcie all the same, though,' McCabe persisted.

'No, I didn't, I fucking didn't.' He groaned as a shot of pain pierced his skull from the blow McCabe had delivered.

'Then why disappear for weeks on end?'

Carter raised his eyes to McCabe who was now standing directly in front of him. He didn't have an answer, and in that moment McCabe realized that Carter had been lying to him. The look in the eye. The flare of the nostrils. The cloud across the face.

And, in turn, Carter knew he'd been sussed.

Just that one question. The simple one. The one that should have been answered with 'I wanted some sunshine.'

Instead, he had hesitated.

McCabe raised the Browning again.

'Where did the money get invested? Tell me, or I'll shoot you now.'

'It never got invested,' he blurted.

'What?'

'It never got invested. Not a penny . . . not as such, anyway.'

'What?' McCabe was incredulous.

Carter tilted his bloody head right back and swore to the heavens, then lowered his chin and regarded McCabe with contempt as he spoke. 'John thought he was dealing with imbeciles, OK? People like Marcie who'd be too thick to realize. So he just kept the money, pretended to pay off interest, but it was really just from the capital. He falsified documents, invested some for himself, of course. He knew it'd come crashing down one day, but he had it all sussed. He and his missus would just decamp to Panama or somewhere equally hot . . . I'm guessing it went tits up sooner than he anticipated, but I don't know. I hadn't seen him for months anyway.'

Fury rose in McCabe's chest like a flame, and he could not hold himself back from crashing the Browning into the other side of Carter's face.

'That,' he growled, 'is for insulting Marcie.'

Carter's head hung over his chest.

'Why are the Yorks dead, Jack?'

'I dunno,' he muttered through a mouthful of blood: the second blow had smashed an inch lower than the opposite one and his teeth had lacerated his inner cheek. He dribbled blood and saliva.

'Like I said – must've all caught up on him before he could leg it . . . I dunno.'

'Is that why you disappeared and then slunk back like a fucking rat?'

'I thought whoever did it might come for me, too.'

'So why did the gyppos top him?' McCabe demanded.

'Again, dunno . . . we had nothing to do with travellers. Why would we? Why would anyone for that matter? They're bad news.'

'So where is the rest of the money, Jack? If it didn't get invested, where is it all?'

'York bought cars, stupid expensive ones. Even bought that Jag outside for me . . . I actually don't know what he did with the money, except all that the police seized from the farm . . . that was a lot.'

'How much did he give to you as a backhander? In cash, not in cars.'

'About half a mill.'

'Which is . . . where?'

No response.

'Won't ask again, Jack.'

No response.

'Is that what you came back for?'

No response. Carter just raised his eyes once more and looked sullenly, yet afraid, at McCabe.

This time there was a response – but from McCabe, who pointed the gun into Carter's face and fired.

'This one, I think,' Diane said, slowing down almost to a stop and peering up the driveway to what she hoped was Jack Carter's house on Shore Road, Silverdale.

'Not bad for a serial bankrupt,' Henry commented.

She pulled up on the road, and they got out and began to walk up towards the house. As they reached the curve in the drive, they saw a car parked on the gravel.

'Maybe we've struck lucky,' Diane said.

They walked up the steps to the front door, but as Diane was about to raise her knuckles to rap on the door, they heard the distinctive sound of a double gunshot from within the house.

Diane glanced quickly at Henry who nodded in answer to the unasked question. She reached for the door handle, expecting the door to be locked.

It wasn't.

She pushed it open and shouted, 'Police officers! Police officers entering the house.' She stepped across the threshold, Henry just behind her and slightly to one side so he had a view across her shoulder.

A figure stepped out of a room at the far end of the hallway. Gun in hand. Raised. Aimed. A man wearing a ski mask pulled down over his face, just eye holes.

Henry pushed Diane to one side and he went the other way, splitting like a zip.

The man fired.

Henry crashed down on to his right knee as he felt the whoosh of the bullet slice through the air above him.

In front, Diane rolled away.

The man fired again and a bullet imbedded itself in the door frame to Henry's right, splintering it.

'Fuck!' Henry heard Diane utter as she continued to roll.

Henry tried to keep one eye on the man, knowing that both he and Diane were horribly exposed and very likely to take a bullet next time. The first two shots had been fired in a rush; the next ones might not be.

But the gunman spun, then disappeared back into the room.

Henry scrambled up to his feet, having to lever himself up with the help of the damaged door frame. Diane was up before him, already creeping down one side of the hall at a crouch with her right arm extended outwards, angled backwards in a gesture that meant 'keep back' to Henry.

'Police!' she called again, still moving forwards, but allowing herself to rise gradually. 'Drop your weapon.'

Then she was at the door from which the gunman had appeared, flattening herself against the wall. Henry slid in behind her. She called another warning and instruction, then added, 'We're coming in.'

She glanced back at Henry and mouthed, *Are we?*

He nodded.

OK, she mouthed, then shouted. 'That gun had better be on the floor, because I'm coming in right now.' On the last word, her fingers tightened for purchase on the door jamb and she used her arm as a fulcrum to swing herself fast and fearlessly into the room, Henry again just behind her.

She stopped abruptly, causing Henry to crash into her, and said, 'He's gone – out of the patio door.'

She exhaled. Henry saw her shoulder shudder as her lungs deflated in relief, then she stepped to one side to allow Henry to see the body of a man tied to a chair, slumped forwards, the wounds to his head catastrophic.

'He has no face,' Diane said.

Beyond him was a patio door, open.

Henry said, 'He'll have transport.'

He wasn't talking about the victim.

SEVEN

Henry and Diane ran through the patio doors on to a wide, paved area and came to a skidding halt. They were having a very hurried back-and-forth conversation on the hoof, working out tactics between them as they ran.

'Do we leave the body?' Diane asked.

'He isn't going anywhere fast,' Henry said.

'Might be another suspect in the house.'

'A chance we'll have to take – but it's your shot, you're the real cop.'

No thought: 'Go after the guy.'

'Where's your PR?' Henry asked.

'In the freakin' car.'

'He's probably gone that way,' Henry said. 'We need to get some backup.'

They sprinted around the perimeter of the house, circling to the front driveway, even though the gunman could just as easily have dived into the thick trees and bushes in the garden and escaped that way.

'Helicopter, roadblocks,' Diane panted, thinking out loud.

'Feet on the ground,' Henry added to the wish list.

'You'll be bloody lucky.'

They ran past Carter's Jaguar and out on to Shore Close. Diane went to her car for her personal radio, but Henry jogged on, only now aware he had twisted his right knee when he'd leapt sideways in order not to take a bullet, and now it was hurting.

He ran to the junction with Shore Road and stopped, looking both ways – right towards the shore itself which formed part of the northern edge of Morecambe Bay, and left up towards the T-junction in the general direction of Silverdale village centre. Henry tried to put himself in the gunman's shoes: if he did have transport, where would be the most advantageous place to wait unobtrusively for Jack Carter to return home? It was only a hypothesis, but it seemed the most likely scenario at the moment: Henry guessed a car on the main road.

Diane caught up with him, transmitting urgent instructions over the radio, calmly and precisely.

As she spoke, Henry gestured that he was going up the road away from the shore towards the junction with Lindeth Road, from which he could either turn towards the village or away from it.

Diane kept up with him, still on the radio.

At the junction, Henry stopped, looking both ways along what was a very pretty country road, tree-lined, nice stone cottages and a few cars parked by the roadside.

'Bugger,' he said, frustrated, then winced as pain engulfed his knee.

Diane finished the dialogue with the comms room operator.

'They're putting up the helicopter, and mobile patrols are en route from Morecambe and Lancaster, including an ARV. Cumbria have been alerted, too,' she added, naming the adjoining police force, the boundary between it and Lancashire only a mile away.

'OK.' Henry kept his eyes roving for movement. The road was still and quiet, but he knew this was probably the best place for the gunman to have lain in wait in relative comfort in a car, maybe; unless he'd come on foot, this was the only access to Shore Road and Shore Close, and Carter must have used this route to drive home.

A car sped past from the direction of the village. A woman and two kids. Then it was gone.

'What're you thinking, Henry?'

'Maybe he was too fast for us, maybe he's gone . . .' Then he heard a car engine fire up down the road to his right. He tensed up and bent low to pick up a stone from the grass verge, about the size of half a house brick, one of a series of stones placed on the edge of the grass to discourage parking. 'Or possibly not.'

In a line of three cars on the opposite side of the road, all facing him, the nose of the middle car, an oldish blue Ford Mondeo, edged out.

Henry looked at Diane. She too had noticed the car.

'Could be,' Henry said. Henry hefted the stone in the palm of his hand and saw that Diane now had her extendable baton in her hand. She flicked it with a whip-crack sound and it opened to its full length.

The two detectives took a few cautionary steps towards the slowly emerging car.

A man at the wheel.

With a ski mask pulled down over his face.

Without hesitation, their cop instinct kicking in – the one where running at a problem is the only way to go – Henry and Diane rushed towards the car. The engine revved harshly and it lurched out of its parking space.

Henry and Diane were now in the middle of the road, still approaching it, though their run had dropped down a gear to a fast walk.

Suddenly, at an angle, the car lurched to a stop and the driver leaned out of the window, gun in hand, and fired two shots at them.

Henry and Diane split low again.

The car revved, the driver released the clutch and, screaming in first gear, the Mondeo gathered speed very quickly and drove at them.

Henry spun sideways to take cover in front of another parked car while Diane went into a defensive crouch on the opposite side of the road.

The car deliberately drove towards Henry, scraping along the car he was sheltering behind, grating side against side, smashing the wing mirrors off as Henry took another step back out of the way and pivoted, preparing to hurl the stone.

The driver twisted and fired at Henry as the car passed him. A hurried shot and it missed, but Henry already had his right arm drawn back, and with as much power as he could gather, he pitched the stone at the car. It bounced in through the window off the centre point – the upright between the front and rear door – ricocheted off that and caught the back of the driver's head.

By the time it connected with the man's skull, Henry knew the stone had lost some of its power, but it had the desired effect of making the driver swerve and lose control. The car veered across the narrow road, missing Diane but ploughing on at an angle into the back of a car parked on the other side of the road, fifty yards away.

The engine still revved and the gears crunched as the driver responded, found reverse and extracted the Mondeo from the crumpled mess while Henry and Diane ran towards it. As the car seemed to wrest itself free from the wreckage, the driver must have seen them coming, put his foot down and accelerated dangerously backwards at them, making them leap apart again.

'Stall it, you bastard,' Henry chuntered under his breath.

But that did not happen.

Somehow the driver slammed into first gear and the damaged car began to roll forward again just as Henry got his finger under the lip of the flip-up door handle. He couldn't quite make it count and the forward momentum of the car made him pirouette awkwardly away, grinding his knee again.

He swore and hopped as he watched the Mondeo drive up towards the village.

Across the road he heard Diane updating comms.

The Mondeo had left behind a trail of mangled metal and oily debris from its underside. Henry was surprised it was still actually moving – but it was – dragging something unrecognizable underneath it, which scraped the road surface, leaving a trail of sparks flying as the metal was dragged along.

It did not get far.

The narrow road wound sharply right uphill and an oncoming vehicle, with the driver blissfully unaware of the mayhem ahead, came far too quickly around the bend, took it wide, straddling the centre line and collided head-on with the Mondeo, stopping both vehicles abruptly. The gunman was thrown against the steering wheel and the driver of the other car, a man in his late fifties, who was not wearing a seat belt, was hurled against his windscreen.

Henry and Diane kept running towards the collision.

The gunman rolled unsteadily out of the Mondeo with his left arm clutching his chest. He picked himself up, brought up the handgun and fired two more rounds at Henry and Diane. He then spun away, seemingly having found his balance, and fired two bullets through the windscreen of the car that had caused the collision into the already injured driver, then he set off running towards Silverdale, leaving the scene of carnage behind him, only to be faced by another car coming round the corner – this time on the correct side of the road, travelling slowly, a Mini Cooper driven by a young woman.

She slammed on the brakes, petrified by the sight of an armed, masked man running towards her.

She stalled the car in her panic and watched in horrific disbelief as the man pointed the gun at her and screamed for her to get out of the Mini, making it seem all the worse because the ski mask did not have a mouth opening and all she could see were his blazing eyes and the line of his jaw moving as he shouted.

He yanked the door open and dragged her out by the hair when she did not respond instantly. She screamed as he flung her on to the road and shot her twice in the legs, then leapt into the Mini, found reverse and executed a sweeping backwards 180-degree spin and gunned the car away up the hill as Diane and Henry reached the wounded woman who was now screaming uncontrollably in agony and terror as she sat up and looked down at the blood streaming out of the gunshot wounds in her lower legs.

Diane reached the woman just ahead of Henry. She knelt down, looking horror-struck at the blood pulsing out of the woman's lower legs in thick gouts.

'Jesus, Henry, we can't go after him now,' Diane shouted.

'I know, I know.' He took in the woman, then turned back towards the driver of the car that had collided with the Mondeo. He was still in the driver's seat, slumped forwards over the wheel. Henry saw the cracked crater the guy's forehead had made on the inside of the windscreen and also the two bullet holes in the glass. 'I need to check this guy,' he said with trepidation and limped over to the wrecked cars. Other people were starting to emerge, and in a few moments the woman from the Mini was being cared for by two other women who knew her, using a first-aid kit from another car, keeping compression on the wounds as the injured woman faded in and out of consciousness.

Henry opened the door of the other vehicle just as the man came to and stared at him with unfocused eyes and a huge circular spider-web wound on his forehead where it had smashed into the glass. Henry was relieved to see that neither of the bullets fired through the windscreen had struck him.

'It'll be fine, mate,' Henry reassured him. 'You'll be OK.'

The man said something unintelligible, his eyes rolled back in their sockets, fluttered closed and he slumped sideways into Henry's arms. Henry managed to take his weight and eased him back up into the seat.

Already in the distance he could hear sirens and, not too far away, the sound of the police helicopter approaching.

As a senior investigating officer on FMIT in the not-too-distant past, Henry Christie had worked long hours investigating murders and other serious crimes. It was a regular part of the job, especially in the early stages of an inquiry when time was of the essence and jobs were being fast-tracked and all manner of resources were being thrown at catching offenders quickly.

So it came as no surprise to him that it was almost midnight when he and Diane pulled up outside The Tawny Owl. It had been a very long day, well into the evening before they had even thought about eating properly, though they had been caffeine-fuelled throughout the day by one of Jack Carter's neighbours who kept coffee, tea and toast coming for all the cops who turned up.

The most difficult thing for Henry, however, was for him to take a step back and let others take charge, particularly when the 'main' other was Detective Superintendent Rik Dean, who was also Henry's brother-in-law. Many years ago, Henry had hand-picked Rik from the ranks of uniformed PCs and facilitated his transfer on to CID. Rik's promotions since then had been of his own doing and he had eventually stepped into Henry's shoes when he retired, something that slightly grated with Henry, though he had tried to let it slide.

The police went through the motions, first by ensuring that the two drivers of the other cars involved were looked after and taken to hospital; both, it seemed, were doing as well as could be expected.

Once this had been done, a huge search was undertaken for the gunman, combining the helicopter with cruising vehicles and checkpoints, but he wasn't apprehended. However, the Mini Cooper he had commandeered was found abandoned on a small car park next to a popular public footpath just outside Silverdale, suggesting that a second vehicle, and maybe a driver, had been waiting for him. The Mondeo he had been using had been seized and conveyed to a secure police compound at force headquarters in order for scene-of-crime and forensic experts to comb it for evidence. Henry had glanced into it before the recovery truck arrived and saw that the chunk of stone he had chucked at the gunman had bounced into the back seat after hitting him. He hoped it might have some blood on it if it had managed to cut through the fabric of the ski mask.

Wearing latex gloves, he had done a quick rummage through the glove compartment, but it was empty. However, he noticed that the registration number etched into the windows of the car for security was different to the actual number displayed on the car. He wasn't surprised.

Diane checked the discrepancy on the Police National Computer and found that the number on the glass referred to a stolen Mondeo from London and the number on the car itself also referred to a

Ford Mondeo, not stolen, but again from London. The car's owner had apparently reported the number plates stolen several months before. Although this was obviously a good start, it suggested to Henry that this car was a product of the stolen vehicle industry and it was likely that all enquiries would lead to a dead end.

Beyond this, as an almost detached observer, Henry pretty much sat back and watched real cops in action at the scene of Jack Carter's murder and the car crashes.

It was all well managed by Rik, then subsequently delegated to an experienced detective inspector whom Henry knew. The guy took over responsibility for scene management.

Diane tried to keep Henry in the loop, but it was a struggle and he understood that. The truth was, he had become an outsider and, if he was honest with himself, it hurt a little.

Support unit officers were brought in – experts at searching and covering vital but more mundane jobs at murder scenes – and, briefed by another DI, they began a fingertip search of the gardens surrounding Jack Carter's house, then moved on to the road, which was sealed off, and then house-to-house enquiries.

'Thoughts?' Rik Dean had asked Henry at one stage.

He did not take a cynical look at his watch, though he guessed it was around eight p.m., a long time having passed since he and Diane had sauntered blindly into almost being killed. And, other than for an occasional nod in his direction, this was the first time Rik had deigned to ask his opinion about anything.

Rik raised his eyebrows to encourage a response from Henry.

'Cleaning up,' he said eventually.

'Meaning?'

'Jack Carter knew John and Isobel York, probably knew about the funny money coming into their possession, may have been part of it even. It's a possibility that Carter might have been killed because of what he knew.'

Rik nodded thoughtfully and said, 'Thanks for that insight. This might not even have anything to do with that.'

'One hell of a coincidence if it isn't,' Henry retorted. 'And you know what I think about coincidences.'

'Yeah, I know what you think.'

* * *

Four hours later, after much standing around on his part, Diane drove Henry home. On the way, he had called ahead to Th'Owl and asked Ginny to ensure there was some supper for him and Diane, though he didn't ask Diane if she wanted to come in until they pulled up outside.

Henry's little finger rested over the inner door handle.

'How are you feeling?' he asked her.

'Well, it's been a busy day,' she said, turning squarely on her seat and looking him in the eye. 'Not had time to think about anything. Stuff happens; you just get on with it.'

'One of the freshest murders you'll ever attend.'

'That bit's true . . . also, it's surprising how quickly you can move when a guy's pointing a gun at you.'

Henry's face twitched. 'I've hurt my knee.'

'I saw you limping. I'm sorry, but I didn't have a lot of spare time to inquire and rub it better.'

'Way it goes . . . Look, I know it's late and you don't have a change of clothing, but there's food on the stove if you're hungry – I know I'm ravenous – and if you want to, you can crash out in the spare bedroom in the accommodation.'

'Actually, I do have a change of clothing in the boot. My new mantra: dib dib dib, be prepared and all that. And I desperately need a hot shower.'

'Good. The full briefing's at ten tomorrow, so maybe we could have a quick sift through the murder files you brought with you in order to lure me back into the field. I may be knackered but I'm still buzzing.'

'Me, too.'

They ate in the living room of the owner's section at the back of the pub. Ginny had left a vegetarian moussaka warming in an earthenware dish in the oven, and they tucked into it with relish, both famished, but now feeling fresher after their showers and a change of clothing, which for Diane included pyjamas and slippers from the stash in the boot of her car. Henry held back from commenting when he saw her, but he was a bit thunderstruck by her appearance and had to swallow.

'Vegetarian?' she said about the food. 'It's as if you knew I'd be staying.'

'Not necessarily staying, but hopefully eating.' Henry already knew she was trying to eat less meat; he himself still ate like a lion but was actually quite impressed by the moussaka.

'Anyway, don't ask me too much about today's events,' she told him. 'Still processing them, but I think I'm OK.'

'No probs . . . me, I was terrified.'

'Uh, yeah, me too, actually.'

They were drinking a nice bottle of Rioja that Henry had snaffled from the wine rack in the restaurant.

Diane picked up her glass with a slightly dithering hand.

Henry's was pretty shaky too, but they clinked glasses and Henry toasted, 'To dodging bullets.'

'May it be a skill we keep for life,' she added.

They sipped the wine, then Diane said, 'Joking apart, what kind of a person are we dealing with here? What kind of *people* are we dealing with?'

Henry inhaled and took another thoughtful sip. 'People we need to be very wary of.'

'I'll drink to that.' She was about to chink glasses again but was interrupted by the ringing of her work mobile which was on the coffee table.

'DS Daniels,' she answered and listened intently to what was being said, her eyes on Henry. He watched her expression change several times until she finally hung up. 'Thanks for that.' She placed the phone down. 'Comms,' she said. 'The driver of the car who our offender crashed into . . . he had a brain haemorrhage. He died,' she concluded simply.

Henry handed her a whisky and sat next to her on the sofa. The news of the death of the driver, the man whose head had smashed into the windscreen, hit them both hard.

'This makes it all the more imperative to catch this man, not that it wasn't imperative anyway.'

Diane sipped the spirit. 'I know.'

'Which means that, whether we like it or not, we should have a quick sift through those files you brought, because I guarantee we won't get a chance in the morning.'

She nodded. Henry walked over to the dining table. Diane followed and they sat next to each other.

'So we start off with me discovering the bodies of John and Isobel York, and they have a ton of money being bagged up in their kitchen. The offenders are members of the travelling community . . .'

'Who also happen to be members of a sophisticated organized crime group using that community to hide their activities.'

'Yep. Anyway, they get arrested, having also helped themselves to the money in the kitchen which we subsequently recover when we make the arrests. Now I don't think – but I might be wrong – that they have any connection with Beth York's murder, or Jack Carter's murder, or the murders of the two young men we found in the garage wall, or that they knew anything about the huge amount of money and the firearms we found there either.'

'But they must have had a reason for killing John and Isobel – which, of course, they won't reveal because every interview is a "no comment".'

'So while there will be some connection along the way, the deaths of Beth York and Jack Carter don't fit in with the way John and Isobel died.'

'Agreed.'

'Find out how they lived,' Henry began.

'Find out why they died.' Diane finished the age-old manhunter mantra for Henry.

'Except for maybe Beth York.'

'Collateral damage?' Diane suggested.

'I'm thinking so.' Henry's lips twisted out of shape as he pondered. He was actually enjoying this in a strange sort of way: the kicking back and forth of theories, the bread and butter of any detective, something he hadn't realized was one of the things he missed. He said, 'She was running away.'

'Straight into her killer's arms.'

'Which poses the question . . .'

'Who is he – obviously – but also what was he doing at Hawkshead Farm that night?' Diane said.

They looked into each other's eyes.

'How do you fancy a walk in the country tomorrow morning before the briefing?' Henry asked her. 'And after that, we go to the prison?'

* * *

Henry did a last walk-through around the pub, checking doors and windows, plus a quick check of the ladies' and gents' toilets to see if anyone was hiding there, then re-entered the owner's accommodation and set the alarms. He walked past the bedroom in which Diane was staying for the night, forced himself not to pause outside the door, and went into his own room along the hallway. He removed his clothes and pulled on a pair of sleeping shorts.

His right knee was extremely painful, throbbing angrily, and he wondered if he had torn the cartilage when he'd spun out of the way of the gunman. He'd had a previous operation on the other knee more than ten years before and recalled that the pain in that was similar to what he was experiencing now.

In the en-suite bathroom, he snaffled a couple of paracetamols and found a crumpled tube of Deep Heat in the cupboard under the wash basin which he took back into the bedroom. He perched on the edge of the bed and began to apply the cream, massaging it in carefully.

He looked up at the tap on the door, hearing his name being called softly.

'It's unlocked.'

The door opened slightly and he could see a sliver of Diane Daniels in the crack. 'Can I come in?'

'Um, yeah, sure.'

She stepped into the room, then closed the door behind her.

EIGHT

Henry rolled out of bed and showered again just before seven a.m. When he came back into the bedroom, Diane had gone. The duvet was still pulled down and he could see the indentations left by her head and body in the pillow and mattress. He was guiltily grateful she wasn't there, even though sleeping with her had been wonderful.

He had a fleeting image of Alison, but then wiped that from his mind.

In terms of Diane, he was far beyond worrying about what other people might think, but what did bother him was the possibility of drawing her into a relationship with an older man – a substantially older man at that. He was just into his sixties, she late thirties, and he didn't want to get her involved in something that had no hope of going anywhere.

'Well, at least you're not skirting around the subject,' she said.

It was a quarter of an hour later and they had met up in the restaurant, which had just opened. A couple of the local gamekeepers were already tucking into large breakfasts in preparation for their day ahead.

Henry and Diane were drinking coffee, and the young waiter had just delivered breakfasts for them. Henry was on a small version of the full English, Diane the vegetarian.

'Look,' Henry said, knowing he had probably phrased things all wrong and got her back up. He sighed as he tried to get it a bit better. 'I think you are amazing, Diane. You're a great detective . . . I think you're beautiful . . . I didn't even think I was capable of getting an erection like that anymore . . .'

She held up her hand – the number-one police stop sign – and said, 'Well, you did. Impressive, too.'

'Thank you,' he said modestly. 'It's just, I like you too much to let you get involved with an old guy with a gammy knee, who probably hasn't stopped grieving for his wife or fiancée – so a guy with psychological issues, too – who, on the one hand, can't believe his luck . . . God, last night was fabulous, Diane . . .' He closed his eyes for a delicious moment, visualizing her rising above him, moving rhythmically, and him trying not to come within about ten seconds. He opened his eyes again, seeing her smirking across the table, and continued, 'And on the other—'

'Stop again,' Diane ordered him.

He did and bit off a chunk of toast.

Their eyes blazed.

'Look, Henry . . . I like you a lot and I'm the one who chose to rub Deep Heat into your knee last night . . . well, at least that's how it started.'

And it was. She had entered the bedroom as he'd been applying the ointment, knelt down in front of him and started to rub it in for him. That was when he realized erection problems were a figment of his imagination.

'But *I* chose to come in uninvited, then *we* chose to sleep together – and that's it! We were both exhausted, we'd both been through a hell of a lot yesterday, and we both needed it for that and various other reasons. But the main reason is that we like each other, isn't it? Fancy each other? Y'know, basic man-and-woman stuff?'

He nodded. That was true.

'Plus I'm no spring chicken,' she admitted. 'Yes, I'm obviously much, much younger than you . . .'

'Isn't that creepy, though? The age thing?'

'If you were twenty years younger and I was twenty years younger, it'd be even creepier, so no. But what about my colour? Is that something that worries you?' Diane's family roots were Ugandan.

'No,' Henry said simply.

'Right, OK, so where are we?' she asked. 'One-night stand or the start of something amazing?'

'Uh, one-night stand which is the start of something amazing?' Henry ventured.

'Done.' She raised her coffee mug; Henry did the same. 'Shall we go for that walk?'

It transpired that Diane had a very well-equipped boot in her Mercedes. As well as a complete change of clothing, including night attire, she also had walking boots, a pair of Wellington boots, an umbrella, overcoats and rainwear, plus all the other things a good detective worth their salt would have: a box of disposable gloves, a first-aid kit, a portable fingerprint kit (which was out of date but serviceable), two torches, a small tool box, a digital camera and a mini scene-of-crime kit which contained all kinds of useful items.

'Where do you put your shopping?' Henry asked.

'Front passenger seat. I shop alone,' she told him.

Henry was already in his walking shoes as he waited for Diane to put hers on. As she did, he turned and looked at Hawkshead Farm, the home of John and Isobel York – and Beth. It was a lovely house, beautifully converted, but now a place that had housed violent death. Henry wondered what its future would be. Would someone have the courage to buy it, should it ever come on to the market? Or would it just be left to rot and deteriorate?

He turned back to Diane who had been perching on the open rim of her car boot while she put her walking boots on. She stood up, slammed the boot shut and hitched on her rucksack.

'Ready,' she declared.

They set off up the driveway towards the house.

They walked between the house and garage, past the large old barn and then over the expansive lawn, the grass now unmown for weeks, up to a low wall at the back of the garden which was the dividing line between it and the moorland beyond. Henry recalled that John York owned quite a lot of this moorland, too.

They stepped cautiously over the wall, and Henry lowered himself carefully down so as not to jar his knee, then began to walk up the steep slope towards the crest of the hill.

The fresh air filled his lungs, and for once in a long time he felt very alive, glancing regularly at Diane who was either alongside him or in front. He could feel the rhythm of his heartbeat and the expansion of his lungs, and although his knee was hurting, despite a couple of painkillers and another application of Deep Heat, all was good.

At the crest, they stopped and looked down the hill at the back of the farm. Beyond that, the view across the valley was stunning in the early morning.

'After the briefing I'll arrange for a support unit team to search this properly,' Diane said. 'Not sure there will be anything to find after a month, but you never know.'

'Tick in the box,' Henry agreed. He scanned full-circle, enjoying the view as much as anything, but also knowing how vital this walk was in trying to relive and recreate Beth York's last minutes alive, even though how she actually arrived at the small lake was still hypothetical at the moment.

'We're presuming she left the house, legged it over the garden wall, then ran up the hill, maybe to where we are now,' Diane speculated. She did a three-sixty turn, then pointed down the hill in the general direction of the lake, which could not be seen from their current position. She pointed to a wooded area in the distance. 'What's that?'

'Azers Wood,' Henry said.

'Oh, yeah, that's where I parked when I came round to see you and Jake. Looks different from up here.'

'And where Tom and I parked for our fishing trip.' Henry was not really familiar with the area and he tried to work out the geography, guessing the lake was somewhere in between where they stood now and the wood. 'So . . .' He spun around. 'Out of the house and up here.'

'Yep.'

Diane had her phone out and was taking photographs. A crime scene investigator would be visiting later and would be asked to do much the same thing, but would get better photographs.

Henry watched her and she caught him looking.

'Stay professional,' she warned him.

'Gotcha.' He forced himself to look away, took a few steps down the hill, then stopped suddenly, looking down into the deep grass at his feet. 'Diane,' he hissed.

He stepped across and looked to where he was pointing.

'Wow,' she said.

It was a strip of duct tape.

'We're definitely on the right track,' Henry declared.

After deciding it would be better to seize the tape now, Diane photographed it in situ, then dropped it into an evidence bag without touching any of the surfaces. Henry continued to look around as she did this.

'Not sure there will be anything of value on it after all this time,' she mused doubtfully.

'You never know. If nothing else, we should be able to identify it as being from the same roll of tape that was found on Beth's wrists or not, plus if the killer didn't wear gloves, it's possible there could be a fingerprint on the sticky side of the tape.' Henry looked down the hill towards Azers Wood, his jaw rotating thoughtfully. A hundred or so yards away was a low wall dividing two fields, which Henry assumed Beth must have crossed on her journey to Rushbed Crag overlooking the lake, over which she had tumbled.

Once Diane had sealed the evidence bag and labelled it up, she put it into her rucksack, and they carried on their journey towards the wall which was constructed of intricately laid dry stone, slotted in expertly like a jigsaw.

The wall was about four feet high and wasn't easy to climb over, but they managed and continued towards the lake, keeping it slow, letting their eyes search the grass as they went.

'If Beth was shot on the edge of the precipice, it might be worth cordoning off an area behind it for a nose-to-ground fingertip search to see if we can find any of the shell casings that might have been ejected from the gun. Again, needle in a haystack and all that, but it needs doing – that's if the gun was an automatic and spent shells were ejected and the killer wasn't holding a plastic bag over the gun to catch them.'

'Gosh, you know a lot about guns,' Henry said.

'I once went on a firearms familiarization day. That's the extent of my knowledge. I found out two things. One, I couldn't hit a barn door from ten feet, and two, firearms scared the hell out of me.' She looked at Henry. 'You've used guns in anger, haven't you?'

'That's one way of putting it.' He didn't elaborate. 'But mostly people have shot at me.'

'I saw the scars,' Diane said.

They continued to walk, up to the moment Henry stopped unexpectedly, turned slowly on his heels, frowning, thinking he had seen something out of the corner of his eye. He looked back towards the wall he and Diane had just climbed over.

He wasn't sure.

Diane had walked on a few steps before realizing she was alone.

'What is it, Henry?'

He shrugged, but then began to walk back towards the wall, then veered left slightly and stopped. He had seen something.

An empty plastic water bottle in the tall grass.

Diane caught up with him and dropped down on to her haunches to look more closely. 'It's got a chocolate-bar wrapper screwed up inside it.'

'What do you think?' Henry asked.

'I'd say that anything we find up here that shouldn't naturally be here, we seize for evidence and examine. Can't do any harm.'

Before touching it, she took a series of photographs of it where it lay, then she picked it up and slid it into an evidence bag, sealed it and signed the label.

She looked up at Henry. 'Should I say "bingo" at this point?'

NINE

The spare car came from a chop shop run from a small unit on the outskirts of White Lund Industrial Estate in Morecambe. It was a dull-grey Vauxhall Insignia and had been constructed and pieced together from sections of three other Insignias, welded together – seamlessly, ironically – then fitted with a set of registration plates relating to a 'clean' Insignia from Scotland so that any cursory police check, such as running the number through the PNC, would fool any nosy cops. A thorough inspection by an experienced traffic cop would probably be a different matter.

It had been left parked up on a small public car park just outside Silverdale with the ignition key on the front offside wheel.

It was only a standby, there in case of emergencies.

McCabe had not wanted to use it. He had wanted the job with Jack Carter to be straightforward, no hassle. Wait for the bastard, get him to talk, kill the fucker.

Then the two cops showed up, the black woman and the old white guy, both of whom moved with surprising speed when McCabe had fired at them. On the one hand, he wished he had killed them. At least that would have given him the time to saunter innocently away from Carter's house, probably unnoticed; on the other hand, and on reflection, if he had killed them, every fucking cop in the country would be after him. They did not like their own being slotted.

So they had burst in on him, he'd fired two wild shots at them and then raced out through the patio windows and back up to his car up on the main road.

Unfortunately, the two cops weren't far behind, and to make it all just that little bit more awkward for him, his car had been facing in their direction. If he'd been facing the opposite direction, he would have driven off without a backward glance. He had momentarily thought about hunkering down in the car in the hope they might not see him, but even as he had that thought, he just instinctively knew that these two cops would have found him and flushed him out, so now, to escape, he had to show his hand, even if it meant mowing them down. His perspective about killing cops changed in that instant.

He aimed for the male cop who somehow managed to jump out of the way.

What McCabe hadn't bargained for was the stone in the cop's hand. McCabe saw only the flash of the guy's hand, but what he did feel a moment later was the impact of the rock as it cracked him on the head. The stun from the blow made him lose concentration, and in that moment he collided head-on with the halfwit local guy coming wide around the bend in the opposite direction.

Then it was all about reacting to a situation that had got out of control and basically doing anything to facilitate his escape, even if he had to put two bullets in that woman's legs and hijack her car. At least he didn't kill her. But he had to ditch her car as soon as possible, and that meant the car swap with the recycled Insignia.

He had arranged for a different car to be waiting in the car park every day he had been keeping watch for Carter and the Insignia was exactly where it should have been, as were its keys.

It was only when he was climbing out of the Mini Cooper to get into it that he removed his ski mask and realized the extent of the cut to his head and that he'd bled profusely down his neck, on to and around his jacket collar and shoulder.

Which meant he would have left traces of his blood on the seat of the Mini and probably in the mangled wreck of the other car he'd been using and had abandoned. The cops wouldn't get anything from the car itself, which could never be traced back to him. The DNA that he might have left behind made him wary, though.

He swore with anger as he gunned the Insignia along the country roads away from Silverdale, slowing as he passed several blue-lighted cop cars racing in the opposite direction. At one point he wiped his head with his hand and it came away covered in blood. He touched the cut with his fingertips to find that his scalp had split good and wide and deep.

He had to think.

He was booked into a B and B in Morecambe, alone this time – no Marcie, no Arthur – and had left some of his gear there. He had paid cash, used an assumed name. It wasn't the most salubrious establishment in town, with a sleazy owner who made his money from housing benefit claimants; even so, to return covered in blood would be tempting fate, as would going to an A and E department in either Lancaster or Kendal. He knew he probably needed the wound stitching because it felt as wide as a valley, but he couldn't chance it; it would have to wait until he saw a private doctor back in London.

He slammed the steering wheel hard and swore repeatedly.

Obviously, he would have been a wanted man for killing Carter, but now he was a wanted man who had made some errors. At least his face hadn't been seen. That would have been the killer.

He knew that the best thing to do for the moment was to lie low.

The B and B was out of the question.

He'd be foolish to keep travelling in this three-piece Vauxhall, not least because it might shudder apart at eighty on the motorway, plus the cops would soon realize he had changed vehicles, and they would be on the lookout for anything in the next two days. He needed somewhere to crash.

He headed for Morecambe and for White Lund, and found the chop shop which had provided the Insignia, drove in through the gates and parked on the apron outside the closed shutter doors of the detached unit, slotting the Insignia into a line of beat-up scrappers.

When he climbed out of the car, he felt slightly woozy from the blow to the head, but clarity soon returned. He went to the office door, which was locked, pressed the buzzer and slammed the side of his fist on the door while looking up at the security camera on the wall above him, making 'Fucking hurry up' gestures at the lens.

Eventually, a man in his mid-forties opened the door. He was small, wiry, wearing a pair of ragged overalls with a welding mask tilted back behind his head.

'Need to crash here for a while, mate,' McCabe said urgently, shouldering his way past the smaller man who could not help but notice the cut and the blood all over McCabe's head and shoulders.

The man who ran the chop shop was called Billy Lane. Although he had provided the standby vehicles for McCabe, obviously he was not privy to what McCabe was doing; Lane assumed he was scoping out property for a high-value burglary. McCabe had paid him well enough to drop off and pick up vehicles from the car park in Silverdale.

Lane followed McCabe along the short corridor, through a connecting door and into the main workshop, which was strewn with vehicle parts, many stacked in metal cages. There was a Maserati up on a ramp with no wheels, no bonnet, no boot lid, no windows, no seats and no engine, just the shell. Lane was midway through the process of 'asset-stripping' this stolen and very expensive car, the parts of which would then enter a supply chain – which had begun when the car itself had been stolen to order in Blackpool the night before and which would continue from the chop house, via various channels, to the Middle East and India. It was a lucrative trade for not much hard work, and all cars stolen and chopped were out of the UK within twenty-four hours.

Very occasionally, Lane pieced different cars together just for fun and a bit of pocket money – that was how he had started in the trade when he was a lad – which is why the Insignia he had provided for McCabe was built from three separate cars.

'Fuck's 'appened?' Lane asked, traipsing in behind McCabe.

'Don't need to know,' McCabe snapped. 'Just need somewhere to crash, sleep for a couple of nights. But' – and here he turned aggressively and pointed at Lane – 'I need you to get some stuff for me, unless you already have it here.'

Lane's face twitched. He was already sensing problems.

He hadn't been that happy providing cars for McCabe in the first place, because that wasn't something he did, but the money had been OK, and now he was struggling to keep the fear off his face. Essentially, he was a one-man band, with his younger brother helping occasionally, such as when delivering the standby cars for McCabe, and he didn't particularly like the thought of anyone jeopardizing his business by bringing their own shit into it. He received orders for cars and parts and fulfilled them, and that was it. Often, he didn't even know who placed the orders. He'd been locked up once recently, fortunate not to be charged with anything, and that was how he wanted things to stay.

'Don't think so,' Lane said bravely.

'Do think so,' McCabe corrected him. Suddenly, there was an ugly-looking gun in McCabe's hand pointed straight into Lane's face. 'I wanna crash. You get me food and drink and some medical supplies, and you won't even know I'm here, OK? Oh, and I need a couple of pay-as-you-go phones, too.'

'There's nowhere here to crash,' Lane whined.

'I've seen your little rest room. That'll do for me, thanks.' McCabe was referring to Lane's grotty office in which there was an old, beaten-up settee stained with oil and grease, plus an ancient portable TV on a metal filing cabinet. McCabe lowered the gun and walked into the office, with Lane behind.

'You can't do this,' Lane bleated.

'I can do what I want,' McCabe responded, basically ignoring Lane's whinge. He spotted a first-aid kit on a shelf next to an old carburettor. He opened it and inspected the sparse, ancient contents. The 'use-by' date had been passed fifteen years earlier and it looked like a rodent of some sort had been using it for a home. He threw the kit down in disgust and turned to Lane.

'Go to fucking Asda, get me some antiseptic cream, some dressings, plasters, towels, paracetamol tablets, two phones, a bottle of whisky, some water and food – sandwiches or something I can stick in the microwave.' He jerked his thumb at the large, old and food-caked microwave cooker on the floor by the old desk. The only thing brand-spanking new in the room was Lane's laptop. 'And before you go, log me into that. I need to keep up with news reports. Oh, and get me a new set of clothes too – jeans, T-shirt and a zip-up jacket.'

'Just what the hell have you done?' Lane demanded tentatively, because he was now very scared.

McCabe looked at him malevolently. 'It's not just what I've done, Laney; it's what *we've* done, you and me.'

'I've done fuck all.'

'You provided me with a getaway car, Laney. That means that whatever I've done, you're as guilty.'

'Guilty of what?'

'Murder, conspiracy to murder, you name it . . . and I suggest you get rid of that Insignia, pal, ASAP.'

'Shit.'

McCabe raised the gun again and pointed it into Lane's face. 'And get me something else, clean, reliable. Understand?'

'You need a hospital,' Lane said.

It was two hours later. He had been to a nearby Asda and bought supplies for McCabe who had wolfed down the meal deal of sandwich, coke and crisps with a hefty slug of the cheap whisky decanted into the coke. Then he sat and watched the local news bulletin which told the tale of the brutal murderer on the run from a horrific crime which had rocked the sleepy community of Silverdale. Details were quite sparse but more were promised for later bulletins, which would include a proper police statement from Detective Superintendent Rik Dean.

Lane's mouth sagged and his eyes flickered nervously across to McCabe, who was watching the TV stone-faced, breathing shallowly.

'You, isn't it?' Lane croaked.

McCabe's eyes slid sideways. 'Us,' he corrected the car man. 'Don't forget the car. It's all piss in the same pot as far as the cops are concerned. Now then' – McCabe had been sitting with an oily rag pressed to the incessantly bleeding cut on his head – 'I want you to clean this up and patch me up, OK?'

'I'm not a nurse.'

'Just do it.'

They went into the cramped toilet – one urinal, one stall and one wash basin. It looked as though it had never been cleaned. Ever. It reeked of piss and shit, indicating the plumbing was not all it should have been.

'Clean the cut, dry it and squeeze on the ointment, then plaster it down and put a bandage over it.' McCabe leaned over the sink and Lane stepped close to him, wetting a cloth with warm water from the tap and began to pat the wound. McCabe had close-cropped hair, and as Lane cleaned it, with his patient hissing painful noises at each dab, it became clear that there were two factors to the injury. First, it was deep. The edge of the stone must have done that. Second, it needed to be stitched or butterflied by a professional, not a man more in tune with dismantling sports cars and applying Swarfega to grimy hands.

'Got me a car sorted?' McCabe asked, his face over the sink.

'Haven't had chance, mate.' With distaste, Lane removed the screw top off the tube of Savlon and squeezed a line of white ointment into the cut, making McCabe wince.

'If I ever get hold of the cop that did this, I'm going to fucking enjoy myself kicking him to death,' McCabe said through gritted teeth. Then he asked, 'Got anything due in?'

'Uh . . .' Lane stalled. He did have a car due in next morning. A Range Rover Evoque stolen from the Lake District. It was due for the chop and the parts would be going onwards to Spain. It had been stolen to order and would mean about three grand for Lane. Easy money.

'Well?' McCabe asked impatiently, sensing the hesitation.

'Yeah, a nice Range Rover.'

'Put on some new plates, and I'll run it to London, then you can have it back. I'll pay you well.'

'OK, sounds good.' Actually, it sounded horrific, and Lane felt himself being dragged even further, kicking and screaming, into McCabe's world.

'When's it due in?'

'Tomorrow morning.'

'That'll do.'

Lane wanted to growl audibly as he cut a dressing to size and laid it carefully along the head wound. He glanced at the pistol that McCabe had placed on top of the broken hand drier next to the sink. Could it be so difficult to use a gun? he wondered. Pick it up, shoot the bastard?

Lane did not have the courage. All he wanted was to get McCabe out of here and away.

He opened the box of plasters, stuck one across the dressing and pressed it into place with his thumb. He did three in a line before declaring the repair complete. McCabe stood up, feeling the work with his fingers.

'Good stuff.'

TEN

Henry and Diane were a few minutes late for Rik Dean's murder briefing. They had waited for the arrival of the crime scene investigator at Hawkshead Farm and briefed her, which put them back a little timewise.

They then raced to Lancaster Police Station, abandoned Diane's Merc in the basement car park, blocking several other cars in, and hustled their way up to what had once been the gymnasium on the top floor but was now a briefing room and major incident room. They tried to sneak in at the back unobserved, but Rik – who had just begun the briefing – spotted them, looked daggers at them, and said, 'As a couple of latecomers have slipped in and I've only just started, I hope the majority of you – who were on time – will indulge me and let me start again for their benefit.'

Several pairs of eyes turned and gave Henry and Diane even more hostile glares.

Henry smiled and leaned against the back wall of the room – which still had a climbing frame attached to it – and took it all in. He recalled the days when he would have been up front, standing on the slightly raised stage, confidently briefing the assembled cops and others; the exciting beginning of a serious investigation, full of promise and the prospect of nailing a killer, someone who had violently taken another person's life. On the flip side, briefings at the far end of an investigation that had failed to find an offender could be very depressing and it could be hard to motivate staff.

As far as the murder of Jack Carter was concerned, and the death of an innocent motorist and the cynical shooting of the woman driving the Mini, this investigation was still in its golden time. That first seventy-two hours when all was possible and detectives were hunting like terriers. After that, if there was no result, everything got much tougher.

Watching Rik speak, Henry could tell he had his audience in the palm of his hand as he regaled them with what had happened the day before, when Henry and Diane had stumbled on a murder in progress while making enquiries linked to the fallout from the deaths at Hawkshead Farm.

Most people in the room were well acquainted with the scenario, but the previous day's events were an exciting add-on to an already complex and potentially wide-ranging investigation.

Clearly, Henry thought, he had taught Rik Dean well. He was a good orator and motivator – maybe even better than Henry had been.

Just before the briefing drew to a close and all tasks were allotted to the detectives and uniformed personnel, Rik caught Henry slightly off-guard when he pointed over the heads of the assembly and said, 'Just before we divvy up the jobs, I'd just like to point out that DS Daniels, whom you all know, and Mr Christie have joined us at the back of the room, and I would personally like to say to them: thank you for your bravery yesterday in pursuing, without hesitation, a very dangerous armed man who had already killed one person and attempted to shoot both of you. You're a credit to this force, although if you're late again, you'll be in big trouble.'

There was a laugh, an 'Oh, yeah' from someone, a whistle of appreciation and then a round of applause which embarrassed both of them, but then quickly faded when Rik added, 'Just so you're not confused . . . some of you may remember Mr Christie. He is a former detective superintendent and SIO who retired a couple of years ago. He is back now specifically to assist this inquiry as a consulting investigator . . .'

'Like Sherlock Holmes?' someone quipped.

'Exactly like Sherlock Holmes,' Rik confirmed. 'So be nice to him.'

Or I'll stick my pipe up your arse, Henry wanted to add – but didn't.

'OK, people . . . DS Tomlinson is the task allocator, so you need to see her at the back of the room to get your jobs and pairings for the day ahead. This, I feel, may be a long investigation, folks, so it might be worthwhile warning your loved ones that they might not be seeing much of you. Thank you.'

They began to break up, chattering among themselves; there was a palpable sense of excitement. A few nodded at Henry. One or two scowled at him. A couple of the local detectives spoke quietly and earnestly to Diane, asking how she was doing and telling her what a great job she had done.

Finally, she and Henry approached Rik who was having an urgent-looking heads-together with a couple of detectives, which broke up as they closed in.

'You were late,' Rik said to Diane.

'For the right reasons.'

'Which were?'

She explained the early-morning hike up the moors, what they had found.

'Too much of a coincidence not to be connected,' Henry said.

'So the CSI has bagged up the bottle and the tape,' Diane added.

'Good. Good thinking,' Rik said. 'How are you both?'

'We're OK,' Diane said, noticing Rik Dean's eyes playing over the pair of them and the slight frown on his face as he tried to work out why they had been together so early in the morning. She could see it in his eyes, but she let him stew on it. Not his business.

'What are your thoughts?' Rik asked them. His eyes, though, were focused on Henry, the man, who obviously knew everything. Henry noticed this and also the slight tightness of Diane's mouth at the unintentional but ingrained snub.

Henry looked at her and gestured for her to do the talking. It was down to her to take the lead, and Rik would just have to lump it.

'Well, I know the financial investigators will be scrutinizing Jack Carter with renewed vigour, and everything that needs doing regarding his death and the motorist's will be done . . . I hoped Henry and I could just carry on with what we were doing.'

'Which was?'

'I was going to take the photographs of the two dead lads we found in the garage wall at Hawkshead Farm and show them around the travelling community for starters, see if anyone recognizes them.'

'Why?'

'We think they might be travellers too, connected to the ones who murdered John and Isobel York. It's just a hunch as much as anything,' she admitted.

Rik looked doubtful. 'Maybe.'

'We'll also make sure the mugshots are circulated around the country to any traveller liaison officers other police forces might have, and councils,' Diane added.

'I do have another idea, too,' Henry said, 'on that subject.'

He didn't elaborate, kept it enigmatic.

Rik nodded and said, 'OK, whatever. Do what you have to do, but keep DS Tomlinson in the loop, please. I'm going to two post-mortems today – Carter and the motorist.'

'Can you keep us posted if anything of interest comes up?' Henry asked him. He tilted his head towards the allocator's desk where there was a queue of officers being given their jobs. 'Has anything come in from the public, by the way?'

'Lots of stuff; don't know how interesting, though.'

Henry glanced at Diane. One of the things he always did when he ran murder investigations was to make time to at least skim through anything coming in via crime hotlines or comms rooms.

'Fancy a look through them before we do anything else?'

Diane nodded. 'Sure.'

'We can get a brew, too.'

They walked towards the desk, but Rik took Henry's arm and pulled him aside.

'When the fuck are you going to pay us a visit? We've been in the house for four months now and we haven't even had a card from you, Henry. Lisa's spitting feathers. Come for tea one day.'

Lisa was Henry's younger sister, married to Rik.

'I will. Soon,' Henry promised.

They brought their coffee up from the canteen and commandeered an empty desk in the MIR. Henry snaffled the message pad on which all incoming messages were logged, even if they never became 'Actions'.

Henry skimmed through them while Diane found the number for the police liaison officer on the Young Offenders Wing at Lancashire prison, near Leyland, to try to arrange a visit with an inmate that Henry thought it would be worth speaking to.

Following the media releases the day before, including a hastily arranged press briefing, hundreds of messages had flooded in. Mostly, they were innocuous – sightings of suspicious men (one, even, from Wales) and vehicles. The task allocator, an experienced detective with an eye for detail, read and graded them. Likely ones were given immediate action and the others would finally get allocated as and when.

Henry had spent many hours sifting through such pads, and one message caught his eye – one that had not yet been allocated, though it had been read. It was one of those seemingly useless, bland messages that probably had nothing to do with anything, but it made Henry frown.

Even though each message was uniquely numbered, Henry left it in the file, lifted the whole folder and carried it back over to the allocator who had just finished dispatching detectives and others to jobs. Henry knew her – an experienced detective called

June Tomlinson – and had used her on a few murder investigations.

'Hi, boss,' she said automatically.

'First names, June,' he corrected her. 'I'm now a member of the great unwashed.'

They had a very brief 'How's it going?' chat, then Henry, having placed the folder in front of her, asked, 'Anyone been to this one?'

She checked and cross-referenced it to her own pad and computer and said, 'Not as yet.'

'Can you give it to me and Diane?'

'We need to be at the prison at two,' Diane told him as she drove through the city of Lancaster. 'They've got a slot, but they're short-staffed so we can have fifteen minutes tops with our guy.'

'Should be enough,' Henry said, 'to scare him shitless.'

'So, where are we going now?'

'Asda.'

'Well,' the lady said, 'just seemed a bit odd . . . well, normally not perhaps . . . and I'd probably never have thought about it, but when I got home last night, I watched the news and saw the police press conference thingy about that terrible incident in Silverdale . . .'

Henry and Diane listened patiently to Edna Moss, a pleasant, slightly plump, hair-dyed-purple woman of sixty-two. Henry knew this to be totally wrong in the world of today, but if he had been asked to describe the type of woman who worked for Asda, he would have described Edna Moss to a 'T' and would not have felt guilty because she was nice, smiley, interested in people and just the sort of employee a supermarket like Asda relied on to make customers feel valued. And although she was a similar age to Henry, she seemed a generation older somehow. It probably didn't help that, in his own mind, he was still nineteen years old.

She talked over her shoulder as she led them through the Asda store situated on the boundary between Lancaster and Morecambe to the security office on the ground floor, opposite the checkouts.

'I know it said that the guy who got away could have been bleeding from a head wound.'

'Did the man you saw have blood on him?' Diane asked.

'No, no, not at all.'

'So why call us?' Diane asked, but in a non-threatening way.

'Because . . . er, I don't know . . . I just thought about it and it seemed odd.' Edna stopped outside the security room door. 'I've already been in here' – she pointed to the door – 'and I've looked at the CCTV stuff again, and yeah, just odd, somehow. He was really furtive.'

She knocked on the door which was opened by one of the uniformed security guards.

'Bob, we've come to have a look at that bit of footage from the camera again,' Edna said to the guy. 'These are two detectives.'

'Yeah, come in,' Bob said. 'It's still teed up.'

Edna said, 'I hope I haven't wasted your time. I know you're chasing a very dangerous man.'

'You won't have,' Henry assured her. 'It was either come and see you or go to Wales and see a bloke who believes he saw the wanted man on the funicular railway in Llandudno.'

'Ah, based on that, I don't feel too bad.'

The three of them shuffled into the office, which was not vast and, for four people, including the security guard, was a tight squeeze. The guard sat at the desk while Henry, Diane and Edna clustered behind him as he logged on to a desktop computer with the footage ready to play. The top of the screen was stamped with the previous day's date and time – 13:45 hours – which was a few hours after the incidents in Silverdale.

'I was on the self-checkout, you know, where customers scan their own stuff.'

'Yeah,' Henry said.

The screen showed a camera shot from above, which encompassed the whole of the self-checkout area, like a small corral of self-scan tills, two lines of eight with the entrance at the far side and the exit just below the camera.

The shot showed Edna with a woman customer, chatting about something. There were no other customers in the area at that moment.

'She's one of my neighbours,' Edna explained. 'And this is him.'

As the two women chatted, a man entered the area carrying a clump of items in his arms rather than in a basket or trolley. The image was good, well defined and in colour. Henry could easily tell the man was wearing a Puffa-style jacket over grubby overalls with work boots on his feet. He wore a beanie cap pulled right down to his eyebrows.

The goods he held consisted of a pair of jeans, a shirt/T-shirt combination, a pair of trainers, a pack of underwear and a short jacket. He was also cradling a pack of sandwiches, a bottle of coke and a packet of crisps, a bottle of own-brand whisky, two pay-as-you-go phones, plus various items from the medical shelves – a pack of bandages, a box of plasters and a tube of Savlon. He scanned the alcohol first, which, with its security tag, caused the red light on a post by the checkout to flash and alert a member of staff to come, remove the tag and approve the sale.

Henry saw Edna pat her friend and approach the man at the checkout, who seemed to jump out of his skin when she spoke behind him.

'I told him I had to take the tag off,' she explained to Henry and Diane. On screen, she reached past the man and took the whisky from the packing area. 'He looked scared. Like he was underage or something. Which he wasn't.'

Edna took the bottle to the control station and removed the alarm tag while the man scanned the sandwiches, coke and crisps, and then began to deal with the clothing. The shirt combo and jeans still had their hangers on them and he made no effort to remove them.

Edna came back. He stepped aside and allowed her to authorize the whisky on the checkout. She spoke to him.

'I asked him if he was OK. He said yes. I asked him if he wanted the hangers and he said no, so I removed them for him. I also asked if he wanted a carrier bag, but he said he didn't. I backed off then. He was curt with me and his eyes – crikey! Like a hunted animal.'

They watched him scan the medical items and two phones in boxes and then pay by feeding several ten-pound notes into the checkout, then gather up his purchases and scurry out, keeping his head down as he went past the security camera.

'That's it, really,' Edna said almost apologetically. 'Now I look again, maybe it's nothing.'

'I got him getting into his car,' the security guard said. He tapped a couple of keys and the screen changed to a shot at the front of the store which recorded the man leaving hurriedly, then cut to another in the car park which caught him going to a vehicle, getting in it, then driving away.

It was a small, white panel van with the name of a company on the side, but this image was less sharp than the in-store one, and it wasn't possible to make out the name or registration number, though Henry guessed the force's tech department could probably get a result by enhancing the pictures if necessary.

'I dunno . . . it was just like . . . something not right . . . an' I'm not saying that's the man you're after. He didn't have blood on him or anything but he seemed to be really jumpy and I just thought, "Accomplice!" That's what I thought. The man you're after must have needed help, surely.'

Henry almost expected her to fold her arms under her bosom and shake with indignation.

'So he paid by cash, therefore no record of a debit card or anything?' Diane asked.

'No. You think there's anything in it?' Edna asked her.

'Maybe he was buying a new set of clothes for the man we're after,' she speculated.

'And even if he isn't, Edna,' Henry said, 'I can honestly say that you have all the instincts of a good detective.'

'Well . . . funny you should say. Thing is, that guy is only little and I saw the tag on the shirt/T-shirt combo was XXL, so it wasn't for him in a month of Sundays.'

'And the man we're after is a pretty large guy,' Henry confirmed.

The security guard had returned to the in-store clip of the man making the purchase. Diane leaned in closer.

'Just pause it there, please,' she asked him.

He hit the button and caught the exact moment the man at the checkout glanced ever so briefly up at the camera so that the two-thirds of his features which could be seen below the pulled down beanie hat were clear to see.

'What is it?' Henry asked.

Diane's honey-coloured eyes sparkled when she looked sideways at Henry and said, 'I know this guy. We ran an operation about four months ago from Lancaster, not long after I was transferred up here – stolen cars and the like – and he was pulled in and given a good shakedown by us and the Major Crime Unit's stolen vehicle squad. He has a chop shop on White Lund.' Diane paused.

'I know White Lund,' Henry said.

'However, when we searched the place, it was totally clean. He had a few bangers for sale and second-hand car parts, but it was all low-class stuff. The SVS were after big-timers – sports cars and the like. So he walked.'

'Name?'

'Billy Lane. Remember him well – a little rat-faced creep – but there was nothing to pin on him.'

'Worth a visit?' Henry asked. 'Or shall we just leave it?'

'White Lund is only just over there,' Diane said, pointing. They were back in her car, approaching the exit to Asda's car park. 'Only just over the road, really.'

'Be rude not to, then,' Henry agreed.

At the car park exit she turned on to Ovangle Road and headed towards Heysham, then did a right which brought her on to White Lund, a huge and expanding industrial and retail estate with businesses ranging from multinational enterprises and huge car dealers all the way down to scrapyards and backstreet shit holes – places like Billy Lane's.

It was a huge, intricate maze of interconnecting roads and dead ends, but Diane knew her way.

It was also a place Henry knew well from his past history as an SIO. He had dealt with a few murders that had taken place here or had connections.

Diane drove into a dead-end road called Eastgate, then turned left off that into another cul-de-sac and drew up outside a very untidy unit emblazoned with a sign, *Lane Motors*.

Which did not seem to have very much going on.

'Looks shut,' Diane said. 'This is the place we raided, though.'

There were a few ropey cars pulled up outside, but the building itself seemed to be closed for business.

'Spin around and let me out . . . I'll go knock.'

Diane swung the car in an arc and pulled in by the roadside. Henry jumped out and went to the front door, tried the office door – locked – and attempted to heave up the shutter door – also locked. He shaded his eyes and tried to peer through a gap in the drawn blinds into what seemed to be a reception area, but it was in darkness. Hands in pockets, he returned to the car and flopped in.

'No sign of life,' he told her. 'How "suspect" was Lane, if you get my drift? Cold, warm or hot?'

'Hot, hot, hot. From the intel, we were surprised he had nothing on him, so to speak.'

'Does he have other premises?'

'One we don't know about?'

Henry shrugged. 'Maybe. Because if he is that good, perhaps this one is a front, a decoy, the one he'll open up to cops if they come sniffing. Meanwhile, around the back . . .'

Diane considered this possibility. 'He could've duped us. Been done before.'

'What about a home address?'

'Can't remember that; I didn't visit it.'

'Custody record?' Henry suggested. 'In the meantime, let's creep around the area, maybe spot his van.'

Diane called into comms via her PR and asked for a check to be made with the custody office, which, she was informed, was very busy, but they would try to get an answer as soon as the custody officer was free.

They cruised the width and breadth of White Lund as they waited for a response to the query but didn't spot any vehicles that resembled the van they'd seen on the Asda security footage. Even though the actual writing on the side of it, or the van's registration number, had not been legible, Henry was pretty sure he would be able to recognize it again, as was Diane.

'He might just have been buying clothes for his bigger brother,' Diane mused. 'If he has one.'

'He might, but I like the way Edna's mind works. If only for her, I'd like to check out this guy. We could do with more people like her.'

'Yeah, I get it.'

Diane turned slowly into another dead end, drove to the turning circle and back up again at a snail's pace.

Henry scanned each premises on his side, and as they passed a detached unit surrounded by a high fence, the gate firmly closed, he said quickly, 'Pull in here.'

As the wheels stopped turning, he was out and walking towards the gate, which was about ten feet high, about the same height as the fence that surrounded the unit. Both fence and gates were made of a tight mesh with thin steel plates attached to the inside to make them almost impossible to see through, but there were some gaps between the struts, and as they had driven past, Henry had glimpsed some cars in the parking area directly in front of the unit and caught the flash of a badge on the front of a car that he recognized instantly.

The three-pronged trident that was the insignia of the Maserati brand. It was just one of those by-products of more than thirty years as a cop, plus an interest in cars in general, that he could identify most models out there even though the modern, bland, cloned designs sometimes made it harder to distinguish between makes.

But he knew a Maserati badge when he saw one.

He had to get his face right up to the crack where the sliding gates met in the middle, and peer through with one eye.

Definitely a Maserati – but just the body shell of one.

He angled his face to try to see more cars.

A Range Rover and a Mercedes G-Wagon.

And also a white van, though he could not quite make out what was written on its side. However, there was that feeling in his gut: it was the one from the supermarket car park. He looked back at Diane and beckoned to her as she leaned across the centre console of the Merc and mouthed, *What?*

He pointed excitedly. 'It's the van. I'm sure of it.'

'Shit.'

She switched off the engine, got out and jogged over to Henry who directed her to peer through the gap as he had done.

'Yeah, I'll have that,' she said.

Henry was inspecting the gates. They were on rollers and met in the middle, secured by bolts and a thick chain threaded through the framework which was fastened by a hefty padlock on the inside. They were very secure and impossible to pull open with just brute strength.

'What do you think?' Diane asked.

'Well, there's someone in,' he said, 'unless there's access at the rear, because the padlock has been locked from inside. Over to you, Detective.'

'I think it might be worth having some hefty cops behind us this time – just in case. Preferably armed, but otherwise brandishing batons and size elevens. I mean, it's unlikely we're going to stumble on a gunman again, isn't it?'

'Highly unlikely, unless they act on the bus principle. You don't see one, then a whole load come along at once. But, just in case, let's have some backup.'

'I'll park down the road a little way and sort something,' Diane said.

They got back into the Merc and Diane drove fifty yards along the road, spun the car around and pulled up on the opposite side to give them a clear view of the gate while she called it in.

'Interesting connection if the gunman has gone to ground here,' Henry mused.

'Yeah, and it'll all get more and more complicated.'

'Something's happening,' Henry said.

He'd seen some movement behind the gate, the shadow of feet, and then the chain was pulled off like a snake disappearing. The left-hand gate began to slide open, pushed by a man.

'Billy Lane,' Diane said, recognizing him.

He was pushing the gate on its rollers in the opposite direction, then he turned and started to push the other half of the gate open, so that he was now facing Henry and Diane in the Merc. He was dressed in the same clothes as his shopping trip the day before – beanie hat, Puffa jacket over grubby overalls.

Lane was concentrating on putting his shoulder to the gate. It did not move easily on its rollers and took some effort, and his face was mostly turned towards the ground until he had finished. Only then did he look up and around. There was just one second of hesitation as his head rotated, a moment he tried to mask.

Henry knew the significance of the moment. 'He's spotted us but is pretending he hasn't.'

Lane stood in the opening, trying to be casual, lighting up a cigarette, blowing smoke up into the air, pretending to be chilling, kicking the ground with his toe-capped boot, but his eyes kept returning fleetingly to the Mercedes parked down the road. From where he was, Henry guessed he probably couldn't see who was sitting in it, just two figures. Out of place, but maybe not a cop car. Mercedes sports cars rarely appeared in this neck of the woods and nor were they usually cop cars, and these things, Henry knew, were puzzling Lane slightly.

Eventually, he finished his cigarette, stomped on the butt and screwed it into the ground before stretching and yawning and getting one last look at the mysterious Merc, then turning around and disappearing out of view.

On her PR, Diane asked, 'Any ETA for this backup, please? There's some movement.'

Comms replied, 'There's an ARV unit en route from the station, be with you ASAP although the city is snarled up with traffic.'

'Anyone any closer?'

'All tied up. The job at Silverdale has got us stretched, I'm afraid, Diane, but I have a patrol making from Carnforth, probably ten minutes away.'

'Roger that.' She looked at Henry and swore.

'We wait,' he said.

'I don't know, I can't fucking tell, can I?' Lane said to McCabe. 'It's just a car that shouldn't be here, but it doesn't look like a copper's.'

'What sort is it?'

'A Merc, SLK, blue-grey, sporty thing.'

'Two-seater?'

'Yeah, yeah, why?'

McCabe swallowed dryly, remembering fleeing from the scene of Jack Carter's murder and running past such a car on the road outside his victim's house.

'Don't look like a cop car,' Lane reiterated.

McCabe's Browning automatic was on the desk. He'd just disassembled, cleaned and reassembled it, then reloaded the magazine with the spare shells he had been carrying loose.

He picked it up, pointed it at Lane's head and fired.

Lane crumbled and fell on the spot, blood spouting from the horrific wound in his face. McCabe stood over him and fired another round into the already damaged head. Lane had been twitching. The second shot put an end to that.

McCabe grabbed the keys for the Range Rover parked outside and went out to it, but before getting inside he had a second thought, found his ski mask and pulled it over his head.

ELEVEN

Henry had a touch of tinnitus. He'd had it years, an incessant hissing in his left ear, something he'd learned to live with and which didn't greatly affect his actual hearing. He'd even had his ears tested and could hear just fine.

Which is why he heard one dull bang, then, a few seconds later, another.

Diane – whose hearing was still sharp and clear – looked at him.

'Hear that?' he said.

'Shots being fired?'

'Sounds like.'

'Or someone dropping a spanner?'

'Shit.' Henry pointed.

The hooded man walked out through the gates and, his shoulders hunched over, he came towards the Mercedes, speeding up as he got closer. The gun was in his hand at his side. And then it was up – aimed at the two detectives.

Diane found reverse on the automatic gearbox, released the handbrake and almost stood on the accelerator as the car slewed backwards.

The gunman increased his speed.

'We need to go faster,' Henry said, the inflection in his voice rising as the man with the gun stopped, dropped into a firing combat stance – quickly bringing up his left hand to support the gun in his right – and began firing at the Mercedes.

Henry instinctively ducked low.

The windscreen in front of his eyes broke as the first bullet crashed through it and missed him by an inch, imbedding itself in his head rest.

Diane's head was low between her arms as another bullet crashed through the glass.

Then another one came in.

Diane screamed.

Henry looked at her, seeing blood pouring from the side of her head where the fourth bullet creased her temple. She released the steering wheel and swooned, but kept her foot down on the pedal.

Henry grabbed the wheel.

The gunman still approached relentlessly, firing.

Henry knew the magazine could hold fifteen rounds.

But he had lost count of how many had been fired at that point – maybe six, but definitely more to come.

Henry screamed, 'Take your foot off the gas!'

Another bullet pinged off the long bonnet of the sports car, ricocheted between him and Diane. The next hit the rear-view mirror, shattering it.

Henry's desperate instruction got through to Diane and she pulled her foot off the accelerator. Henry dragged the gear stick out of reverse and found drive even though the car was still moving backwards.

'Now put your foot back on!' he shouted again.

Another two bullets.

One of which smacked into Diane's left shoulder, obscenely jerking her back into the seat, the impact tearing into her flesh and joint and splattering hot blood over Henry.

The gunman came on relentlessly, moving in that irresistible stance, powering on, firing.

Henry shrieked, 'Foot! Accelerator!'

Something clicked with Diane – a primal response – and, despite everything, she forced her right foot back down and the car lurched forwards with Henry gripping the wheel and aiming at the gunman who suddenly stopped, realizing what was happening: a fast, heavy, quickly accelerating sports car was bearing down on him.

Henry swerved the car directly at him, but he stood his ground with the gun up, seeming to take aim at Henry who tried to keep his body profile as low as possible.

The gunman fired twice more, but Henry kept hold of the wheel, determined to annihilate him. But just as he thought the gunman would disappear under the front wheels, two things happened simultaneously.

Diane fainted and the gunman leapt aside.

But her foot stayed jammed where it was for a few more

moments as the car sped past him. He pivoted and fired all of his remaining bullets into the side and the back of the Mercedes.

Henry heard each one smash into the car and expected at least one to hit him, but that did not happen.

Another struck Diane in her back. Henry knew this. Saw her jolt violently with its impact.

And now, directly ahead, Henry realized the car was hurtling towards a large rubbish skip on the road side and he couldn't prevent the car from crashing headlong into it, an impact which hurled him head first through the open space where the shattered windscreen had once been, sending him slithering along the bonnet towards the skip.

He could see it coming.

Even in those micro-moments, he knew that colliding with it would at the very least break many bones, at most kill him. With a massive effort brought about by self-preservation, he twisted and spun off the bonnet, hitting the ground and rolling just inches away from the skip, coming to an untidy stop, realizing he was still conscious, still alive, still functioning.

He came up on to one knee, his bad one, knowing he had to power though the pain in that joint, then propelled himself towards the gunman who was sprinting back through the open gates of Billy Lane's industrial unit.

Henry's mind was working fast, assessing the situation. Making judgements which he knew even then would later, in the cold light of day, be shredded by his betters.

Diane had been shot. She needed urgent treatment – that was obvious. She was *the* priority.

But that needed to be balanced by the immediate necessity to neutralize the man with the gun who they had stumbled into once again. If he was not stopped now, he could easily be back with a reloaded gun to finish the mayhem he had started.

So Henry ran, spurred on by his second surge of adrenalin, arms driving him like pistons, but also knowing he was unarmed, unprotected, an easy target. He went through the gate into the yard only to be faced by the black Range Rover he'd seen through the gap in the fence a few minutes earlier.

The gunman was at the wheel, still masked.

The big, heavy car was moving, bearing down on Henry.

Henry stopped in its path as it picked up speed.

He knew he had lost this round and that it was imperative to stay alive. At the very last moment, he threw himself sideways and the car screamed past, and just for a second the gunman looked at him and he looked at the gunman, locked eye to eye, and Henry knew he would never forget those eyes, even though the man was looking at him through slits in the ski mask.

Henry clocked the registration number, logged it in his brain, then ran back to Diane.

There were already four people – all men – grouped around the Mercedes, all looking shocked and nonplussed, having been drawn out of their workplaces on the cul-de-sac by the sound of shooting and cars crashing. One was on his haunches at the open driver's door, looking in at Diane. Two stood back, stunned. The fourth was on his mobile phone.

'You calling an ambulance?' Henry yelled at this fourth man.

'Yeah, yeah.'

'Cops as well!' Henry also shouted.

Henry didn't go directly to Diane but stopped at the boot of the car, having to wrench it open because the impact with the skip must have twisted the chassis and bodywork. He grabbed the first-aid kit and blanket he had seen among all the other stuff Diane kept in there, which Henry had noticed and remarked on the day before, prior to their walking expedition.

He was fiddling to open the kit as he went to Diane and said to the man squatting there, 'Out of the way, but stay behind me to help, yeah?'

'OK, mate.' The man, who was in paint-splattered overalls, stepped aside gladly.

More people were emerging from the surrounding premises.

Diane was slumped over the steering wheel. She was breathing. Blood covered her head and shoulders. The wound in her left shoulder seemed to pump blood steadily rather than gush it out. Henry couldn't see the wound in her back properly, but peering down he could see that blood drenched her clothing and the car seat, and it looked as though the bullet may have entered around the liver area, though Henry could not be certain. What he did know was that it was a serious, life-threatening injury that needed urgent treatment.

'Ambulance coming!' the guy with the phone called out.

Henry gave him a sort of wave of acknowledgement.

'Diane, Diane, can you hear me?' Henry asked her.

He got no response.

He tried to control his own breathing and rising panic, wondering if he should try to move her out on to the blanket. Or would that make things worse? He saw Diane's PR had dropped between her feet, was now just under the two foot pedals. He reached for it and called in.

'Henry Christie to comms on DS Daniels' radio.'

'Go ahead. What's happening, please?'

'DS Daniels has been shot . . . seriously wounded . . .' As he spoke, he handed the first-aid kit to the man he'd moved out of the way. 'Open this,' he said. 'Bandages and dressings, get 'em out.' Into the PR, Henry said, 'Offender – male, wearing a ski mask, believed to be the suspect for yesterday's shooting in Silverdale. He's driving a black Range Rover, registration number . . .' Henry lifted his thumb off the transmit button, his mind suddenly blank. Then he remembered the number and gave it to comms. 'Please confirm ambulance attending and assistance, please,' He paused. 'Diane's been badly wounded,' he concluded briefly.

A flurry of calls then clogged the air as patrols responded and were deployed.

Henry tossed the radio aside and turned his attention back to Diane who was losing copious amounts of blood. Because she was still breathing and did not require CPR, he made the decision not to move her. Instead, he took a large dressing from the terrified man and told him, 'Go get your first-aid kit from where you work, please.'

The man did not reply.

'First-aid kit?' Henry prompted.

'Yeah, yeah.' He legged it to wherever he was employed.

With the dressing laid flat on the palm of his hand, Henry gently moved Diane forward a little and slid his hand down her back, trying to locate the entry point of the bullet, but then realized, as he looked, that there was also an exit wound just below her ribcage.

'Jesus,' he said under his breath.

Diane groaned. 'Gonna need him.'

'Not on my watch, babe,' Henry said determinedly, with a grim expression on his face and tears forming in his eyes. But even as he said these words and continued to speak softly to her, told her help was coming, held the bandages firmly over her wounds, she convulsed, coughed and blood splashed out of her mouth, and Henry knew this was a terrible sign.

TWELVE

Henry sat back and closed his eyes, reliving the past eight hours.

He had climbed into the ambulance to be with Diane on the short journey from White Lund to the A&E department at Royal Lancaster Infirmary. He had stood back, wedging himself into the corner of the vehicle, giving the paramedic space to work feverishly on Diane who was losing blood at an alarming rate. And then came that horrendous moment when her heart stopped, and the haggardly, worried expression on the paramedic's face told Henry that everything, bad as it already was, had just taken a turn for the worse.

Henry watched the young woman – God, she seemed too damn young to be doing this, fighting to save someone's life – reach for the defibrillator and apply it to Diane's chest. Then the wait – only a second or two – to check on the vital signs again: had the pulse of electricity worked or hadn't it?

No.

Henry gasped.

Then the reapplication of the device, the recharge, the shock and the obscene writhe of Diane's body.

Then another agonizing wait.

'It's back!' the paramedic said coolly, but her expression changed to one of relief as she started working on the gunshot wounds again.

Henry wiped his face with the back of his blood-streaked hand and wedged himself tighter into the corner so he would not collapse, because he wasn't certain his legs were strong enough to hold him upright anymore.

'You're going to be all right,' the paramedic said as she worked feverishly. 'Yes, you are. Come on, Diane, let's do this.'

Pulling off White Lund, then heading towards Lancaster, the ambulance almost immediately hit standing traffic.

Henry heard the driver shout obscenities as he began the precarious in-out-in swerving through the tailback into the city, slamming on, veering, forcing oncoming vehicles to brake hard, pull out of his way, and even though he got to the infirmary as quickly as he possibly could, it doubled the journey time, doubled Diane's chances of dying.

A team of nurses and consultants waited to meet the ambulance as it bounced to a halt outside A&E. The rear doors were yanked open, and within seconds Diane was being wheeled through the emergency entrance, straight to the trauma unit.

Henry followed and had to fight his natural instinct to be with her as she was taken in. He knew he would be in the way, would be an unnecessary distraction for the medical staff, so he hung back, let them do their job of saving Diane's life.

He found a bench further down the corridor, sat down and said, 'Fuck.'

The wait began.

'Here.'

Henry looked up. Rik Dean was holding a takeaway coffee for him. 'C'mon, have it. You've been here for a full shift and haven't eaten or drunk anything.'

That was true. Henry could not have kept anything down. He would have vomited, but now he realized he needed some sustenance and, with a dithering hand, he took the offering.

'Americano. Out of a machine.'

'Thank you.'

Even though Henry had not moved from the hospital, he had done everything he could to help the fast-moving investigation – nay, manhunt – that was taking place outside, across the country. Detectives had been to speak to him and he had given his all. A family liaison officer had even been to see him for a chat. Henry had been as polite as he could be with her, then fobbed her off just as politely. Rik Dean had been in and out, but he'd been conflicted by the requirement to be the senior officer on call for

Diane's progress and to run the strategy for catching a killer. Henry had been straight with him and told him to concentrate on the job, and that he, Henry, would remain at the hospital. He had Diane's PR with him, had been given fresh batteries and could listen in to any local developments.

It had been a couple of hours since Rik had shown his face at the hospital.

'Any news, Henry?'

He shook his head. 'Still in surgery . . . six hours now.'

'Jeepers.' Rik sat down next to him. He had a coffee, too. 'The chief constable is aware of the situation and she's asked for regular updates. She'll be out to see how things are here soon, I imagine.'

'Yeah, good,' Henry said without rancour.

'She knows you're here.'

'Yeah, I get it.' He took the lid off the coffee and sipped it. Rik had laced it with sugar, which was not normally how Henry would have taken it (sugarless), but it gave him a little burst of energy and reminded him he hadn't eaten since breakfast. 'Where are we up to, Rik?'

The detective superintendent emitted a deep sigh and shook his head. 'Nothing so far.'

'Hang on – the guy drove away in a fucking big black Range Rover with personalized plates on it, Rik. Cops were converging on the scene. Checkpoints were in place within minutes . . .'

'I know all that . . . but it's not an exact science, is it?' Rik said, clearly feeling the pressure.

'So this guy has murdered at least two people that we know of in the last twenty-four hours – Carter and this guy Billy Lane – and he's possibly also murdered . . .' Henry paused here, made a weak gesture towards the operating theatre, then got a grip. 'Maybe also murdered a police officer.'

'I said I fucking know, Henry.'

'So there's a country-wide search going on for him, for this very fucking obvious car, and he slips through the net . . . how, exactly? Tell me now.'

'Hey, mate, I know you're upset.'

'Upset? I'll tell you something, Rik, I am experiencing anger right now that I haven't experienced in a long, long, long time.' Henry rammed the flat of his left fist against his chest. 'Right fucking here. Fury!' His fingers were tightening into a fist and opening repeatedly. 'And I feel so bloody useless . . . and guilty . . . Jeez.'

'Hey, she's an experienced cop, Henry. You know that. And the fact is you were holding back, waiting for backup and the guy just came at you. You couldn't have known this would happen.'

Henry shook his head despondently, took a sip of the sweet coffee, then uttered a deep groaning noise, like a wounded animal.

'But at least we've managed to salvage some of the guy's clothing with blood on it,' Rik said.

'What do you mean?'

'Looks like there had been a fire in an oil barrel at the back of Lane's unit and some clothing had been burned in it, but we salvaged some which was blood-stained, and we found some rags and tissues with blood on them in a bin in the toilet, so it looks like he was cleaning the head wound you must have caused when you chucked that brick at him yesterday. Going to be DNA for sure.'

'Are you fast-tracking it?'

'Absolutely.'

'When I say "fast-tracking", I don't mean sending it through the "channels",' Henry said, tweaking the first two fingers of his left hand to represent air speech marks. 'I mean physically taking samples to the lab and standing over the scientist while it's analysed – the DNA and the bullets. That's what I mean.'

'That's exactly what will happen. SOCOs are packaging up what we've got so far, and I'm sending two traffic cars, with a detective in each – one to the forensic lab, one to the firearms people in Manchester. They'll be on the road first thing tomorrow and on the lab steps as soon as they open for business.'

'Good.'

Rik's mobile rang. He stood up to take the call and walked away from Henry who heard him say, 'Yeah . . . yeah . . . OK . . . where? When? Right, right . . . and somebody's with her now?'

Henry cocked his head to listen but couldn't quite work out what was being said at the other end of the line, but he did clearly hear Rik Dean say, 'Shit, shit, shit,' as he hung up.

He spun to Henry. 'You're not going to believe this.'

But what Rik was about to say or reveal was cut off as the door to the operating theatre opened and the surgeon Henry knew had been operating on Diane stepped out, removing his gloves and mask.

There were stages in the journey that McCabe seriously thought he would never get through. As he sped away in the Range Rover, he barely expected to get off White Lund before being surrounded by a plethora of armed cops and made to get out, lie flat and be arrested – and probably, definitely, have the shit kicked out of him for shooting a cop.

However, he did make it.

He also made it on to the M6 motorway and began heading south, moving into the outside lane and gunning the big car at around the ninety-five mark, and didn't see a single police motorway patrol.

He made it all the way through Lancashire without mishap and into Cheshire. There he reduced his speed – he knew not to push anything too far – and cut back to about seventy. He began to think that a car swap would be a good thing, which is why he took the chance to come off the motorway on to Sandbach services between junction sixteen and seventeen. He parked up as far away from the café as possible, leaving the Range Rover stuffed between two heavy goods vehicles, then sauntered across the car park to the café, grabbed a brew, sat by the window and waited for his lift to London.

Rik Dean's mouth clamped shut as Henry rose hesitantly from the bench and looked at the weary-faced surgeon.

'Mr Christie? You came to hospital with Miss Daniels, I believe?'

Henry nodded and said a dull, 'Yeah, how is she?'

'Critically ill, I'm afraid.'

'I'm Detective Superintendent Dean,' Rik cut in. 'I'm Miss Daniels' boss.'

'Do we have any close relatives here – next of kin?' the surgeon asked.

'I've been trying to make contact with her brother,' Rik said, 'but he's out of the country. Her father died a few years ago and her mother's in a dementia care home.'

'OK.' The surgeon closed his eyes briefly.

'So we're it, really,' Rik said. 'We're her family at the moment and we'll do everything necessary.'

'Fine, OK . . .' He looked at Henry. 'I'll keep it simple – one bullet entered her back just above her waist on her right side and drove a path through her abdomen and exited close to her navel. On the way through it struck her liver and stomach, causing severe internal bleeding, which has been very difficult to pinpoint . . .'

'But you have done?' Henry interjected.

'I think so . . . Another bullet entered her shoulder and struck her clavicle and acromion, which is a bone attached to the scapula.' He touched his shoulder to indicate exactly where he was talking about. 'Fortunately, this is not that serious a wound. And a third bullet grazed the side of her head – a deep gouge, but it did not penetrate.'

'And the prognosis?' Rik asked.

'She is on life support to assist with her breathing, and although this is one of those corny lines, her life is in the balance – not only from internal bleeding but because of the damage to her organs. She's being closely monitored and cared for, I promise you . . . but she may die. The next few hours are critical.'

'Odds?' Rik asked.

The surgeon took a deep breath. 'Seventy/thirty in favour of death. Tough question, though.'

'Shit,' Henry said. His chest tightened and his eyes filled with tears.

'We'll keep you updated,' the surgeon said. He turned to go back through the double doors into theatre, but paused and turned back to Henry. 'I believe you performed first aid at the scene?'

'Yeah, basic to say the least.'

'Basic was good. If you hadn't done it, she wouldn't be in a position to fight for her life now. Well done.' Then he went through the doors.

'My fault,' Henry said hopelessly, sitting back down. 'My fault.'

'No, it's not, and you know it isn't.'

'She didn't tell me her mum had dementia,' he said, on a different thought track suddenly.

'Why would she? It's not like you're close or anything, is it?'

'No, no, guess not.' He inhaled deeply, exhaled a very long breath. 'So what were you going to tell me?'

* * *

McCabe dawdled at Sandbach service station, watching everyone carefully, trying to pick his target, until things finally came good for him. He was in the café overlooking the car park when he saw a car with one occupant pull off the motorway, meander around the car park, which was quite full, until a space was found on the edge between two vans, a fair way from where he had parked the Range Rover.

There was a youngish woman at the wheel, a professional type. Smart, going places, McCabe guessed. She spent a few minutes parked up in the driver's seat talking on her mobile phone, then she got out and went to the boot of her car.

By twisting his head, McCabe was just able to see her as she raised the boot – and here, he thought, *Boot is good.* From the way she seemed to rise a couple of inches in height, she had replaced her flat-soled driving shoes with high heels. She slammed the boot down and, locking the car with the fob, walked to the café, talking on her phone all the while.

On high heels. Not flats. Maybe mid-twenties, in a knee-length skirt and jacket in grey, with an open-necked blouse underneath.

She was good-looking, well coiffured, with good legs accentuated by the way in which her heels tightened her calf muscles. McCabe liked the look of her. He also liked the fact she was so into herself and her appearance that she could not face the total ignominy of walking from the car to the shops in flat shoes.

Which meant she would have to reverse the procedure when she left.

McCabe's face twitched with a little smile. He pulled down the peak of the baseball cap he'd stolen from Billy Lane's office and looked into his coffee, praying that no cops would roll into the service area and clock the Range Rover.

He kept an eye on the woman.

She visited the loo, then queued for coffee, all the while with her phone glued to her ear, having intense conversations, presumably with business associates. At the counter she ordered a large latte and a panini, which instantly frustrated McCabe who wanted her to leave immediately. The longer she stayed, the more chance he had of being discovered.

To his annoyance – and he almost lost it for a moment – she collected her food and drink and took them to a table and began to pick listlessly at the panini while she talked and now laughed on the phone.

Husband. Boyfriend, maybe.

C'mon, bitch, McCabe urged her. *Eat your food.*

Then – *Fuck!* – he saw a double-crewed police motorway patrol drive on to the services in a liveried Range Rover and start to cruise around the car park.

Moments later they'd spotted the Range Rover, stopped across the front of it; one of the cops got out and approached it warily.

The woman pushed her half-eaten panini away, then, with her coffee in one hand, her phone to her ear in the other, she left.

McCabe rose. He was only feet behind her.

She didn't even notice him. He could hear her wittering about unpaid invoices now. He kept as close to her as he dared, hoping that anyone seeing them would think they were together.

At the Range Rover, way across the other side of the car park, he could see the traffic cops were both out of their car now, calling it in.

McCabe's heart began to pound as he and the woman got closer to her car, at which point McCabe swerved away and went down the side of the van that was parked alongside the car.

He paused.

Needed to time this just right.

He had to move quickly, violently, effectively.

He gave her a few seconds to get round to the back of her car, open the boot . . . then he went for it, pulling the Browning from his belt at his lower back and peeping around the corner of the van. The woman did have the boot lid open, which was good, fitted in with his plans. He heard her say, 'Fuck you,' into the phone, which she tossed into the boot, then bent her left leg up so she could reach her shoe and take it off.

As far as McCabe was concerned, she was perfectly positioned.

One last glance – there was no one in this vicinity to witness this – then he spun out, four strides to cover the distance, and he crashed the barrel of the Browning on to the back of her head, stunning her. Before she could slump to the ground, his hands were under her armpits and he heaved her in one fluid lifting manoeuvre into the boot. He folded her in like a foetus and then, in a fury and for no reason, he crashed the barrel of the Browning on to her head again and again until he was sure she was dead.

He grabbed her keys and phone, then closed the boot and jumped into the car. It fired up first time and he moved off, passing within yards of the two cops who had made one of the discoveries of their careers and who didn't even look in his direction as he tootled past them and re-entered the motorway.

It was a good car, fast and smooth.

Rik Dean said, 'Two motorway cops found the Range Rover on Sandbach services on the M6 in Cheshire. The services were locked down and fifty cops descended on them, but he'd scarpered.'

'On foot?' Henry asked.

Rik shook his head, bit his bottom lip. 'A car was found burned out in north London an hour ago . . . It's taken this long to join the dots.'

'OK, so he stole another.'

'Yeah, but not quite.'

'What does that mean?'

'He did steal another, but kidnapped the owner in the process, stove her head in and shoved her in the boot.'

'And set fire to the car while she was in the boot,' Henry guessed.

Rik nodded. 'It's not yet known whether she was dead before the fire, but we think she was.'

Henry did not say anything. Inside, though, as cold as his rage was, it actually burned him. He rubbed his eyes and paced the corridor, then stopped dead in front of Rik who was handling another phone call.

When he finished, Henry said, 'I want this.'

'Want what?'

'I want this. I want to be able to pick up where Diane and I had got to, I want to follow any leads, and I want someone behind me with a gun and muscle.'

'I can't authorize any of that; you know that,' Rik guffawed.

'Yeah, you can. First of all, swear me back in as a constable so I get all those powers back. I only need to stand in front of a magistrate to do that. Then assign someone to be my running partner.'

'Such as who?'

'Jake Niven. He used to be a firearms officer.'

'But he isn't anymore. He's a rural beat bobby.'

'Get him requalified, reauthorized, give him a Glock and let him run with me.'

'Not possible.'

'Anything's possible . . . give us a plain ARV car with a gun safe. He can keep it in there, doesn't have to carry it in a holster. Confidentially, let every force in the country know what the situation is . . .'

'Henry! Come on, man. Have you heard yourself?'

'I'm hearing myself loud and clear, Rik. Me and Diane, more by bad luck than judgement admittedly, were on the trail of this guy, and it makes sense for me to pick it up and run with it. I've got a feel for this bastard now and I know what I'm doing. I used to be a real detective, remember?'

'There's a whole murder squad on it.'

'Let 'em keep on it. This is a complicated inquiry and there's lots of angles to be coming at it from. If someone else gets lucky, then good. I'm not in competition. I just want a fair crack at catching this guy. What do you say? I promise I'll earn all that money you keep chucking at me.'

Rik Dean swallowed. He actually liked the idea, but knew it flew in the face of process and procedure to have a loose cannon like Henry running around the place with armed backup. It was unlikely to be sanctioned.

'I can only speak to the chief,' he sighed, 'and see what she says. I imagine it'll be a very big no, and if it is, you'll have to live with it.'

'She'll have a soft spot for me,' Henry guessed.

'What the hell does that mean?'

'Just ask her if she remembers me and watch her blush,' Henry said.

'Wow – Mr Legend, eh?'

Henry didn't expand on it. 'I have someone else I want to call, too.'

'For what?'

'Uh, serious, off-the-record backup. The muscle I was talking about.'

'I hope it's not who I think it is,' Rik said with dread.

Henry told him the name and he saw Rik's Adam's apple rise and fall as though he had something as big as a house brick stuck in his gullet.

Diane was transferred from the operating theatre to the critical care unit, and Henry was allowed to see her. He walked into the unit with trepidation, terrified by what he was about to see. His legs turned weak at the sight of her there, heavily sedated, surrounded by monitors and drips, with lines running in and out of her. He edged close to the bed, seeing the ash-grey pallor of her skin, so very poorly looking, so ill, her chest rising and falling, the death rattle in her lungs rasping audibly as she clung to life.

'Diane . . . it's me, Henry.'

He wasn't so naïve as to expect her eyelids to flutter open or fingers to twitch at his voice. All he could do was hope that, at some level, his words would penetrate, mean something to her, even though he doubted that, too.

'Diane, I'm going to get this man and I will bring him to justice, darling. And you know it's not just because he hurt you so badly – although that is a big part of it, admittedly. I'm going to bring him to justice for everything he's done. I promise you.' He kissed the tips of his fingers and brushed them gently against the back of her hand. He looked at her for a few moments longer, having to purse his lips tightly to prevent his face from crumbling, to stop his whole being from falling apart.

Then he became aware of someone behind him.

It was Jake Niven who had witnessed Henry's kiss-touch of Diane's hand.

Jake nodded sagely.

'What are you doing here, Jake?'

'Come to give you a ride home, mate.'

'That's good of you.'

'Come on.'

Jake stood aside and allowed Henry to pass, patting him on the shoulder gently, and both men took one last glance at Diane who had not moved. They left the infirmary and went on to the restricted car park close to the ambulance bay. Jake indicated a car to Henry, a slate-grey BMW 5 Series which looked sleek and fast.

'What's all this?' Henry quizzed Jake. 'Where's the Land

Rover?' Henry was referring to the battered old vehicle Jake had been allocated for his rural beat duties.

'Second question first – the Land Rover's at headquarters garage; first question – this is a top-of-the-range BMW fast-twat that, somehow, Rik Dean has managed to snaffle from the firearms operations department.'

'Um, right, why?' Henry was still flummoxed.

'Because Mr Dean has pulled me from my normal duties for a few days and told me I am working with you.'

'Has he now?'

'And this car has a hidden gun safe in the boot.'

'Empty, I presume?

'At the moment, but first thing tomorrow – actually, later this morning now,' Jake said, checking his watch, 'I will be requalifying for my handgun ticket at the HQ firearms range, and if I pass, I'll be having a Glock personally issued to me, after which you're going to brief me as to what the actual fuck is going on!'

'Wow, babe, that is so deep, it's making me queasy.'

Marcie Quant looked with distaste at the wound in McCabe's scalp. She had bravely removed the dressing that Lane had applied and was almost sick at the sight of the open cut, but she carried on dabbing it with a face cloth as though it might bite her.

'Yeah, well, a fucking rock hit me, didn't it?'

McCabe was in the bath, immersed in hot water and surrounded by bubbles, allowing the stress of the last couple of days to evaporate. He had met Marcie on a council estate in north London, having used the phone belonging to the woman he'd kidnapped in order to arrange the tryst, then he'd jettisoned the device on the M1. He had driven on to some spare land after calling into a petrol station he knew, where, if necessary, they would happily delete any of their CCTV footage for him for a backhander. He'd filled a petrol container, driven on to the spare land and doused the car, not remotely bothered by the kicking and banging from his captive in the boot; he thought he'd killed her, but obviously not. He flicked a match to the petrol, stood back and watched the flames whoosh up and engulf the vehicle and the woman in it.

Marcie had been waiting for him on the nearby estate.

'It needs stitching up properly,' she told him, her face a picture of revulsion. She was kneeling by the bath as she tended him.

He had given her sparse details of his escapades in the north but didn't feel inclined to say much because he was tired and stressed and just wanted to relax, chill, eat a curry, drink some beer.

'I know. We'll get Doctor Grey out. Just you bandage it up for the moment.'

'OK.'

Marcie sat back on her heels as McCabe slithered down into the water with a sigh.

'Missed you,' she said.

'Same here, babe.'

Marcie leaned forwards again. Her right hand caressed his chest, then began to inch down across his body and her fingers gently encircled his cock which was erect in anticipation. Her hand began to move slowly, speeding up with the frequency of his gasps of pleasure, then pure ecstasy.

Jake dropped Henry off at The Tawny Owl. The place had closed for the night, so Henry had to let himself in through the locked front door with his key, entering the bar area which had already been cleaned immaculately by Ginny and the staff; when the cogs began rolling in the morning, there would be nothing to clear up.

Henry went through to the owner's accommodation where he found Ginny and her boyfriend, Fred, in the lounge, feet up, eating a curry and drinking lager.

'I'm back,' Henry said brightly. 'Just gonna open the bar and grab a double.'

Ginny leapt up and shot to him, embracing him. 'Are you all right, love?'

'I'm OK,' he assured her.

'How is . . .?' Henry had kept Ginny up to date with developments.

'Not good but being well-cared-for.'

'Have you eaten?'

'Not since breakfast.'

'Let me sort some of this curry out for you – it's good. Rice and some naan.'

'That'd be good . . . I'll get that Scotch, then I'm just going to sit in one of the bays,' he said, meaning one of the windows in the main bar. 'Just grabbing a shower first.'

He did – hot and long – purposely keeping his mind blank, just revelling in the hot jets beating into his tightly wound shoulder muscles. Then he changed into a T-shirt and jogging bottoms before going into the bar, helping himself to the whisky with a little water, before wandering over to the window and sitting at one of the bar tables to gaze at the view across the village green.

He sipped the whisky, but knew this was the only one he would be having. He wanted to be able to turn out immediately if there was any news from the hospital. He also wanted to be ready to go in the morning.

Ginny appeared with a bowl of curry as promised, which she placed on the table.

'Do you need to talk?' she asked him.

'No, I'm fine, sweetheart. It all just got a bit hectic, and me and Diane just stumbled across something that went very bad, very quickly.'

'How is she – really?'

Henry's mouth became very tight, his eyes moistened, and he had to bite his bottom lip again to stop it from quivering. He admitted, 'I don't know . . . just that she's very poorly.'

Ginny leaned over and hugged him.

'Maude's been asking for you,' she said as she stood up.

'Bugger.'

'She's nice, Henry. Genuine, too.'

'I know what you're saying.'

Ginny nodded. 'Bed for me. Up early, as you know. We've got eight in overnight and we'll be almost full tomorrow night,' she said, referring to staying guests.

'Can you manage?'

'Got it covered. Goodnight.'

She held out her hand and Henry squeezed it, then she was off.

Henry looked at the steaming curry, knowing he was famished but not really wanting to eat. However, after the first forkful he scoffed it quickly and dipped broken-up chunks of naan into the sauce, and was glad he had.

Then he sat back, feet up on the bench seat under the window, and looked out, sipping the whisky, mulling over his plans for the day ahead.

Although Rik had been able to OK Jake Niven's reauthorization as a firearms officer and his temporary transfer to assist Henry, Henry knew it was unlikely he would be able to convince the chief constable to give the nod for Henry to take the attestation to become a constable again. That was really Henry just throwing it out there in the heat of the moment, but he wasn't too concerned.

If he had Jake at his side, he had all the powers he would need. Plus a gun.

Also, if Henry's other idea came to fruition, he would also have someone else alongside – or hidden in the shadows – who did not need the encumbrance of anything enshrined in law.

But the important thing, above all, was for Henry to decide how to push the investigation forward and get results quickly.

He believed that the best plan would be to keep to what he and Diane had decided to do before running into the gunman at Lane's establishment.

Starting with a prison visit.

He sipped the whisky.

In the shadows of the woods across the stream, Henry saw movement. He dropped his feet to the floor and rocked forward to peer.

Definitely something moving. Something big.

His guts tightened with anticipation. He kept watching and then his lips twisted into a grin as Horace, the huge red deer stag, emerged, leapt across the shallow stream, mounting the bank and moving into a circle of light cast by a lamppost on the edge of the green.

'Bloody hell,' Henry said.

Horace seemed to be basking under the glow as though it was a spotlight, tensing his huge, rippling flank muscles like a self-obsessed bodybuilder.

Suddenly, the magnificent animal's head swivelled as a vehicle came down the hill towards the village. Turning on a sixpence, he spun and leapt back over the stream and disappeared into the trees.

Henry felt deflated and annoyed by the car, which he watched skirt its way around the perimeter of the green and drive on to the car park at the front of Th'Owl.

A man got out. Tall, broad-shouldered, probably good-looking. He stood and surveyed the pub, finding his mobile phone in his pocket and making a call.

Henry's phone rang moments later.

'Henry,' came the familiar voice. 'Steve Flynn.'

THIRTEEN

'This is still not a good situation,' Marcie said. In the nursery, Arthur was screaming his lungs out, but there were two closed doors between him and her, so the noise was muted but still annoying. She and McCabe had completed their third very satisfactory fuck since he'd returned home, managed to get some sleep between each bout and now, the morning after, Marcie was reflecting on everything. She had taken charge of the sex and, following an outrageous climax, had slid sweatily off McCabe, lit a cigarette and pondered. McCabe, still exhausted from his killing spree in the north, had immediately dozed.

'What?' he said groggily.

'Not a good situation. This.'

'Whatever.'

'OK, I mean you've done great up there. The Yorks are dead . . .'

'Which I didn't do.'

'OK, right, I get that . . . some fuckin' gyppos did it and saved us a job, but then you've taken care of Jack Carter and snuffed out any link to us. Now we have to convince Dunster Cosmo that all his money has gone to that great investment house in the sky and, hopefully, if I plead innocent, he might back off from us . . . I say "might", which is why this is still not a good situation . . . plus you had to shoot a cop, so we need to lie extra low for a long time until that shit fizzles out. Maybe scoot abroad?'

'It was something I had to do,' McCabe complained.

'I know, I know – you did good. We just have to hope they don't come knocking,' Marcie said. 'But as for Cosmo . . . he's going to take some real convincing. I'm more worried about him than the cops.'

'I know what you mean, babe.' McCabe closed his eyes and instantly fell asleep again.

When he next woke up properly, he was tied to a chair, his ankles taped to the legs, his arms bound behind him.

His head drooped, his chin on his upper chest.

His eyelids flickered and he knew both his eyes were swollen. His face hurt, zinging with agonizing pain, and something dribbled out of his mouth. Blood, saliva.

He groaned and heard another groan next to him – and sobbing.

He tried to look sideways, but his eyelids wouldn't open fully and what he could see was just unfocused blur. He knew instinctively that there was someone alongside him in the same predicament and that someone was Marcie.

But before he could recover his senses, he was drenched by a powerful, freezing wall of water, hitting him with such brutal force in the centre of his chest that he was thrown bodily, chair included, and hurled backwards on to a floor of cold, hard concrete where the jet spun him round and round until it finally subsided and he was lying on his side, desperately gagging as he tried to breathe again.

It could never be said that Henry Christie and Steve Flynn had an easy relationship.

Their animosity dated back many years to when Henry was a DCI and had been asked to investigate Flynn, then a DS on the Drugs Branch, who, with others, was suspected of stealing a huge amount of money from a drug dealer following a police raid.

Henry had been unable to prove any wrongdoing on Flynn's part, but there was a big whiff of suspicion over his head, and Henry had made Flynn's life so uncomfortable that Flynn left the police under that cloud. Other things going on in Flynn's life also added to his decision to skulk out of the force and head south to Gran Canaria where he eked out a fairly meagre existence as skipper of a sportfishing boat.

In the intervening years, Henry and Flynn, through various circumstances, had come into contact with each other a few times and eventually arrived at a mutual understanding, especially when Flynn proved his innocence to Henry, who had begrudgingly accepted it. They had become friends of sorts, or maybe just a couple of guys who tolerated each other.

The thing about Flynn from Henry's point of view was that he was big and tough, relatively intelligent, and someone Henry would be happy to have behind him if he ever needed any muscle. Flynn was no youngster, but years of hauling in fighting sailfish from the Atlantic Ocean had kept him incredibly fit, and that was why Henry had speculatively given him a call, expecting nothing.

Flynn, though, was intrigued, if deeply suspicious.

Henry said, 'Didn't expect to see you.'

Flynn shrugged. 'I was passing through on family business. Up here to see my son.'

Henry nodded. Through the retired cop grapevine, he knew Flynn had become embroiled with some shenanigans involving Albanian gangsters, but he didn't know how that scenario had ended. Presumably because Flynn was here, all was good.

'Heard you got caught up with some shite,' Henry said.

Flynn shrugged again. He wasn't the verbose sort. 'So why ring me, Henry?'

'Because I'm caught up in some shite, too, and I need someone to watch my back, someone who can operate off the radar a bit and – uh, how can I put this? – someone unencumbered by the legalities of a situation.'

Flynn blinked. 'You lost me at unencumbered.'

'OK, in simple terms: protect me if necessary. There's something I want to do, and do it quickly, and I think it might ruffle the feathers of a bunch of people who are also unencumbered by legalities.'

'A bodyguard?'

'In a way.'

'What's in it for me?'

'The pursuit of truth and justice?' Henry said loftily. Seeing the cynical look on Flynn's face, he added, 'And two fifty a day, maybe some expenses, free board and lodgings here . . . although there won't be any Alison for you to lust after.'

Flynn said, 'I heard about that. I'm sorry.'

It was Henry's turn to shrug. 'So what do you say?' Henry had thrown the £250-a-day figure at him because he himself would be drawing £1,000 a day. He'd have to pay income tax on that, but

Flynn could hide his take from it tax-free. Henry didn't care. Henry said, 'I'll guarantee you seven days' minimum, even if what I'm doing doesn't last that long. Cash in hand.'

Flynn nodded. For him it would be handy money as his fishing business brought surges of cash, followed by many fallow months. If nothing else, £1,750 would buy him food for a few months.

'So what's going on?'

McCabe shivered, the cold biting; he could hardly breathe, his teeth were literally chattering like cogs in an old gearbox. He was completely naked now, the chair back upright, his hands and ankles still bound. Alongside him was Marcie, her head drooping. Like McCabe, she was naked, but she had not yet had the cold water treatment; even so, she shook with cold.

McCabe raised his head slowly and squinted through the slits that his swollen eyelids allowed him.

He saw shadowy figures standing in front of him, although he couldn't quite work out how far away they were from him. They were unfocused, blurred, maybe eight feet apart.

Another figure joined them, stood between them, then walked right up to McCabe.

McCabe raised his face higher and knew he was looking at Dunster Cosmo, who said, 'I think it's time we three had a discussion.'

The first figures to appear from the gloom that morning were a vicar standing behind a terrified-looking woman carrying a shopping bag. But there was no weapon in evidence.

So although Jake Niven swung the Glock towards them, he did not shoot the vicar or the woman.

The figures clattered away out of sight.

Still holding his breath, Jake took a few tentative steps forward.

A man holding a shotgun stepped into view, the double barrels aimed at Jake's body mass.

Jake double-tapped him – bang-bang – two shots, quick succession, so fast they sounded almost like one. Both hit the gunman's chest, shredding his heart and lungs. He would have been dead if he'd been real.

The figure flicked out of sight.

Jake felt the dribble of sweat from his hairline, dared to take a breath, then moved on a few more feet, dropping into the cover provided by a low wall just as two more gunmen appeared from either side, weapons brandished. Jake took one of them out dead-centre chest – great shooting and another double tap – but only managed to put one bullet into the other, in the middle of the head. Show-off shooting.

Jake calculated: five shots gone, eight remaining.

He rose to his feet, adopting the combat stance, and moved on slowly, knowing he was required to make progress. He angled across the ground, his gun sweeping sideways, back and forth, expecting many problems. The next figure to appear was a kid with a baseball bat resting on his shoulder. Jake sighted on him instantly; his brain computed what he was seeing. It might look like a shotgun, but it wasn't and that was his decision to make. So, no threat.

He swivelled away as another kid came in from the opposite direction, and in that split second Jake had to make another life-and-death decision because this 'kid' was carrying a gun and it was pointed at him.

Jake screamed a warning. Loud. Clear. Unambiguous. 'Armed police! Drop your weapon or I will shoot you.'

Still he came.

Jake shot him – another double tap, centre body mass. Classic shooting. You didn't aim to kill, you aimed to stop. The killing was incidental.

Six bullets remaining.

And then, moments later, having made a further series of instant life-and-death decisions, Jake's Glock was empty and he stopped, raised the weapon and shouted, 'Empty.' He released the magazine into his left hand and held both gun and mag up high.

It was over.

Henry Christie removed the ear defenders, as did Rik Dean. They looked at each other, nodding their heads in admiration, having just watched Jake Niven's firearms requalification shoot from the back of the firing range.

'He can still cut the mustard,' Rik said.

'Certainly can.'

Having finished the shoot, Jake had been debriefed at the far end of the range by a trainer who, on the face of it, had given him quite a bit of grief initially, but finished by patting him on the shoulder and shaking his hand.

'He still uses shotguns a lot,' Henry told Rik. 'He's a member of the local rough shooting club in Kendleton and spends a lot of time with gamekeepers.' Henry knew it had been a while since Jake had been an authorized firearms officer – that had come to an end when he became the Kendleton bobby – but he'd jumped at the opportunity to requalify on the Glock when Rik had approached him about the job Henry wanted him to do. Jake's wife, Anna, had been less than enthusiastic but had accepted it.

Rik asked, 'Anything come of that other name you mentioned?'

Henry knew he was probing about Flynn, but he decided to be a bit cagey. He wanted Flynn in the background, knowing his presence was one of those last-resort things. 'I left him a message but he's not got back to me yet.'

'Just as well,' said Rik, searching Henry's eyes for the lie, then turning towards the firing range where Jake and the firearms trainer were on their way back up from the sharp end.

'Score?' Henry asked.

'Ninety-eight,' Jake said, wincing.

To requalify on any shoot, the lowest score allowed was a very stringent ninety-four per cent. Ninety-eight per cent meant Jake had dropped one shot, but his score, while still a very good 'pass', annoyed him; when he'd been an AFO, his requalification scores had always been a hundred per cent.

'That's good,' Henry congratulated him.

'I'd like one more run,' Jake requested of the trainer, then looked at Rik Dean. 'Still feeling rusty, boss.'

'Fine by me, but you'd better make it quick. Henry wants to be on the road as soon as. He needs to be at Lancashire prison soon.' Rik glanced at Henry. 'Your rearranged appointment.'

'I'll be quick,' Jake promised.

Dunster Cosmo's 'about time' in reference to his discussion with Marcie and McCabe didn't happen until several hours later.

Instead of having an immediate chat, he decided to let the couple stew – or chill – for even longer on the chairs in the middle floor of one of the numerous small industrial units he rented around London. This one was in Neasden in north London and was destined to be used as a holding pen for the human beings he helped other criminal gangs to traffic into the UK.

Today it was not in use. All there was today were two people bound and gagged in chairs, two armed men standing a few feet behind them with masks pulled down over their faces, and in the office in one corner of the unit, a cold, hungry baby boy crying.

Cosmo entered the unit by way of a staff door and walked diagonally across to Marcie and McCabe, stood in front of them, hands clasped in front of him like a priest.

'Now then, where do we go from here?' he asked.

Wearily Marcie raised her chin. 'I need my baby, Dunster,' she pleaded.

'Mmm, not sure about that.'

'Why? Why? What's he ever done to you?'

'It's not what *he's* done to me, Marcie; it's what *you've* done to me.'

Her head drooped and she started to sob. 'I didn't know they were ripping us all off,' she bawled. 'I woulda sorted it, but the gyppos killed 'em before I could speak to 'em.'

'Mmm, gyppos,' Cosmo murmured with contempt, his mind wandering into another subject which filled him with anger. 'They'll be getting their dues. Anyway, that's a whole different ball game.'

McCabe had looked up. 'Let her get to the baby, Dunster.'

Cosmo leaned in. 'You honestly think I give a flying fuck about that baby, that I won't just bury it when I bury you two?'

'You can't mean it,' Marcie cried.

Cosmo pivoted and directed his ire back to Marcie. 'Ten million quid says I mean every single fucking word.' He paused, stood upright, clasped his palms in front of his face as though he was about to pray. 'So, who's going to speak first?'

'See, I'm not all bad,' Cosmo said.

He looked paternally down on Marcie, who was still naked but covered by a grimy old blanket over her shoulders and now had tiny Arthur clasped to her bosom, having fed him, calmed him and warmed him up. She was no longer shivering, although she was still cold. She had been released from her bonds, but McCabe had not. He was still naked and tied to the chair.

Dunster had ordered his two men to drag McCabe on his chair across into the office in the corner of the industrial unit, then do the same to Marcie but to cut her ties, give her a blanket and return Arthur to her.

The two heavies then lounged at the back of the office.

Marcie and McCabe were sitting on one side of an old, tea-stained table and Cosmo was sitting on the other side.

'No, you're not,' Marcie agreed.

Cosmo smiled. 'Right, glad you agree. Now, about my money.' He kept smiling. 'The thing is, Marcie, I gave Brendan – your dearly departed husband – a great deal of my money to invest and I continued to do this well after his death, except I gave that money to you. You then invested this money with John York, a name I'd never heard Brendan mention, incidentally, and you told me this John York was the person Brendan had been investing through all the time and you would continue to do so. But the sad thing is that John and his wife came to a particularly sticky end – which is a whole other story – but just because they are dead doesn't mean to say I still don't want my money, because I do. And since their unfortunate deaths, all you seem to be doing is stonewalling me, making excuses, fobbing me off, and now I've begun to suspect that – maybe – there is something you're not telling me. So . . .' Cosmo leaned on the table. 'I want every single penny that Brendan and then you invested in cash, underneath my bed. I don't want it in some fancy, foreign, offshore bank. I want every penny back under my mattress, so that when I'm fucking my girlfriend, I'll get extra hard when I'm ramming my cock home, thinking about all that lovely dosh underneath her arse. So, the fact that John York is dead shouldn't alter a thing. You know where the money went; I want you to get it back.'

As he spoke, his eyes were focused on Marcie's tits but she couldn't even be bothered to cover up. Finally, he looked up and smiled at Marcie and McCabe. 'The alternative to not giving me my money is pretty appalling, I can tell you.'

It was a relatively short drive from headquarters to Lancashire prison near Leyland and through the gates of the separate annexe that was the Young Offenders Wing in which young men under the age of twenty-one were kept segregated from the mainstream prison population next door.

The young man Henry had arranged to see that morning was called Jamie Costain. He was a member of the well-known Costain family who dominated the criminal skyline in Blackpool but was now on remand awaiting his Crown Court trial on a charge of accessory to murder. His co-accused, Tommy Costain, one of his cousins, had been charged with the actual murder of a drug dealer in Lancaster (and other very serious matters all connected in some way to the double murder of the Yorks), but Jamie, now sitting stone-faced in an interview room, was on the periphery of all this and had just been acting as a lookout for Tommy as he kicked his victim to death in an alleyway.

While investigating the murder of the Yorks and other brutal crimes (including the shooting of their dog) which had resulted in Henry arresting Tommy Costain and others, he and Diane had accidentally encountered Jamie, and Henry had ruthlessly coerced the lad into speaking off the record about Tommy; in so doing, Jamie had inadvertently put himself in the frame for the accessory charge.

Jamie's face contorted with contempt when the interview room door opened and Henry entered alone.

'I am not speaking to you,' he said instantly. 'You're a twat.'

Henry sat down across the table from him. 'Thanks for that.'

'I should never o' spoken to you in t' first place.'

'I'm told you've made no admissions of guilt,' Henry said, 'so it's not as though you dropped Tommy in it, did you?'

Actually, Jamie had provided Henry with information about Tommy's location by pointing it out on a map, although Tommy did not know this.

Jamie's face twitched.

Henry knew that if Tommy – who was essentially second-in-command of the Costain crime clan – knew this, then Jamie's time on planet Earth would be very limited. Tommy was being held on remand in the adult section of this prison, as was Conrad Costain, the old man who was the godfather of the clan, but Henry was sure that Tommy had enough clout to be able to get someone on this side of the wall to stick a blade into Jamie.

Jamie fidgeted. 'Even you coming to visit me here . . . If Tommy gets wind, then I'm goosed. And anyway, fuck d'you want?'

'He won't find out, promise you,' Henry said. 'And even if he did, I've come here to help you – and him – sort of.'

'I very much doubt that.'

Henry placed the file he'd brought with him on the table.

'I said I wasn't talking to you.'

Henry winked at him. 'As we both know, and although I know you had nothing to do with it, those two people on the farm, John and Isobel York, were butchered by two travellers called Roche and O'Hara. Two killers, two assassins, brought in by Tommy Costain to give one or more London gangs a bloody nose for not allowing the Costains into some county-line operations running out of the capital . . . that is more or less what you told me last time we spoke.'

Jamie's eyes remained blank.

'But you never told me who ran the London gang or gangs, and that's what I'm here to find out, Jamie. I want names.'

Jamie suddenly leaned forward. 'I don't know who they are.'

'OK, that's fine. I'm not saying you do.'

'So why are you here? Putting me in danger of gettin' a shiv between me ribs.'

Henry continued, 'You'll probably have heard that a lot of cash was recovered from the farm – and I mean a lot.'

'Yuh – millions.'

'Yuh,' Henry mimicked him. 'And firearms and ammo – and two dead bodies. Two young guys, shot in the head.'

'I didn't do it. Didn't even keep nix,' Jamie joked. 'You i'nt gonna pin that one on me.'

'I know. I thought about trying,' Henry teased him, keeping a straight face.

The smirk on Jamie's face vanished very quickly. 'So what you doing here? I get it you're investigating the money and the dead guys, but other than what I've told you, I know eff-all. I'm just a gofer.'

'Yes, but you see things, Jamie. Hear things, take things in. People think you're unimportant, but I don't. You're a valuable guy.' Henry slid his fingers into the file. 'I want you to look at these photographs and also the mock-up pictures of the two men we found murdered at the Yorks' farmhouse. The photos are pretty gruesome, Jamie, and the mock-ups are what the police think the dead men may have actually looked like before they got their faces blown off. Can you do that for me? That's all I'm asking – do you know these men, or not?'

'Why would I?'

'Just look, eh?'

Henry slid out the four sheets, spun them around and pushed them towards Jamie who, at first, would not even glance at them. Henry kept his own eyes on Jamie because he knew that if the lad did look and did recognize them but claimed he didn't, it would leak through his facial and body language. If he didn't recognize them, it would also be obvious.

Studiously, Jamie kept his eyes firmly on the ceiling.

'Just look, Jamie.'

He scowled at Henry, then reluctantly did as asked and his eyes immediately told Henry he knew the two men. There was the moment of realization, the flaring of the nostrils, the denial from the nervous shake of his head.

Henry said, 'Who are they?'

'No idea.'

'Wrong answer.'

Jamie sighed through his nostrils, then relented. 'I don't know – but I have seen them, OK?'

'Names.'

He shook his head. 'I seen 'em talking to Tommy and Conrad once.'

'So these two guys were talking to Tommy and Conrad?'

Jamie nodded.

'What about?'

'Di'nt hear.'

'Guess what about.'

Jamie shrugged. 'I'd guess summat to do wi' the county lines kickback from London, but that's all I know.'

'So they're gypsies?'

'Travellers.'

'From where?'

'Peterborough, I'd guess, but I don't know for certain – and I'm only saying that because Roche and O'Hara were from there. That's my guess.'

'You saw these two talking to Tommy and Conrad?' Henry wanted to confirm.

'Like I said.'

'What did these guys do? Y'know, what was their job?'

'Muscle.'

Henry frowned, trying to work this out. Two travellers from Peterborough are brought in to murder John and Isobel in some kind of retaliation for the Costains not being allowed to have a percentage of a county lines drug-running operation organized by one or more London gangs. Then another two, as yet unidentified, young men, who would seem to be from the travelling community, end up in a wall space at the farm.

Coincidence, Henry thought. He liked coincidences because to him they meant clues.

The world of John and Isobel York was really not a good place, Henry also thought. In so many ways it seemed they had bitten off more than they could chew. They just didn't run for cover early enough.

'Is that it?' Jamie asked.

Henry nodded. 'For now.'

'No – forever. I won't be talking to you again. You're going to get me knifed.'

Dunster Cosmo stood behind McCabe and pushed a .38 revolver into the back of his neck. McCabe could feel the 'O' of the muzzle.

Cosmo's two men had dragged Marcie and Arthur to one side of the room and they stood either side of her and the baby all watching the brutal scene unfold in front of them.

Cosmo said, 'This is what I mean by appalling,' as he screwed the barrel into McCabe's skin, angling it up slightly. 'A bullet going in here and then exiting via your face . . . and just in case you're wondering, yes, they are soft-tipped rounds so they will remove most of your face.' He leaned in close to McCabe's ear. 'Now, you've been a good boy for me, Darren, put a lot of people in the ground for me on a freelance basis, but that doesn't mean you can't take one for the team, does it?' He tapped the muzzle hard against McCabe's temple, then stood back, rolled his shoulders, set himself. He curled his forefinger around the trigger. It was a double-action revolver, and as the hammer began to roll back, the cylinder started to rotate.

'I can get your money for you!' Marcie screamed.

Cosmo relaxed, smiled and stood upright. 'I knew you'd see sense.'

'Any joy?' Jake asked Henry as he climbed into the car. Jake had been waiting in the prison car park while Henry was inside talking to Costain.

'Meh!' Henry responded. 'No names, but he remembers seeing the two men with the high-ranking Costains, Tommy and Conrad.'

'Is it worth speaking with either or both of them two?'

'They're not the most chatty people where I'm concerned.' Henry had a long, antagonistic relationship with the Costains. 'Could be worth a try, but I'll have to arrange to speak to them through the prison liaison officer anyway.'

He strapped himself in just as his mobile phone rang.

It was Rik Dean. 'Henry, where are you?'

'Just about to leave the prison.'

'Don't! You need to get back. There's been a stabbing.'

FOURTEEN

'I need a week. Give me a week,' Marcie begged.

'Five days,' Cosmo said.

'Seven . . . come on, man, seven. Please.'

'Six.' He relented.

They were still in the office within the industrial unit. McCabe had been released, his clothes flung at him. He had dressed hurriedly, still shivering, furious with Cosmo, his eyes blazing at the older gangster. Cosmo caught the look and went up to him, grabbed his face between finger and thumb, squeezing his cheeks hard.

'Don't get any dumb ideas about what you want to do to me, son. I see it in your eyes. I see the hatred, the humiliation, but I also see that you're alive and well and don't have a bullet in your head, so just remember that.' He cocked his head towards Marcie who was scrambling into her clothes. 'If she comes good, you'll both be breathing, and that pug-ugly kid of yours might live to have parents.' He flicked McCabe's head away and pointed at him. 'Do not try anything.'

'We won't,' Marcie called, hitching her jeans over her hips.

Henry and Jake ran to the security gate, Henry thinking, *Shit, I've just got someone stabbed.*

'There's been a stabbing,' Henry told the prison officer at the reception, the same one who had allowed him in earlier. 'I've been asked to return.'

The officer said, 'Yeah, but you're in the wrong place – you need to be on the adult side, there's nothing happened on this wing.'

'Really? I thought . . .' Henry's assumption had been that the incident was connected with his visit to Jamie Costain who, he'd thought, must have been set upon as soon as he'd returned to the bowels of the YOW.

'But we can take you through, if you like.'

'Have you any details?'

'Not as yet.'

Henry became slightly deflated. He had no desire to be sidetracked, but felt that even though he was no longer a cop as such, he had some responsibility to cover and protect the scene until the actual investigating officers landed and took over.

He and Jake were led quickly through the interconnecting corridors until they were finally allowed into the last secure chamber, which reminded Henry of passing through an airlock into a spaceship in a science fiction film. No prisoners were ever allowed through it, either way, for any reason.

They were handed over to a pair of tough-looking prison officers – a man and a woman of equal dimensions – who led them through further corridors, up on to landings, past locked cell doors and into a short section of corridor leading to a shower and toilet area.

Henry guessed that whatever had happened had taken place in the showers. It was a bit of a cliché, but the truth was that many assaults in prisons did take place in such areas where inmates were often at their most vulnerable and unprotected; more often than not because of well-meaning but misguided privacy laws, there was a lack of security cameras and direct supervision.

The corridor had been cordoned off at either end.

A prison officer stood guard at each end, too. There was a hubbub of activity and stressed-out faces on the staff, but particularly on a woman in a smart trouser suit who Henry knew was the prison governess. She looked likely to explode at any moment. Her eyes lit on Henry and Jake; although she had met Henry when he'd been a cop, she showed no sign of recognizing him, but she did nail them as police.

'Officers, so glad you could make it so quickly.'

'We were on site,' Henry said.

'And you are?'

'Henry Christie.' He didn't bother to go into the intricacies of how he wasn't in the police anymore.

'Jake Niven.' He didn't reveal he wasn't a detective, although he was in plain clothes.

Henry had glimpsed the body of a naked man between other people's legs. He also saw blood. 'What's happened?' he asked the woman. He hadn't been able to recall her name, and she hadn't introduced herself either, but her ID lanyard swinging around her neck reminded him that her name was Daphne Crossjack.

'A stabbing. I'm afraid he's dead – confirmed by our in-house medics. A blade from behind, in the ribcage underneath the arm; stabbed many, many times. He'd bled out before any of our staff even found him, which could only have been a matter of a few minutes.'

'Has the offender been detained or identified?' Henry asked, already dreading the answer.

Crossjack shook her head. 'This has always been one of the weak points in the prison. It's usually well supervised,' she added, then looked as though she would like to eat her own words.

Henry picked up on that. 'I sort of wish you hadn't said that.'

'I'm sure it was just an accidental oversight,' she said defensively.

'Or a deliberate one,' he countered, 'but that'll be something for the investigation team to look at.'

When something was 'usually' done and then it wasn't, it 'usually' meant that people were looking away when they shouldn't have been.

'May we have a look?' Henry asked. 'We'll keep to this side of the tape until we get suited and booted.'

'Yes, go ahead,' Crossjack said. Henry could almost see the cogs of her brain whirring as she mulled over the implications of a murder on her patch. Some very important, searching questions were going to be asked.

Henry eased his way through, with Jake just behind, until they were at the tape stretched across the corridor at waist height. It was only a fairly short, narrow passageway, a link from the landing into the showers – maybe six feet wide, twelve feet long – meaning that someone had timed, planned and executed an ambush to perfection.

He looked at the body, which he hoped – apart from an inspection for vital signs by the medical staff – was more or less in the position in which it had fallen.

And from what he could see and surmise, because the body was lying with the head towards him, he had been attacked leaving the shower and returning to the cells.

A white male, completely naked, with a blood-drenched towel just covering his feet. He was face down, ironically in the recovery position, with one knee drawn up and in a wide pool of blood from the multiple stab wounds into the ribcage just below his right arm.

The hair was blond and blood-stained.

Henry glanced over his shoulder at Crossjack who had come with him. She looked pretty queasy, although Henry wondered if that was more to do with the prospect of her career plummeting than anything else.

'No sign of a weapon?' he asked.

She shook her head. 'By now it will have passed from prisoner to prisoner and been disposed of or hidden for next time. I hold out little hope . . .'

'Where there's *some* hope,' Henry said. He looked back at the body and frowned. He could not see the young man's face, yet there was something vaguely familiar. 'Who is it?'

'A prisoner on remand. Thomas Costain,' Crossjack answered.

Dunster Cosmo's mobile phone beeped as a text landed. He removed it from his pocket and glanced at Marcie and McCabe, who looked like two folk who'd been dragged backwards through the proverbial hedge.

'I've been waiting for this,' he said, pressing the key to open the text menu.

'We'll go, then,' Marcie suggested.

'No . . . you'll wait.'

Cosmo read the text and then looked at the four graphically violent photographs that had arrived, his face registering increasing pleasure as he scrolled through the images a few times, enlarging a couple of them with his finger and thumb to inspect detail. Finally, his face broke into a wide smile of triumph, until he looked at Marcie and McCabe again, and his humour disappeared and his eyes became stone-cold grey.

'This man – one of a gang – tried to muscle in on some of my business,' he said, jiggling the phone. 'Two of that gang are already dead . . . they'd been foolish enough to come down here and threaten me, so I did what needed to be done with them.'

'The ones we disposed of for you?' Marcie guessed.

'Correct-a-mundo,' Cosmo said. 'But what I want to point out to you is this.' Cosmo turned the phone screen towards the couple. 'I don't want you to go thinking you can leg it or diddle me out of my money, because I have a very, very long reach. I can get into places only a cockroach can get into. This man is another member of that gang, one of its leaders. He was in prison. Now he's dead. So let that be a warning.'

Marcie took the phone and held it so McCabe could see the screen, too. She flipped through the photographs with her fingertip, then handed the phone back to Cosmo who split the device in two and removed the SIM card. He dropped the phone on to the floor and stamped on it with his heel before snapping the SIM card and placing the two halves in his pocket. He intended to dispose of those bits later.

'Now go! Shoo!' he instructed the pair. 'And be back in five days, bearing all my money.'

'We agreed six,' McCabe pointed out.

'Did we? Well, it's five now. I'm unpredictable like that, so you'd better get a move on.'

'You need to isolate Conrad Costain, this guy's grandfather. He's also on remand here,' Henry told Crossjack urgently. 'Get him into solitary or something. He's in danger – if he hasn't already been stabbed.'

'No can do.'

'What the hell do you mean?'

'He isn't here.'

'What? Where is he?'

'We transferred him out yesterday. He was causing too much trouble, was on his third warning.'

'He's eighty fucking years old,' Henry exclaimed.

'And a total bastard to supervise.'

Henry and Crossjack had moved back from the throng around the body and were in a huddle further along the landing.

'He was almost impossible to control from the moment he arrived, obviously in cahoots with his grandson. We had to split them up, even though they were being kept in separate cells here. He was causing real ructions, pretending he had Alzheimer's, for one thing, even though he clearly hasn't.'

'So where is he?'

'Manchester.'

'Strangeways?'

'As was,' Crossjack confirmed.

'You need to get on to them now, get them to lift him out of the general population and bung him in solitary – but don't tell him why or allow him to find out about this.' Henry was doing some calculations in his head.

'Why ever not? Bastard that he is, he should still be told. This is his grandson.'

'I get that – but let me do it. Get Manchester to grab him, lock him down, no access to phones, TV or any communication devices – and I'll be there in less than an hour.'

'But his human rights—'

'Should've been shelved when he ordered the murder of a man and his wife who had done him no harm, just because he was feeling peeved. I can be there in under an hour, so can we just get on with it, please?'

Crossjack pursed her lips. 'Why?'

'First to save him from the same fate as his grandson; second to use Tommy's death as a lever for vital information,' Henry explained. 'Look – he'll be incommunicado for less than sixty minutes, that's all.'

'I'll do it now,' she said and strode away, presumably to her office.

'Thank fuck for that,' Henry said. He turned to Jake. 'We need to get moving.'

Jake was one of those fantastically practical street cops who had done almost every available 'hands-on' course, from a basic driving course to advanced, security escort driving, an HGV course, even – plus all the courses related to firearms, short of being an instructor.

So, having led a fairly sedentary life in the backwoods of Kendleton for a few years, driving the rickety old Land Rover (that he'd come to adore), being behind the wheel of something that had legs was a pleasant change.

He put his foot down, aimed the BMW at the M61, entering at Bamber Bridge, and sped towards Manchester while Henry worked his phone.

The first call was a quick one to Steve Flynn who had been sitting in Henry's Audi in a layby about a mile away from Lancashire prison, awaiting instructions. Henry told him to begin making his way to Manchester prison, no further explanation given.

Next, he spoke to Rik Dean, bringing him up to speed with the situation he had just left in his wake, and asking for the prison liaison officer to warn Manchester that Henry was en route.

Rik was cool and efficient, said he would do this.

Henry said, 'It's taken a bit of a twist, this.'

'You're not kidding.'

'Let's just keep on its tail,' Henry said, 'Follow it down the hole.'

'Yeah, OK. Look, I have some updates for you regarding DNA, but you get Conrad sorted first and see if he comes up with anything.'

Henry's interest was piqued by the DNA teaser, but he decided not to ask. Instead, he asked Rik to instruct the telephone unit to contact mobile phone providers and see if any calls had been made from the prison around the time of or just after Tommy Costain's death. He said he would.

Next, Henry called Flynn again. 'Location?'

'Right behind you.'

Henry glanced at Jake, who grinned. The speedo showed a hundred miles per hour. Then he looked over his shoulder to see his Audi almost on the back bumper of the BMW with Flynn at the wheel, who gave Henry a little wave.

Henry flipped to face front again and made another call. This time to Royal Lancaster Infirmary.

They were at Manchester prison twenty minutes later. Ten minutes after that Henry was being shown into an interview room where he sat and waited for Conrad Costain to be brought in.

While a cop in Blackpool, Henry had had extensive dealings with the Costain family of miscreants, a family that had become an organized criminal enterprise, but he had never encountered Conrad in that time. Not that it particularly surprised him. The Costains were a widespread, extended family, and many were involved in the criminal side of things. Henry had wanted to dismantle and disrupt them before he retired, but he held his hand up: he had failed.

Along the way he had arrested many of them, chipped away at them, had one as an informant even, but he had never successfully managed to crack the hierarchy.

Even when old man Costain came into the picture.

He had been involved in contracting the two 'hitmen' travellers who had murdered the Yorks, but beyond that Henry knew very little about Conrad, other than realizing that he was probably the kingpin of the whole organization. Even though the guy was actually over eighty, he was still fair game for Henry, who was eager to be having another shot at the family as a sideshow to the investigation he was embroiled in.

Henry's whole career had been built around defending the rights of, and fighting for, the dead, and he wished no one the kind of demise that Tommy had just suffered, but he hoped that his death might prove to be the catalyst for opening up Conrad Costain's old, thin-lipped mouth.

The door opened.

Conrad, his wrists bound by handcuffs, was led in. The cuffs were removed, and he was pushed on to the chair across the table from Henry, the feet of which were screwed to the floor. Henry gave a nod to the prison officer, who retreated to the corner of the room and put in earphones to listen to music but kept a wary eye on Conrad.

Conrad looked considerably older than when Henry had first met him, which was only about a month ago at the time of his arrest. Henry could see the physical decline of the older man even in that short space of time. Life inside was hard for a guy his age, even if he was a tough guy. His cosseted existence in a luxurious static caravan (under which Henry had discovered the cash stolen from the Yorks, plus an escape tunnel) on a fairly quiet, under-the-radar travellers' site had been taken from him. He was now in a small prison cell, banged up for eighteen or more hours each day, and even if he threw his weight around and was a disruptive fucker, he had lost everything. Chances were, if the police successfully prosecuted him, he would spend the remainder of his days stewing behind bars.

Conrad stared at Henry as though he was a turd. 'You again.'

Henry nodded.

'I always knew of you,' Conrad told him. 'Even though you never knew of me.'

'I was a famous cop.'

'You were a pain in the backside.' Conrad shrugged. 'But just one of those things to endure. A nosy, annoying cop. Never intimidated by us. That half impressed me, although it did make me think you were perhaps a bit simple.'

'I was famous for being simple.'

Conrad leaned forward. 'But do you know one thing?'

'What would that be?'

'I once put a contract out on you.'

Henry heard the words. Ingested them. Understood them. His mouth went dry.

'But I rescinded it,' Conrad said. 'Not because I wanted to – I really thought you should be dead – but because Troy Costain begged me not to have you mown down like a dog in the street.'

'That was kind of him . . . and such a classy way of killing someone.' Henry could feel his heart thumping as he regarded this dangerous old man while also thinking about Troy Costain, who had – unknown to the Costains – been Henry's informant way back.

'I didn't know why he didn't want you dead.'

'Practical reasons, I would guess.'

'Because eventually it was his relationship with you that got him killed – ironically.'

Henry didn't comment, but it suddenly felt as if he was the one on the back foot here, as if he was the one under scrutiny. Interview rooms were his hunting grounds, places he controlled, where, more often than not, with patience and skill, he nailed wrongdoers to the wall – metaphorically speaking. Now he felt as though he was losing his touch. Retirement must have blunted his cutting edge.

Conrad had a smirk on his lips. 'Perhaps I'll put that contract out again.'

'You might have a problem with that, Conrad.'

'How would that be?'

'You're running out of people capable of delivering even a newspaper for you.'

Conrad folded his arms, sat back.

Henry placed the file he had taken in for Jamie Costain to look at on the table between them. Conrad looked at it for a moment.

Henry then put his mobile phone on the table.

'You're boring me, Henry. I'm too old to be bored. Or intimidated – if that's what you're trying to do.'

'No, it's not. Look, Conrad, I'm truly sorry about this and if you really do know anything about me, you'll know this is true. I *am* sorry.' Henry picked up his phone and found the photo file. 'Though I'm no longer a cop as such, I'm doing some work for them and I was asked to attend an incident earlier this morning at Lancashire prison.' Henry decided to keep more or less to the truth. 'On my arrival, I accompanied prison officers up to a corridor leading to a shower area where there had been a fatal stabbing.' Henry paused. He had delivered more death messages than he could count. There were many different causes, but one thing he knew, one thing that had stuck in his mind ever since his initial training all those years ago, was that, however tenderly or forcefully the message was delivered, there had to be no uncertainty. You could not tell the recipient that their loved one had 'passed on' or 'gone to a different place' or mince words in any way that could be misinterpreted. They had to know for sure that death had occurred and that the person would not be walking back through the door. Ever. 'I'm sorry to tell you, Mr Costain, that your grandson, Thomas Costain, was the victim. He has been stabbed to death and I am genuinely sorry.'

'Lying fucker!' In a sudden reaction, Conrad angrily crashed his fists on the table.

Henry didn't flinch. The prison officer yanked the earphones out and put a hand to his baton. Henry indicated for him to keep cool.

'This is a lie. Part of a conspiracy. You've moved me here so you can manipulate us to get us to talk to you, to confess. I suppose there's cops over there saying the same thing to Tommy right now – that his grandad is dead. You're a bunch of toss-bags if you think I'm going to fall for that.'

'Conrad, it's true. I've seen his body, I'm afraid. He's been stabbed multiple times.'

'Liar.' Conrad wasn't having any of it.

Henry tapped the screen of his phone. Now for the really brutal bit. 'I have some photographs. They're unpleasant and they're not staged. You can see them if you so wish, but what I'm telling you is the absolute truth. Tommy is dead.'

'OK, show them to me.'

'You're sure?'

Conrad nodded.

Henry set up his phone and slid it across the table.

Conrad took it and swiped slowly through the photographs several times before placing the phone back down and shoving it back.

In the space of seconds, Henry had watched him wither even more.

'I'm sorry.'

'Did they get who did it?'

'Not yet. It looks as though he was ambushed on his way from the shower.'

'Jesus.'

'Who could have done this, Conrad?'

The old man's head twitched. A tear rolled down his cheek.

'Who ordered it?' Henry probed.

'Don't know what you mean.'

'OK. In that case, who ordered the killings of these two young men?' Henry pulled the photographs out of the file. 'These are photographs of the two young guys I found up at the Yorks' farmhouse. You haven't seen them yet because you've been so uncooperative, but I'll lay odds you know who they are. Both were shot in the head.'

Ruthlessly – and he knew he was piling it on – he shoved the photos across, the actual ones of the dead men and the mock-up drawings done by a police artist.

Conrad looked at them with a glower, but it was obvious that emotions were churning inside him. He said, 'Is it really true about Tommy?'

'Yes, it is.'

Conrad nodded, then looked more closely at the images.

As with Jamie before, Henry studied Conrad's face and, even if he tried not to show it, Henry could tell that he recognized the two men.

'Found in a wall space at the farmhouse.'

'I'd heard.'

'Who are they?'

'I can't tell you that.'

'Or won't?'

Henry kept watching him. He could see the old man was fighting to keep control of everything.

'These men were brutally murdered in what looks like a gangland-style execution,' Henry said calmly. 'This morning Tommy was also brutally murdered in what looks like a targeted attack.'

Not, of course, Henry thought, *that you yourself don't order people to be just as brutally murdered.* The two men who had murdered John and Isobel York had been ordered to do it and had committed an horrific crime, one of the worst Henry had ever seen in his life, as well as killing the family dog which was additionally unforgivable. Henry was pretty sure that had all been done on the orders of this old man sitting opposite him.

So, in some respects, he had no sympathy for him.

In others, Henry's inbuilt conditioning to bring killers to justice made him desperate to bring Tommy's murderer to book, as well as whoever had killed these two men.

Plus, as part of this whole, complex scenario, a good cop was lying on the brink of death because of something that involved Conrad Costain.

Henry said, 'This all has to stop, Conrad. Whoever is behind all this – the Yorks, these guys' – he indicated the photos – 'Tommy, too – it all has to stop. And I'll bet you have the key to it. OK, maybe you can't or won't tell me the names of these men, but what you have to do is give me a name, the name of the guy you're at war with in London over the county lines thing . . .'

At that Conrad looked up sharply.

Henry said, 'Yes, I know what all this stems from; what I don't know is who is involved, and you need to tell me now, Conrad.' He went on, laying it on thick, and concluded by saying, 'But what I *do* know is that there is every chance you too will get a knife in the ribs, because even in here, even if you're isolated, in solitary, someone will get to you. All you have to do is give me one name and let me take it from there.'

Silence.

'The thing is, Henry, retribution is a two-way street,' Conrad said.

'Maybe, but you're a sitting target in here, and I'll guess that there are at least one hundred men in here willing to shiv you to death for a couple of grand in their family's coffers. But he is out there – whatever his name is that you won't reveal; a moving target, probably with protection. And he's already shown how to deal with a situation he doesn't like, by getting someone in a prison two hundred and fifty miles away from London to kill.'

Henry tapped the photos, tapped the phone.

He added, 'And part of me thinks that if you hadn't been moved from Lancashire prison to here, you would probably have been knifed to death sitting on the bog this morning. So no, you were moved here because you are a disruptive fucker, not so we could manipulate you. You got lucky this morning. Your luck won't last, Conrad.'

Costain looked at Henry. 'One name. I say it once. If you don't hear properly, I won't say it again. Understand?'

FIFTEEN

'Dunster Cosmo.'

'What sort of a name is that?' Steve Flynn asked Henry.

Henry smiled, then gave Jake Niven the nod.

On leaving the prison, the three men had convened at the McDonald's restaurant on the A56 on the way out of Manchester. Henry had bought each of them a Big Mac, and as he nodded, he bit into his burger with relish. He was very hungry, but he knew this meal would not satisfy a very empty belly.

Jake had his work-provided iPad in front of him and had logged on to the restaurant's internet, confident enough in the encryption and antivirus software on it to begin a search for the name Cosmo via a secure link to PNC and other police intelligence databases.

Flynn looked on contentedly, munching his food, but asked, 'What's the update on DS Daniels, Henry?'

'I phoned on the way across. I'm down as first contact until we unearth the brother's location.' He paused. 'Not good. Still under heavy sedation; seems the internal bleeding hasn't stopped so they're going to operate again later today.'

'Shit,' Flynn said, suddenly not enjoying his burger as much.

'I know,' Henry agreed dully. When he took a sip of his coffee, his hand was shaking slightly. He didn't like thinking about it, but the worst-case scenario kept creeping into his mind – and also that maybe he should be by her bedside instead of gallivanting around like a knight in shining armour, trying to bring an offender to justice. But he knew this is what Diane would have wanted him to do. And he took some comfort in the knowledge that Diane's colleagues from Lancaster nick were ensuring someone was with her most of the time.

Jake raised his eyes to check if Henry was OK. Clearly, he wasn't. He returned to the screen of his computer. The search seemed to be taking forever.

Henry called Rik Dean and gave him Cosmo's name. 'Jake and

me are just having an energy boost before heading back.' Henry eyed Flynn, who chuckled to himself. 'We're just checking Cosmo on PNC, see if we can find anything.' He told Rik about his face-to-face with Conrad, culminating in him naming Cosmo, then clamming up and saying nothing else. Henry then asked, 'What have you got for me? You mentioned DNA.'

'Something has come up, but maybe we can talk when you're back.'

'Tell me now.'

'OK, in brief. I've fast-tracked the DNA search, as you know, but we've had no direct match in police records for the shooter from the samples we managed to get.'

Henry swore in frustration.

'But all is not lost,' Rik said. 'I got the chief to authorize a familial DNA search, which she did . . . Hang on, let me backtrack slightly, first. We did a DNA search on the items you found with Diane up on the moors, the water bottle and the tape, and obviously from the other crime scenes – at Jack Carter's house, at Billy Lane's chop shop . . . and actually, best of all, a guy running a B and B in Morecambe came forward to say he'd had a suspicious guy staying in one of his rooms for a few days, who suddenly didn't return and left some items in the room, including toiletries – which are rife with DNA. Still with me?'

'I am. Did they all match?'

'Short answer is yes. Matches from all the scenes – so that also puts this guy in the vicinity of Beth York's body,' Rik informed him. 'Got a detective and an e-fit artist with the owner of the B and B who, interestingly, says the man stayed there before – get this, with a woman and child. He should be a good witness, hopefully.'

'Things are starting to come together . . . So, the familial search, why?'

'Because we have a partial match, but the chief, as you know, has to authorize a full search based on that to get a result that actually names names.'

Henry was momentarily stunned. 'That's fantastic.'

'Isn't it just? But look, you do that check on the name Conrad gave you, then head back here and we'll have a proper sit-down.'

Henry hung up and looked at Jake who said, 'Dunster Cosmo.'

* * *

Rik Dean took Henry to one side, furious with him.

'You said you couldn't contact him.' Rik's eyes shot sideways to look at Steve Flynn, who gave him a little wave.

'Fibbed.'

'He hits people.'

'Which is why I'd like him at my back,' Henry said. 'I can control him if needs be.'

'He needs putting on a leash,' Rik said. He knew Flynn well, had been involved with him when Flynn had become embroiled with Albanian mobsters, but was very wary of him being drawn into this scenario. 'I thought you didn't even like him?'

'I never said I did like him.'

'Not really happy,' Rik whispered.

'Give him a pass so he can come and go into police buildings when he needs to,' Henry said. 'He's staying.'

'Whatever . . .'

Shaking his head, Rik turned back to the major incident room at Lancaster where Henry and the two others had returned after their Manchester trip. Rik had locked down the room so there would be no interruptions and just three other people were present – DCI Wellburn, DS McManus and DC Khan, all members of FMIT and Rik's core team for this investigation.

Tables had been rearranged and pushed together, and they sat on three sides of the rectangle, leaving the fourth side – which faced the front of the room – free. The large interactive whiteboard on the wall was on and displaying the blank home screen from a laptop in front of Rik.

'OK, folks,' Rik said, his eyes taking in everyone, but lingering slightly on Flynn. It wasn't that he had any major animosity towards the guy, he just didn't want him along for this ride. Yes, Flynn was effective and fearless in the right circumstances, but he was a bit of a sledgehammer. 'First of all, an update on Diane: she's currently undergoing more surgery to try to find and stop some internal bleeding; she remains very poorly.'

Each person took in the news.

'OK,' Rik went on. 'Some other updates first, after which we're expecting a Skype connection with an officer called Ted Sandford from the National Crime Agency in London regarding a name that's just come into the frame – a certain Dunster Cosmo.

'First update: the DNA samples of the offender from the crime scenes we've been dealing with – Beth York, Jack Carter and Billy Lane – all match, so we have one offender for all three, although he is not on the DNA database, which is a shame. However, we've now done a familial DNA search and got a hit. There are close similarities between our offender's DNA profile and this individual, which leads the analyst to believe this guy is the offender's brother, or even his twin.'

Rik tapped a key on the laptop and photographs of a male in his mid-thirties appeared on screen, all obviously mugshots from custody, front and profile views. He looked thin, ragged and had a black eye.

'Gerald Daniel McCabe, thirty-three, on the sex offenders' register for life for the abduction and rape of two nine-year-old girls when he was just eighteen. Released six years into a fifteen-year sentence for that offence – don't ask – but has continued to reoffend regularly, though most of the offences are minor, if you will – flashing, harassment – though he is also suspected of a series of rapes of old women via burglary. So far he's managed to wheedle out of any charges; this photo relates to an indecent exposure in a shop for which he was arrested and charged and is now awaiting a court appearance.'

Rik paused, let them take it in.

The DCI said, 'So this is the shooter's brother?'

Rik said yes and, anticipating the next question, said, 'We've checked his antecedents but there is no mention of a brother. At present he is on court bail with conditions and has been ordered to live in a bail hostel.'

'Where?' Henry asked.

'New Cross, south London.'

'That's handy,' Flynn commented dryly.

'There's more,' Rik said. 'As we know, Beth York, Jack Carter, Billy Lane and Diane were all shot by a gun loaded with nine-millimetre bullets, and again with some major fast-track work by the Firearms Database folk in Greater Manchester, we can say with certainty that all were fired from the same weapon.'

'I saw it,' Henry said. 'A Browning.'

Rik nodded. 'So, unless the weapon has been passed around in a very short space of time, we are definitely looking for one offender – this guy's brother.' He pointed to the mugshot on screen of Gerald McCabe.

Henry's anus contracted, but this pleasure was interrupted when Rik's laptop began to ring as a Skype connection came through from the National Crime Agency.

'Hi, Ted. Thanks for joining us,' Rik said, making the Skype link.

'Pleasure.'

Rik introduced everyone present in the room, then projected Ted Sandford's face up on to the interactive whiteboard and turned the laptop around to get all the individuals into shot so Sandford could see whom he was addressing.

'Shall I get right down to it?' the NCA guy asked.

'Please,' Rik said.

'Dunster Cosmo – Dunster Erasmus Cosmo, to be precise,' Sandford began, 'is quite simply one of the biggest, most feared gangsters in London. He's been operating at the top of his game for some time now.'

'What's he into?' DC Khan asked.

'One of those "You name it" answers,' Sandford said. 'Began his career long ago with armed robbery as a teenager – banks, shops, cash in transit – but that became old hat. Gravitated into drugs – dealing, supplying, trafficking; now involved in trafficking people and also has a base of porn, brothels, betting shops, and runs some well-organized county lines. Very happy to use violence and firearms. Relatively clever with it, too.'

'How do you mean?' Henry asked.

'We all know crims use pay-as-you-go phones. He does but rarely takes direct calls. He has a system of phone operators, all using pay-as-you-go, who take his calls, phone him, then destroy the phones. He's pretty hard to track that way. That said, he does occasionally take some direct calls. Also clever in respect of people trafficking. We think he's a conduit in that he provides staging posts for other people bringing in illegal immigrants. He short-term leases or rents warehouses around London through a series of business firewalls and uses them as clearing houses for just a few days, then shuts them down and moves on after the "goods", shall we say, have passed through.'

There was much more, and Sandford was on the line for another half hour. His final parting shot was to reveal that there was very little footage of Cosmo because of the way he operated, but that he could share some long-range, but good-quality, shots taken of Cosmo attending the funeral of a man some four years before; the man was believed to be one of Cosmo's business associates who had, as is often the way with business associates, been killed in a drive-by shooting in Liverpool.

The man's name was Brendan Quant.

Henry pleaded with Rik Dean, but even as he spoke the words, he knew they were falling on ears that were hard of hearing. Henry was desperate to keep moving, force issues, speak to people and nail them down by fair means or foul.

He wanted to head down south, locate the sex offender called McCabe and interview him about his brother, as yet nameless. He also wanted to bowl headlong into Dunster Cosmo's lair and shake the shit out of him.

He wanted to do it now. In his mind he kept saying, *All connected, all connected.*

His blood felt boiling hot in his veins. His breathing became laboured as he made his pitch to Rik. He started to pour sweat. His limbs dithered and shook. His sight became unfocused.

They were still in the MIR.

'You've got to get this thing moving, Rik. We need to be heading down to London, get things underway . . . don't you see?'

Rik backed off under the onslaught. 'Henry,' he began reasonably, unable to keep his eyes off the wall clock which showed just after seven p.m., 'we are not going anywhere at this time of night, OK? Certainly not down south.'

'What? Why not?'

'Not going to happen . . . I've got to make lots of phone calls; there are people I need to speak to, arrangements to make, intelligence to gather . . .'

'Analysis to paralysis,' Henry scoffed. He and Rik were toe to toe. 'We move now, we get into position,' he argued.

'Hey, man.' Steve Flynn took gentle hold of Henry's bicep. He could see Henry was about to detonate.

Henry shrugged him off roughly. 'You don't touch me.' His eyes glowered hard at Rik Dean's, then he jabbed him in the chest, but Flynn wasn't having any of that. He grabbed Henry's finger and stepped between the two men.

'Back off, Henry,' Flynn said. 'I see where you're coming from. I get it; we all get it.'

'I really, really don't think you do.'

Henry then shrugged himself away from both men and stormed out of the MIR, although even as he tried to slam the door behind him (which was impossible because it was controlled by a pneumatic arm which did not allow slamming), he did feel a bit silly.

He stalked up to the infirmary, perhaps a half a mile away from the police station, and made his way to the critical care unit to try to find out where they were up to with Diane.

The lady behind the reception desk said, 'She came back from surgery about half an hour ago.'

'And?'

'I'll try and contact the surgeon for you.'

Henry took a seat in the waiting area, feeling quite empty and powerless in so many ways. He sat with the palms of his hands together, his elbows on his thighs, staring at the tiled floor, not sure how long he had been there until he was suddenly aware of someone standing in front of him.

'Mr Christie?'

He looked up to see a middle-aged Asian man in slacks and wearing a shirt with the sleeves rolled up. He had an ID lanyard around his neck.

'That's me.'

'I'm Mr Masood. I believe you've been enquiring about Miss Daniels. You're her next of kin?'

'I am enquiring, but I'm a friend and colleague. I was with her when she was shot. We're trying to locate a relative but struggling at the moment, so I'm first call.'

'That's fine. You were the one who performed first aid on her?'

'Yeah. And who are you?'

'I'm a vascular surgeon. I was brought in to see if I could locate exactly where Miss Daniels was bleeding from internally.'

'And have you?'

'Well, to cut a long story short, I think I have managed to repair the damage. The bullet nicked the superior mesenteric artery in her abdomen, as well as all the other damage done to her, but we found that and repaired it. She has lost a lot of blood and has had a lot transfused back into her. She remains very weak and certainly not out of the woods yet. We will be keeping her under close observation, but if the blood loss has been stemmed, bearing in mind she is a very fit and healthy woman, I think her chances of recovery are now good. The next few hours will tell.'

Henry had been holding his breath as the surgeon spoke. Then he exhaled with relief. 'Thank you. Can I see her?'

He sat by the bed and looked at her, talking quietly, making promises, telling her about the progress of the manhunt, that there were good leads and, God willing, collars to be felt, and that he would not rest until the shooter was behind bars or in the ground.

Finally, he felt a hand on his shoulder. Rik Dean.

Henry stood up wearily and said, 'Sorry, pal.'

'Understandable.'

The two men went out into the corridor where Steve Flynn waited.

'So what's the plan?' Henry asked.

'Plan is, you get a half-decent night's sleep, then you, Jake and Flynn here tear down to the Smoke and see if you can locate the shooter's sex-offender brother. I'm thinking maybe a five a.m. set-off. I'll be staying up here, coordinating stuff. How does that sound?'

'Fair. Sensible,' Henry conceded. 'And thank you.'

'I've already sent Jake home; he'll be ready to roll at five. I suggest you guys go eat, get your heads down and, traffic permitting, you can be in London by nine tomorrow morning.'

Driving Henry's Audi, Flynn motored them back to Kendleton where The Tawny Owl was still open and bustling.

Henry spotted Maude in the bar but didn't want to talk to her, or anyone for that matter, other than Ginny, so he and Flynn went straight through to the back where they each grabbed a shower and reconvened in the lounge where two steak-and-ale pies were waiting for them.

The food tasted incredible and was filling – unlike the burgers earlier in the day – and was accompanied by a pint of Stella from the bar, brought through by Ginny.

Henry gave her a swift overview of the day and what was planned, and she said she would get up extra early to ensure they had a good breakfast to travel on. Henry said no, but she insisted, and he backed off, knowing that was a battle he wouldn't win. Not long after, he went to bed, but Flynn went into the bar for an extra half hour before he, too, retired into the spare bedroom.

Rik Dean worked through until eleven p.m. The last thing he wanted was for any representatives of Lancashire Constabulary to bowl into London and upset the local cops. Through his contacts, he laid the ground for Henry and the two others to be able to go knocking on doors and kicking them down if necessary, though he hoped it wouldn't come to that.

By the time he logged out of his computer, he could hardly keep his eyes open and he was relieved to be heading down in the lift to the upper ground floor and walking across to his car, a rather splendid Lexus hybrid, where he folded himself into the luxurious driver's seat and pulled almost silently off the car park.

He had fairly recently moved to live in Lytham St Annes and knew he had the best part of an hour's travel ahead, but he was looking forward to it and actually getting home.

He was no music buff but he did have a liking for Frank Sinatra's 1950s run of albums, so he found *Songs for Swingin' Lovers* on his in-car selection and sailed towards the motorway.

What he completely failed to see was that as soon as he had driven off the police car park, a car further down the street had moved away from the kerb with two occupants on board and followed him.

SIXTEEN

They were actually on the outskirts of London by eight a.m. Progress down the motorways had been unusually swift and hassle-free, although the pace slowed considerably when they passed over the M25 and drove towards the city.

Henry and Jake were in the BMW, Flynn in the Audi. They'd

decided on two cars so their options would be more fluid once they were in the city, although actually keeping each other in view was difficult enough. With the backup of smartphones and GPS, they hoped they wouldn't go too far wrong and lose each other in the masses.

They followed the M40 as it morphed into the A40, then cut down south along the A320, towards the Thames.

Henry, who didn't know London well, perked up when he saw they were travelling down Edith Grove, which he knew, as a bit of a Rolling Stones nerd, was where the fledgling group of Jagger, Richard and Jones had been cooped up in a tiny, grotty flat for a while, living hand to mouth in the days prior to great wealth. He wondered if the property had a blue plaque on it but wasn't sure what the number was and imagined it would have changed since 1962. He didn't spot one anyway.

Next, they merged on to Cheyne Walk by the Thames embankment where he kept an eye out for the present-day Mick Jagger who, he seemed to remember, had a house somewhere along here.

He didn't spot him either.

When they reached Vauxhall Bridge, they turned across the Thames, passing the iconic MI6 building on the South Bank and following the A202 as it circumnavigated the Kennington Oval cricket ground and continued in a south-easterly direction along Camberwell New Road, then Peckham High Street and into New Cross, where they found Amersham Road on which the bail hostel was situated.

They looked at it quickly and then drew in sharply to the left of the road where there was plenty of roadside parking; craning their necks, they were able to see the front door of the hostel. It was in a long terrace of big three-storey houses, and Henry knew it was divided into eight small flats for the occupants. At least that is what his quick internet research had thrown up. Previously, of course, it had been a private residence, but over several decades it had gone through many hands and refurbishments from a bed-and-breakfast to a DSS dosshouse, to student accommodation and, finally, its most recent reincarnation as a bail hostel, or Approved Premises, for sex offenders. It was owned by the local council, run by a private management company and housed people on police bail pending court for serious sex offences. Henry could only imagine the happy reaction of the other residents in the road on hearing the news of its opening.

Behind Henry and Jake, Flynn climbed out of Henry's Audi, stretching his long legs, rolling his shoulder muscles, and sauntered up to them on the pavement, bending down at Henry's window.

'I need food and drink. I spotted a sandwich shop just back there advertising breakfast sarnies and hot drinks. Interested?'

They had driven with only one toilet break, although they'd begun the day with the promised breakfast prepared by Ginny, and the last hour of the journey – from reaching the outskirts of the city to arriving in New Cross – had made all three thirsty and hungry again.

Henry and Jake nodded eagerly and gave Flynn their orders.

'I'll bob down.'

'Keep your phone handy,' Henry told him.

'Why, what's the plan?' Flynn wanted to know.

'Wait for a while, see if there's any activity; if not, we'll knock on the door and ask to see him. There is a warden on site.' Henry was reluctant to speak to McCabe in his flat, only because if he did kick off for any reason, he might have backup from other residents and things could get untidy. Henry envisaged pinning him against a wall outside or preferably taking him to a local cop shop to speak to him, not under arrest, but on police turf.

Flynn said OK and sauntered down the road, glancing across at the hostel as he went, but not making his interest too obvious, he hoped.

He walked down on to New Cross Road, turned left and crossed over to a row of shops with a bakery in the middle. The aroma emanating from it hit his nostrils immediately. It sold a range of breakfasts from straightforward bacon and/or sausage sandwiches to vegan rolls.

There was a queue. He took up his position at the back while perusing the menu on the wall behind the counter. Eventually, his eyes dropped and looked without interest at the customers ahead of him; as they entered the shop, they split into two queues in front of two tills and serving points at the counter.

Flynn had taken his place in the left-hand queue. There were four people in front of him.

In the queue to his right were six people in total, one at the counter, five waiting behind. At the head of that queue was a young woman with dyed red and blue hair. Flynn, for his own amusement, tried to guess what her vegan order might be, although as soon as he began that process he knew he would be stereotyping her as a political activist or, as he called them, 'a tree hugger'. No doubt he would be wrong.

Next his eyes moved to the man standing behind her.

Who – unless he was actually with this woman – seemed to be just a tad too close to her for comfort. He was right up behind her, although she did not seem to be aware of his presence as she chatted to the server and looked in her purse.

Flynn had an oblique view of the man's profile from his position a few feet to the left and maybe eight feet behind. It didn't help that the guy was wearing a floppy, fur-lined trapper-style hat with drop-down earmuffs like a deerstalker. The broad muffs hung down over the side of his face, masking most of his profile. He was also wearing a scruffy-looking parka jacket which came down to just above his knees and he had his hands in the pockets.

At least that is what Flynn initially thought and what the whole world would be deceived into believing, because the reality of the situation suddenly dawned on Flynn as the man moved slightly, getting even closer to the woman at the counter. Flynn realized that the sleeves of the parka were stuffed into the jacket's pockets, but the man's arms were not actually down them – they were in front of him, free under the coat.

It was an old shoplifting trick: pretend you're wearing a large outer coat while being able to snaffle goods from the shelves and stash them in the inner pockets.

But in this man's case it was also a good flasher's trick.

Because the man, so close to the girl that she should surely smell him, had his penis out. It was erect and he was masturbating rapidly.

Flynn flew across at him with a roar, but the man – probably skilled in and ready for such situations – saw him coming and contorted away from Flynn's outstretched hands, his cock ejaculating, though this did not stop him from moving quickly and spinning out of the shop.

Flynn was a big guy, broad, fit, but not particularly sprightly, and he lost his balance slightly as he turned, clawing for the man's arm but missing, although his fingertips did just manage to get hold of one of the flaps of the man's hat and pull it off his head.

Flynn recognized him immediately.

Gerald Daniel McCabe. The man they had come all this way to talk to.

Flynn went after him, but as he emerged from the shop, McCabe was already twenty yards ahead, heading for Amersham Road.

As he ran, Flynn pulled out his phone and speed-dialled Henry's number at the same time as running across the road and dodging traffic. There was an instant connection.

'Yo!' Henry said.

'McCabe . . . running up Amersham Road in your direction,' Flynn said. 'Green parka. Just caught him wanking off in the bakery.'

'Gotcha.'

'He's running,' Henry said to Jake, quickly getting out of the car and looking down the road to see McCabe hurtling towards him, but on the opposite side, with Flynn some way behind.

Henry could see McCabe's top coat was flapping like Batman's cape with the sleeves trailing behind like wind socks, while at the same time he was trying to rehouse his cock.

With Jake at his heels, Henry started to leg it across the road, having to weave through the traffic which slowed them both down. McCabe was moving quickly, and before Henry could head him off, he had vaulted over the low wall of the front garden of the bail hostel and crashed through the front door, slamming it shut behind him.

Henry, still with his phone to his ear, shouted for Flynn to veer right and go around the back of the row of houses in case McCabe went straight through, out the back of the premises, and disappeared.

Henry and Jake were at the front door just seconds after it was shut. McCabe must have known it would be open for him, or maybe he'd purposely left it ajar for just such circumstances. Whatever, the door was now firmly closed and locked.

Henry banged on it with his fists and pressed the doorbell which he could hear ringing through the house.

* * *

Flynn bore right on to Parkfield Road, sprinted across it to the alley that ran behind Amersham Road. It was an untidy place, overgrown with grass and blocked by a grey van some thirty yards up.

Flynn settled to a jog, but then saw McCabe appear through the door in the wall of the back yard behind the hostel and jump straight into the driving seat of that van.

Flynn now slowed to a walk but, on his way, scooped up a house brick from a stack of them behind another wall. He heard McCabe turn the engine, which didn't seem to want to fire up, coughing and wheezing.

Then the van started and McCabe crunched it into gear.

Flynn stopped in the middle of the alley, maybe twenty yards in front of the van. In his left hand he held his phone to his ear; in his right he gripped the brick, wondering what the next move was going to be, because if it was in McCabe's head to set off and mow him down, it was going to require some quick thinking and fancy footwork on Flynn's part – first to hurl the brick through the windscreen and then to get out of the way. There wasn't much room on either side of the vehicle – maybe four feet either way.

The engine revved.

Then Henry and Jake bowled out through the back-yard door, and Henry grabbed the driver's door handle to try to wrench it open.

McCabe had locked it.

He had also applied his foot to the floor.

The van moved and quickly picked up speed, with Henry clinging to the door handle, Jake just behind him with nothing to grab.

Flynn had almost no time to come up with a coherent plan, but whatever it was had to be spot on in terms of timing; otherwise, he would be flattened.

The van accelerated.

Grew bigger, got closer.

Flynn drew back his right arm.

Henry, who had to release his grip on the door handle, twirled down the side of the van and crashed into Jake.

Flynn pitched the brick through the front windscreen, causing it to shatter and crumble, but the van still continued to drive at him and was just feet away from running him down. In order not to let this happen, Flynn had to decide what to do in that split second.

The van was almost on him.

He could clearly see McCabe's wild face behind the wheel, grim, determined.

And with timing skills honed by years of bringing marlin to the gaff, he managed to get the toe of his right foot on the front bumper as though he was using it for a springboard and jumped over the steeply angled bonnet, through the space where only seconds before the windscreen had been. He crashed into the cab and thudded untidily on to the passenger seat alongside McCabe who, for a moment, was stunned as Flynn tried to rearrange himself so he could go for him.

McCabe kept his foot pressed down. He was very quickly over the shock at finding he had collected a new passenger and with his left hand he started to slash out with a rusty, long-bladed, machete-type knife he kept tucked down the side of his seat for such emergencies.

Flynn saw it flash and drew back against the passenger door. The knife just missed slicing his face off.

Flynn himself retaliated instantly, grabbing McCabe's left wrist in a vice-like lock, twisting the whole of his forearm as he tried to disarm him. McCabe screamed in agony and tried to yank his arm free, but Flynn did not release it.

At the same time, McCabe still had his foot on the accelerator, his right hand gripping the wheel, and the van was still careening down the alley with Henry and Jake running behind.

When the van reached the point where the alley joined Parkfield Road, it did not stop, but shot straight across, mounted the pavement and ploughed into the gable end of the house opposite. The impact propelled Flynn back out through the windscreen, across the bonnet and smashed him into the wall.

McCabe hit the steering wheel hard with his chest.

But he was a man conditioned to keep running at all costs.

Despite the pain in his chest – he thought he'd cracked too many ribs to count – he shouldered open the driver's door and tumbled out on to the footpath on to his hands and knees, almost in a starting-block position, which was good because he was ready to sprint away.

Henry and Jake came across the road as McCabe came upright, transferring the knife from his left to right hand and turning to the cops in a threatening gesture.

'You stay there and put that knife down now,' Henry yelled, but came to a halt just beyond its range.

'You're under arrest.' Jake followed that up by flashing his warrant card.

'No fucking way.' McCabe started to run. Jake stepped into his path and said, 'You're going nowhere, pal.'

'Get out of my way,' McCabe warned him, ducking sideways and slashing the knife at him, at which moment Henry bowled into him from an angle, coming in on the blind side, encircling McCabe's upper body and arms with his own arms in a bear hug. McCabe struggled violently, kicking and writhing, but Henry held on as Jake, timing it right, stepped in, grabbed his right wrist and squeezed, making him drop the knife. Jake got out his rigid handcuffs as Henry wrestled McCabe to the ground, pulled the guy's hands around his back and applied the cuffs.

Henry released McCabe as Jake dropped on to him and pinned him down.

Henry turned to Flynn who stood up, clearly in agony.

'You OK?'

Flynn nodded and breathed out, but he had been hurt probably more than he wanted to admit from his impact with the brick wall. At least he hadn't hit it head first.

The two men clustered around Jake and McCabe who was being held, squirming and complaining, by the officer.

'Wouldn't have noticed him,' Flynn said, rubbing his neck and rolling his shoulders, 'except that he had his dick out and was masturbating over the girl in front of him. Fortunately, she wasn't aware. But he saw me, I saw him and he legged it; then I recognized him.'

'You did good,' Henry said. 'At least we don't have a problem about where to speak to him anymore. An interview room will do nicely.'

Jake, still kneeling on McCabe's back, was already phoning the local police.

The van in which McCabe had tried to escape was now embedded in the side of the house, but because it had mounted the pavement at a slight angle to the road, it was not causing any traffic snarl-up other than that caused by rubberneckers who crawled past, gawping at the incident.

Flynn, still rolling his muscles to ward off the pain, had walked to the rear of the van – a Ford Transit with panelled sides and double doors on the back. The impact, although pretty much head-on, had crumpled the length of the van and put it out of shape. The rear doors had twisted on their hinges and unlocked themselves, but because they were out of shape, Flynn had to jerk hard to open them and look inside.

For him, it was one of those moments that poured dread into his whole being, like molten metal being tipped into his soul.

He knew he was looking at the inside of a torture, rape and murder van.

A large plate of thin steel had been fitted behind the front seating area to completely separate it from the rear section. The interior panels had all been lined with egg cartons to muffle noise. Four chains had been riveted to the upright struts, and at the end of each chain was a pair of shackles. A series of hooks along the sides had a variety of clothing on them, including several ski masks. There were tools in an open box along with rolls of masking and duct tape.

And, on a grimy mattress stained with piss, shit and semen was a young boy, maybe nine years old, half-covered by a dirty blanket. His wrists and ankles were in the shackles. Tape covered his eyes and mouth. He was not moving, and Flynn could not tell if he was alive or dead.

'Henry! Get back here,' he shouted and clambered in, suddenly forgetting any of his aches and pains.

'They reckon four,' Henry said. He was on the phone to Rik Dean. 'This could have been number five. He'd been taken from the street last night. He's been raped and drugged and would probably have been murdered sometime today, like his other victims. It's a good job Flynn spooked him; otherwise, we could have been happily chatting to him and never known about the kid and the van.'

'Bloody hell, well done,' Rik said.

'Down to Flynn,' Henry reiterated, 'although I never did get my breakfast order.'

'Maybe I misjudged him.'

'Maybe we all did,' Henry said, thinking of all those years when he couldn't think of a single good thing to say about the guy. 'He has hurt himself, though. Being flung through a windscreen into a wall isn't good, even at a relatively low speed.'

'Give him my thanks anyway. What's your next step?'

'To talk to this guy about his DNA brother if we can get in for ten minutes. Obviously, the local cops are all over him now, but we have been promised a window.'

Once the police had arrived, McCabe had been transferred from the scene of the crash to Lewisham Police Station and from that point on, as the Metropolitan Police murder investigation team descended en masse to assume control – which they were quite entitled to do – Henry, Flynn and Jake had been pushed to one side, other than to make statements, and McCabe had begun the ride of his life.

It was frustrating but understandable, and Henry got it.

The trio dutifully wrote their own statements, then were told to wait.

It was six hours before Henry, accompanied by a Met detective called Halsall, was allowed to speak to McCabe for a few minutes.

'You guys did good. We've been pulling our hair out for the last four weeks, one kid going missing after another, two boys and two girls, all turning up raped and murdered. Obviously, the same offender, all offences committed in the same locality, but the picture build-up was quite slow. It was only last night we got intel of a grey van possibly being used.'

They were outside the door to the interview room.

'He's not saying anything,' the detective went on.' He's got a brief and it's all "No comment . . . no comment", but that'll be his downfall eventually.'

'Usually is.'

'How do you want me to introduce you?'

'Er . . .' Henry hadn't thought about that. 'Just Henry Christie from Lancashire, I reckon. Keep it vague and simple, just like me.'

They chuckled as they entered the room.

McCabe was now in a forensic suit and elasticated shoes. He

had the hood tugged over his head and was sitting with his chair pulled up close to the table with his face just inches above the surface as though he was inspecting the grain of the wood. His solicitor sat alongside him.

He didn't look up once, though after the detective had introduced Henry, but not the reason for his visit, he said, 'No comment.' Clearly his default position.

'Mr McCabe, what I want to speak to you about does not concern any of the reasons why you are in custody,' Henry began. 'This is just me asking you some questions which will not be recorded or used against you.'

McCabe maintained his position, his head hovering just over the tabletop.

'I'm investigating some very serious offences committed in Lancashire which involve murder and the use of firearms. You're not involved, but through your DNA you are connected.'

Henry paused to see if there was a reaction.

Nothing.

'Several people have been killed or seriously injured and, as I say, there is some connection to you, Mr McCabe.'

Still nothing.

Henry liked to be cagey in interviews. Sometimes it was prudent to lay all your cards on the table, but more often than not it was better to drip-feed information. Although this wasn't a suspect interview, he had to be cautious as to how much he revealed because he did not know what this man's relationship was with his brother. If they were close, he would somehow try to warn him that the cops were on his trail; if they were estranged or hated each other, maybe he would be happy to reveal all.

'Can I ask – how do you and your brother get along?' Henry probed. It was a problem not knowing the brother's name, so Henry had to wing it slightly.

This did get a reaction.

McCabe raised his head and looked at Henry with a crooked smile on his face. Henry could not help but notice that sometime between this man's arrest and now he had acquired a very big, swollen black eye.

Henry took a punt. 'Not well, I guess?'

'Cunt,' McCabe said.

'Me or your bro?'

'Him.'

Another punt: 'I take it he wasn't . . . isn't . . . sympathetic to your interests in life.'

'Like I said, cu—'

Henry cut him off. 'Yeah, I get it . . . so, big fallout?'

'Mr Straight Guy,' McCabe sneered. 'Army, fuckin' army – snooty twat – but that didn't last long because he might be straight but he still likes hurting people.'

'What d'you mean?'

McCabe raised his right hand, pointed his forefinger at Henry and went, 'Bang!'

'So you and him don't get on?'

'Bigger, stronger, harder 'n me, but my kid twin brother could not handle what I do.' McCabe tapped his forehead. 'That did his head in. I mean, once' – McCabe leaned forward confidentially – 'years back, this, I even snatched one for him and brought her home in the back of another van I had.'

A chill shimmered through Henry.

Next to him, he felt the Met detective touch his leg with a finger.

'You brought one home? Who would that be?'

'Some poxy kid from Wembley . . . I gave her to him on a plate . . . tied her down, pulled her legs open and said, "There you go, brother of mine," and instead of being grateful, guess what?'

Henry didn't respond. Just waited for McCabe to fill the gap he had made.

'Kicked the shit out of me.'

Henry felt the detective tap again. Henry knew he would be much more interested in the kidnapping and maybe the murder of a child a few years ago than any problems McCabe had with his brother, especially now he had started to talk for the first time; once he started to talk, like most prisoners, he would never stop.

But Henry wanted a name and possibly an address because he had his own fish to fry. The least the Met could do – as thanks for catching a dangerous sexual predator and murderer – was allow a few minutes with him.

So he ignored the Met guy's now incessant tapping.

'He's one of those holier-than-thou people, is he?' Henry asked.

'Oh, yeah. But he likes hurting people. Difference between me and him is that the people I go with actually love me, even right up to the end, and I love them . . .'

Henry's toes curled up.

'What's your brother's full name?'

'McCabe. Darren McCabe.'

'Where does he live?'

'Near here. Up in Greenwich.'

'Address?'

'Up on Norman Road, I think. Look I haven't seen him for ages, y'know? But I think he lives up there with a bird and a kid now.'

Henry stood up and said to the detective, 'He's all yours.' To McCabe, he said, 'I hope you rot in hell.'

SEVENTEEN

Henry left the interview room relatively pleased with what he had achieved, but he needed much more and quickly.

His first port of call was to the custody desk to ask for the mugshot of Gerald McCabe taken when he had arrived at the station – one hard copy and a digital copy sent to his phone. He met up with Flynn and Jake outside the police station and they decided to drive in one car the short distance to Norman Road in Greenwich, which they found quite easily.

However, they parked on Greenwich High Street and strolled to a café with internet access.

From there Henry phoned Rik Dean who was in the MIR at Lancaster. He opened the conversation by saying, 'Now they think it's many more.'

'Wow. I allow you to go to London and within hours you've nailed a serial killer. Pretty good going.'

'Team effort.'

'I've been to see Diane, by the way.'

Henry went cold. Rik's voice sounded ominous. 'And?'

'No change . . . which in some ways is a good thing. Seems they really have managed to stem the internal bleeding.'

'Good.' Henry blew out his cheeks. 'Now then . . .'

Flynn and Jake were at the counter buying drinks and sandwiches. They returned with two full trays to the secluded alcove in which Henry was seated and distributed the food.

Henry checked to see if it was possible that they were being listened to by anyone, but the café was quite empty and the alcove made things fairly private. He placed his phone on the table between them and switched on the speakerphone so Flynn and Jake could listen in.

'Ricky boy, I need someone to get into army records and see if we can unearth a photograph of one Darren McCabe' – he gave him the date of birth – 'who apparently served in the forces for a short time. Also, I'm going to send you a mugshot of his twin brother, Gerald. Can you see if you can get it blown up first of all and then get the artist to do a quick drawing from it so it's similar but not exactly the same, if you get my drift. Only thing is, I want it as soon as, because we're going to do some basic coppering tomorrow morning.' Henry looked at Flynn and Jake. 'Aren't we, guys?'

They nodded less than enthusiastically.

'I'll sort it,' Rik promised, 'and send it to you.'

'I've booked three rooms at the Travelodge in Greenwich for us tonight and tomorrow night just in case, so I'll access their internet and then see if I can get what you send printed off behind reception. Time's getting on, so we'll start fresh in the morning.'

'All charged to LanCon?' Rik asked.

'It's the right thing to do.'

'OK, no probs, I'll get on with this.'

'How's the prison job coming along?' Henry asked.

'Oh, marvellous. We have a couple of hundred suspects and not one wants to talk to us. Strange, that.'

Henry ended the call, looked from Jake to Flynn, and at the food and drink in front of them.

'Thanks for today, guys.' He was about to say something a bit slushy and motivational when his phone rang. It was Rik Dean again.

'Henry, know how I was saying we were getting nowhere with the prison job? Well,' he said excitedly, 'we got a ping!'

Going back up through London took a very infuriating ninety minutes, all the way from Greenwich to Willesden, just south of the point where the M1 juts into London and becomes the A5. Henry drove his Audi because Flynn was feeling the pain of his wall-smash increasing all the time, and although he was convinced that he hadn't done any actual damage to himself, he was beginning to struggle. He'd snaffled four Nurofen tablets but they seemed to be having little effect.

Jake followed in the BMW.

Finally, and with the assistance of satnav, they drove on to a large retail park near to Church End where they met up with the National Crime Agency officer they had spoken to previously, Ted Sandford, the guy who had briefed them via Skype on Dunster Cosmo. Sandford turned out to be a fifty-eight-year-old former detective superintendent who had retired from the Met and joined the NCA.

They met him at the quiet end of the car park, outside a Toys R Us that had closed down a couple of years before. They all shook hands.

'Hear you've struck gold already,' Sandford said.

'More by luck than judgement,' Henry replied.

'My sources tell me the Met have very red faces . . . under their noses and all that.'

'Well, they shouldn't have,' Henry said and meant it. Catching serial killers was hard and it often took a lucky break that opened the floodgates.

'Mmm, whatever,' Sandford said. 'Anyhow,' he continued, 'I've spoken to Rik Dean, as you know, and he's put me in the picture about the "ping" from Lancashire prison.'

He was referring to the fact that the telephone unit at Lancashire Constabulary HQ, in liaison with mobile phone providers, had eventually discovered that a text had been sent from a mobile phone in Lancashire prison just after Tommy Costain's murder. This was known as a 'ping'. It was not unusual for texts or calls to be made, obviously; most were legitimate and related to staff-owned phones, and just local calls or texts anyway.

The one thing different about this was that it had been made from a pay-as-you-go mobile bought from a supermarket in Preston which had only ever been switched on one time (as indicated by the 'pulse' from the phone), used to send one text, switched off and never used again.

One phone, one text message: end of story.

And although the body of that text could not be read, what could be shown was the number of the phone it had been sent to and its location within a radius of ten metres.

The message had been received by another pay-as-you-go phone that had been purchased just the day before, switched on for just one morning, then switched off after the text had been received and never used again.

Another phone, used once.

'We can jump to conclusions, obviously,' Sandford said, 'and it might be that the text was sent by a prison officer, not a prisoner – but what we do know is those facts: one message sent, one message received, both phones no longer in use.'

'Which stinks,' Flynn said, still rolling his neck muscles.

Sandford regarded him. 'Who are you, exactly?'

'Hired help.'

Sandford's eyebrows met in the middle as he frowned, then he turned back to Henry.

'So possibly reporting a job well done?' Henry surmised. Then he asked Sandford, 'Why are we here?'

'First because of Dunster Cosmo who, as you know, is always on our radar, and although he's pretty clever with his phone use, as I already told you, he might just have slipped up on this occasion. The location in which the text from Lancashire landed is right here, more or less – on an industrial estate just across the way, near the railway depot at Neasden.' He pointed and went on, 'And because the signal was so precise, we actually pinpointed the industrial unit where it landed.'

Sandford reached into his car and brought out an iPad which was already logged on to an aerial view of an industrial estate. He put the device on the bonnet and all four men crowded to see.

'It's called Gladstone Hill Industrial Park, maybe a mile from here as the crow flies. It's a big one with many nooks and crannies. Mostly legitimate, but also a lot of rogues on there, plus many unoccupied units.'

Looking at it reminded Henry of White Lund in Morecambe.

'The text message landed here.' Sandford placed his finger on the image.

Henry peered at it. It looked quite a large unit.

Sandford then chose 'street view' and dragged what looked like a very unwilling cartoon image of a person across the screen and released them so that the map changed to an actual ground-level view of the unit in question.

'Formerly leased by a haulage company. It's been empty since they went bust, maybe eighteen months ago, and it's on the books of a commercial estate agent in Cricklewood,' Sandford explained. 'As soon as we got the message from Rik Dean, we went to have a discreet drive past. It's surrounded by a high fence, as you can see, not overlooked by any other units, very private, and also the units either side are empty, too. It's got big gates that you can only glimpse through – if they are closed, that is.'

Henry looked sharply at Sandford.

'When we drove past, the gates were open and a couple of vans were parked inside.'

'Legit?' Jake asked.

Sandford shook his head. 'The discreet drive past wasn't so quick as to prevent photos being taken,' Sandford said, adding, 'My people are good.'

He selected a file from the tool bar of the iPad and tapped to open it. It showed photographs of the industrial unit obviously taken from a passing car. Several were taken through the open gates towards the unit itself and a loading bay. Two vans were parked by the bay, the wide, sliding door of which was open and revealed the interior of the unit. Two men were caught on the photograph.

'Have you spoken to the letting agents?' Henry asked.

Sandford shook his head. 'Not yet. We thought we'd hang back on that just in case we spooked anyone, although we did make a quick call to them asking if the unit was available for rent and we were told not until next week.'

'Yet we're not sure if this has anything to do with Cosmo,' Henry said. 'Just because the text landed here.'

'I agree. However . . .' Sandford expanded one of the photographs and zoomed in on the faces of the two men. Although the image became less defined, their features remained quite clear. 'We know these guys: Derry Brand, an Irish fella, and Liam Gorst, and they are Cosmo's closest associates, if you will – known in the trade as lieutenants, heavies, sidekicks, enforcers . . . whatever. They do his bidding and the big question, apart from the one about the text from the prison landing here just after a murder was committed, is what is going on here?'

Henry said, 'This all fits in with Cosmo's MO, doesn't it . . . short-term leases, et cetera.'

'People trafficking,' Flynn said.

'Could well be,' Sandford agreed. 'Which is why I've got surveillance teams, a firearms unit, dog patrols and a couple of strike force vans in place already, to see if anything goes down tonight. It looks to me like these guys could be waiting for people to arrive . . . so you're all welcome to tag along and see what transpires.'

'We're up for it,' Henry said. He looked at his colleagues. 'Aren't we?'

Two hours later, Henry, Flynn and Jake were squeezed uncomfortably on to the back seats of a police personnel carrier somewhere – Henry did not have a clue as to exactly where he was, geographically speaking – within striking distance of the industrial unit which may or may not be the subject of some action.

Each man had been provided with a hi-vis singlet to wear over their jackets with the word 'Observer' imprinted on the back, and they'd had specific instructions not to get involved in anything that might happen, and just to watch. They'd each signed a risk assessment form – even Jake, the only real cop of the trio – to acknowledge the possible danger they might find themselves in and to indemnify the Met from any claims further down the line. A back-covering exercise.

Sitting in the van with them were seven cops – one sergeant, six constables – attached to a special operations unit which Henry understood to mean cops who kicked down doors and did other exciting things. They were geared up in overalls, stab vests, boots and crash helmets, as if they might be going into a riot situation.

A variety of tools were spread among them, including crowbars, sledgehammers and door openers, as well as the usual accoutrements such as batons, CS spray and Tasers. None were tooled up with firearms, but Henry knew there was a firearms unit parked up somewhere nearby.

Henry was quite enjoying this. The feeling of anticipation, ready to pile out and wade into whatever could be addictive.

And, as always, the waiting was accompanied by laughter, non-PC jokes, and the obligatory fart that sounded as though it might follow through.

Very little had changed over the years in that respect.

Cops were still a pretty crude bunch.

By midnight nothing had gone down. The loading bay of the industrial unit was still open and the two guys with the vans were still inside the compound. They'd mooched around a little, made calls on their mobile phones, smoked a lot, but little else.

It was pretty clear, though, that they were waiting for something.

Just after the witching hour, another car drove into the yard, accompanied by three smaller vans.

Over the radio on a specially encrypted channel, which Henry could hear in the van, Sandford – who had eyes on the premises – said, 'Looks like it's getting interesting, not least because the car that has just arrived with the three vans is Target One's own vehicle. We might have caught him napping here. In other words, Cosmo has arrived.'

In the van, Henry and the two others glanced at each other, their eyeballs glinting in what light there was from the street lamps.

Sandford went on to say, 'Could be a night for the arrival and distribution of goods.'

Nothing further happened for another hour other than updates from Sandford who kept up a running commentary from his location relating to the movement of the men who continued to mooch, chat and smoke.

'They're waiting for something,' Sandford said.

Ten minutes later, his voice became more animated when he said, 'It's here! An articulated HGV pulling a container unit has just pulled into the yard and is now reversing up to the loading bay. The goods have arrived, ladies and gents and others, the goods have arrived.' His voice was dramatic.

In the van there was a palpable surge of excitement as the officers sat up and prepared themselves for some action.

Even Henry's heart started to pump a little more quickly.

'It's a tight space, but the driver's doing well,' Sandford said as he watched the HGV. 'He's backed up to the loading bay and stopped now. He's getting out and talking to Cosmo . . . Seems to be some sort of disagreement . . . gesticulating . . . waving of arms . . . arguing. Someone's not happy . . . One of Cosmo's guys is opening the container . . . I think we need to hit this now,' Sandford said, 'catch them in the act . . . All units go!'

With a lurch, the personnel carrier jumped forward, and about thirty police officers secreted in various locations close to the target premises moved in quickly.

'They've come down from Harwich,' Sandford said sombrely, his voice trembling with emotion. In fact, he was close to tears. 'Sailed across on the ferry from the Hook of Holland. And somewhere along the way, the air-flow system stopped working.'

The flatbed trailer with the container on it was still backed up to the loading bay and the doors of the container were wide open.

Henry and Sandford stood side by side looking into the container which was now lit brightly by emergency scene lighting from a mobile incident unit.

'How many?' Henry asked. He was feeling both nauseous and enraged.

'Twenty-four, including two babes in arms.'

Henry's insides twisted into a knot of fury as he looked across the illuminated shapes of the dead people in the unit. Some were in tight embraces, others curled up in foetal balls, trying to stay warm and alive.

None had succeeded.

They had shivered their way to suffocation and a miserable, lingering death.

'Fuck,' he said.

'They seem to be Asian in origin,' Sandford told him.

Stepping carefully over and around them were two crime scene investigators clad in forensic suits, taking photographs, recording the scene with still cameras and video. The flashes from their cameras seemed to add poignancy to the tragedy they were studying.

None of the bodies had yet been moved. So far all that had happened was that a Home Office pathologist and her team had been called to the scene and rechecked every single body for signs of life to confirm what paramedics had already done and to pronounce death. She had left the container unit in tears to go and prepare the mortuary for the arrival of their bodies in due course.

Henry himself could not even begin to fathom the tragedy he had played a part in unveiling. The money paid to the gangs who promised a better life in the UK; that people would be able to claim benefits straight away, then get a guaranteed job and begin sending money back home to their dependants. Who, he thought angrily, still believed that shit?

Even now, with the worldwide problem of people trafficking and modern slavery under the spotlight, Henry could not believe the gullibility of admittedly desperate people who put their trust and cash into smugglers' hands to make that hop across the Channel to the land of plenty.

He wondered at what point the air supply stopped working and when the people trapped inside the container began to realize that something was seriously amiss, that the air was getting thinner; when the breathing became more and more difficult, and then panic set in, the banging on the sides started, the screaming, and when a baby no longer drew breath.

He forced his mind from these bleak thoughts and images, and tried to work out the kind of money involved. The figures blew his mind.

'Well, at least we've got Dunster Cosmo and his crew,' Sandford said, cutting into his thoughts, 'even though it's no consolation for these people and their families.'

'Yeah, at least we got them,' Henry said.

The police operation, despite being hastily convened, had gone remarkably well, but because Henry, Flynn and Jake had been told to hang back, they hadn't witnessed much of it, only being called in after the arrests had been made of Cosmo and his associates, plus the lorry driver.

All of them had attempted to flee as the police descended, and there had been some Keystone Kops-like chases around the exterior of the industrial unit. A couple of police dogs had sunk their fangs into the buttocks of two of the men, one being Cosmo himself.

Henry was sad to have missed that, because even though he had never met or interacted with Cosmo, he knew he hated him.

All the suspects were taken away quickly in a fleet of police vans that Sandford had arranged to be on standby, and all were lodged in separate police stations to ensure there was no way they could communicate with each other.

In the container unit, a CSI bent low and took a flash photograph of one of the victims, lighting the face of the young girl eerily.

'Jeez,' Sandford said. He had his hands on his hips, his eyes raised to the heavens, then he looked at Henry. 'I can't believe how gutted I am.'

'I can, because I am, too.'

Henry could not look any more. He turned away and walked into the industrial unit which would have been used as a cattle pen for these people before they were dispersed to other locations in the UK. There, he guessed, they would simply have been dumped on the streets and left to fend for themselves.

He thrust his hands in his pockets and walked around the edge of the concrete floor, scuffing his feet in the dust. At the far end of the unit he walked into the office in which he saw some chairs and a table, probably left by the previous occupants. Something on the floor by the wall caught his eye. He crossed over to it and saw he was looking at a mobile phone in bits. He bent to look. The back had come off and was in two pieces, the screen was cracked but it looked salvageable.

'What're you looking at?' a voice from behind asked. It was Jake Niven.

'Broken phone. You got a pair of disposable gloves?'

Jake delved into a pocket and handed a pair to Henry who fitted them and picked up the pieces.

'No SIM card,' he said. Henry turned the phone in his fingers. The back of it was still on the floor, snapped into two halves. Henry was looking at what was exposed in the phone with the back and battery removed: the slot for the SIM, the place where the battery fitted and a small circuit board. He would call it the gubbins. Next to what he thought was the circuit board was a small sticker with various identification numbers printed on it, including the FCC ID, the SSN and the IEMI number, and a bar code, and he just knew that what he was holding had to be the phone on which the text from the prison had been received and which had then been stomped on.

Henry held it up to the light to see if he could make out any fingerprints; there were smudges on the screen which could be useful.

He took the phone over to Sandford and showed the pieces in the palm of his hand.

'Oh . . . promising,' the NCA guy said.

'No SIM card, though. However, I'll bag it up,' Henry said. 'There's a smudge of a print on the screen.'

'Can it be reassembled?' Sandford said. 'Or at least could the battery be put back in and powered up?'

'Don't see why not.'

'If you can switch it on, then unless the text was deleted before an attempt was made to break the phone up, it could still be on the phone, even though there is no SIM card.'

'I know that,' Henry said.

The battery did slot back into place. Henry held it there with his thumb and pressed the power button and was surprised to see the display on the screen light up. He pressed the menu button and selected the message icon. And held his breath.

Had Cosmo got careless?

There was one message in the inbox from, it said, an unknown sender.

'He hasn't deleted it,' Henry said in disbelief.

'Probably because he didn't expect us calling tonight,' Sandford said.

Henry selected the message and saw the text was still there.

It read: *U got 1 dead man.*

By scrolling down, the number from which it had been sent was also there, plus the date and time received, which linked in nicely with Tommy Costain's murder. The message showed that there were attachments to it. Henry selected one and a photograph appeared on the screen – Tommy Costain's body lying in a pool of blood. There were three more taken from different angles.

He showed them to Sandford, who said, 'Wow. Just wow.'

However, Henry's elation was tempered by glancing into the back of the container unit just as the CSI took a series of flash photographs of twenty-four dead people who had lost their lives chasing the dream of a better life.

He knew he would have to take his place at the back of a very long queue of law enforcement officials wishing to talk to Dunster Cosmo.

EIGHTEEN

It was four thirty a.m. by the time they arrived back at the hotel in Greenwich and got to their rooms. They were exhausted, and Flynn was still in agony from his earlier encounter with a wall. Henry thanked them both and they arranged to meet later in the morning in the restaurant on the ground floor.

Henry thought he would not sleep. His mind was buzzing, but as soon as his head touched the pillow he went out like a light until eight a.m. when his phone rang and he scrambled across the wide bed to answer it.

'Hope I haven't woken you,' Rik Dean said.

'No.' Even that word was thick, and it was obvious to Rik that he had done just that.

'Anyway . . . what's happening?'

Henry shook his head and put his mind into gear. 'Twenty-odd migrants dead in the back of a lorry.'

'Yeah, it's all over the media. And?' Rik sounded confused. 'Been too busy to take it in really. Tell me.'

'That's what I was doing last night, following up the "ping". It got kinda complicated, but Dunster Cosmo's been arrested, plus a few members of his organization. Unfortunately, it means we're at the back of the queue to talk to the guy, but we did manage to find the mobile phone, minus the SIM, on which he received the text from the prison. There's more work to do on that, but it's a trail to follow and he won't be going anywhere soon, if ever.'

Henry spent a few minutes bringing Rik up to speed with last night's operation and how it had panned out just from the 'ping' from the prison.

'Brilliant work,' Rik said.

'So why have you rung?'

'Just to say I'm sending you the work done by the police e-fit artist on the pictures you sent of McCabe's brother.'

'Brilliant . . . but could you chase up the army? They should have a photo in their records. I know it'll be one from a few years ago, but it may be helpful.'

'I will. So, today? You're planning to go door to door down that street?'

'I am.'

'You need to take care, Henry. If you come across this guy, you know what he's like. He won't be a pussy cat. He'll just shoot you dead you know that.'

'He'll have to shoot Steve Flynn first.'

Henry made another phone call after this, then dragged himself unwillingly out of bed, showered, dressed and made his way down to the restaurant where he helped himself to too much food and a large coffee, then sat at a table close to the wall-mounted TV which was showing a news channel that seemed devoted to the police operation last night in north London. The sound was low but the scrolling news banner told of the tragedy of twenty-four deaths of people believed to be from the Far East and the arrest of seven men believed to be members of a people-smuggling gang.

Henry watched an exhausted-looking Tom Sandford give a quick press briefing and promise more details as and when they were available and appropriate.

Already there were stories emerging of desperate texts sent from the container, some family photographs of the people believed to have died and even an interview in China with the father of one of them. When news broke, Henry thought, it broke fast these days.

Flynn and Jake joined him around nine fifteen, grabbed breakfasts and coffees, and with eyes on the TV screen, they ate.

The first thing Jake asked was, 'Diane?' assuming Henry would have made the call to check on how she was.

He had. 'No change but no worse.'

Jake nodded.

Henry explained his phone call from Rik and that he was expecting some mug shots to be sent to his email which he then wanted to get hotel reception to print off.

'Then we go knocking on doors, see if we can find a killer behind one of them.'

Norman Road was only a couple of minutes away from the hotel on foot and when Henry saw it he sighed with frustration. It was a pleasant enough road but seemed mainly to consist of low-rise apartment blocks with access to them restricted to tenants by way of security keypads. There was one block that looked older than the others and could possibly have once been owned by the local authority way back, but the bigger picture was that it would be difficult to gain entry to any of the blocks and go knocking on doors and flashing the photographs that Rik had sent to Henry.

Henry felt despondent, but then his day brightened when he saw a Post Office van pull to a stop alongside one of the blocks. A postman got out and went into the foyer of that particular block with a handful of letters.

Henry hurried up to catch him as he came back out empty-handed.

'Excuse me, can I have a quick word?'

The postman looked immediately suspicious and a little wary of the three big men bearing down on him. Henry saw the look and wondered how many times the poor guy had been robbed.

'Hey, nothing to worry about,' Henry assured him. He still did not look too convinced. 'Just a few seconds of your time, if you don't mind.'

'Right, OK.' Still not happy.

Henry unfolded the photographs he'd had printed off on A4-sized paper, one of the actual Gerald McCabe and then the speculative e-fit of what his twin brother, Darren, might look like based on a combination of the mugshot and the description taken from the B and B owner, but with the face slightly cleaned up, a bit more flesh around the gills, the bags under the eyes less prominent.

'We're police officers . . . just curious if you know this man, or maybe someone who looks similar and lives here in Norman

Road. We think he lives here with a woman and a young child.'

The postman screwed up his face and again looked suspiciously at Henry and his two companions. 'You sure you're police?'

'Yeah, of course.' Henry indicated to Jake. 'Show him your warrant card.'

Jake did. The postman read it carefully and muttered, 'Lancashire Constabulary, eh? Long way from home.'

Henry nodded.

'Where's your ID?' the postman asked Henry.

'Look, I'm a civilian employee and it's not come through just yet . . . thing is, do you know this guy or not? If not, fine. But if you do, or think you do, we need to know because he's wanted for some very serious offences up north, which is why we're down here in London, and we're simply trying to track him down and make an arrest.'

Finally, the postman seemed to accept the tale.

He studied the photographs and said, 'There is a guy . . . looks a bit like this, I suppose, but not completely like him, if you get my drift. He lives with a woman and they've got a pretty young kid.'

'Where does he live?'

'There.' The postman pointed across the road to the red-brick block of flats that Henry had already tagged as possibly having once been council-owned. 'That ground-floor flat.'

The block was divided into ten flats over three floors, so they were quite large units, built in the 1960s before space became such an issue in London and everything became smaller and more expensive. There was a ground-floor flat on either side of the entrance foyer, and the front doors of the properties could only be accessed through a security door leading into this foyer. There was the obligatory keypad plus doorbells for each flat with scribbled name plates relating to each flat. All had names with the exception of Flat 1, the one on the left of the entrance foyer.

'Four-zero-eight-five,' Henry said, regurgitating the keypad code the postman had given him which, he also informed Henry, would only get him into the foyer. The postman had this number only because the letter boxes relating to each flat were in there. The lift and the stairs required another number which he did not possess.

Henry was fine with that because it gave him direct access to the front door of Flat 1.

He tapped in the number, heard the click of the door being released, then stepped through with Flynn and Jake behind him. He knocked on the door, but there was no response. There was still nothing from further knocking. He would have liked to have been able to shout through a letter box, but there wasn't one. The door was just one piece of solid wood without any glass, just a peephole. He turned to Flynn.

'How are you feeling today?'

'Well enough to kick a door down,' he said enthusiastically.

'Be my guest.' Henry had a quick look at Jake who had a slightly worried expression on his face about the legality of entering the flat in this manner. Henry said, 'I can smell smoke, can't you?'

He stood aside, allowing Flynn room to operate.

Flynn lined up with the concentration of a rugby player about to convert a try. He sniffed. Rolled his shoulders. Measured the distance. Worked out where best to flat-foot the door (just below the Yale-type lock). There may have been bolts on the other side, but if the flat was empty, they would obviously not be in place. His eyebrows twitched. His body wound itself up to deliver a powerful blow.

The first kick did not seem to have any discernible effect.

The second clattered the door open and almost smashed it off its hinges.

They had gone and all the signs pointed to not returning in the near future.

Henry looked disconsolately around the main bedroom, seeing swathes of clothes strewn across the bed as if laid out and a choice made.

'Henry?'

Flynn had entered the room holding a framed photograph, a nice one of a couple and a child. Smiling. Happy. Proud. 'This was on the fireplace.'

The man in it looked very much like a smarter version of Gerald McCabe and very much like the speculative e-fit.

But not quite. It was his twin brother who looked quite sweet and normal. The gunman.

Jake then entered bearing several unopened letters he had retrieved from the letter box in the foyer. They were mainly flyers and circulars, and it was hard to say how long they had been there. 'Addressed to a Mrs Marcie Quant.'

Henry took this in, the surname sounding familiar, and then he looked at the photograph in Flynn's hands.

'I've seen this woman before – and the man,' he said.

Jake peered at the photo over Henry's shoulder and simultaneously all three men's eyes locked as they realized where they had all seen them both before.

'Surveillance photographs,' Flynn said. 'The ones Ted Sandford showed us. The ones taken by the NCA at that guy's funeral, the one who'd been gunned down in Liverpool. Dunster Cosmo was in attendance. She's the dead guy's widow and this fella' – he tapped the photo – 'was there, too.'

'That's it!' said Jake. 'She's called Quant and the funeral was for Brendan Quant, the guy who got whacked in Liverpool.'

'Cosmo seems to be the common denominator in all this,' Henry said, 'and looking at this guy' – he tapped his finger on McCabe's face in the photograph – 'I'd say he was Gerald McCabe's better-looking twin brother, Darren, and one thing's for sure, we're hot on his tail.'

'Why don't we get a proper warrant and a search team in here?' Jake suggested. 'Do it by the book.'

Henry took out his mobile phone and took a photograph of the framed photo, then called up Ted Sandford.

Henry found the remainder of the day to be frustrating but necessary.

Through Ted Sandford, he managed to rustle up a search team from the Met which seemed to want to trash the flat and get out as soon as possible. It took a lot of patience and the application of some discipline by him to keep them on track.

In the end, after a four-hour search, they found seemingly little of importance and nothing much was seized other than a few more photographs and some documents. There was no computer in the flat, although it did have broadband connection. Henry guessed any computer would be with the couple, wherever they were.

When the search was over, Henry ensured the property was sealed up securely and a notice with phone numbers on was slapped on the front door saying this was now a police crime scene. Two police cordon tapes were strung across the door.

Finally, everything that had been bagged up was transferred to a secure property store at Lewisham Police Station.

By the time all this had been done, it was five p.m.

Henry checked on the status of Gerald McCabe to find he was still being interviewed, and the buzz was that he had now admitted to twenty abductions/murders in the Greater London area in the last fifteen years, plus numerous break-ins where he had raped elderly occupants, male and female. His recollection of the number of indecent assaults and indecent exposure offences – as well as the stranger rapes he had committed where he had not abducted or murdered anyone – was hazy.

Henry also checked on Dunster Cosmo's progress but struggled to get any update. He was very much being kept under wraps, which Henry understood. There was a very good chance that if he cracked, a whole multi-million-pound criminal enterprise could be brought down.

After this he, Jake and Flynn returned to the hotel in Greenwich where they had booked rooms for another night.

They split up, with plans to meet up later and get an evening meal in Greenwich. Flynn headed straight for a hot bath to ease his aching muscles and then bed for a couple of hours. Jake went to grab a shower, then call home. Henry hit his room and showered too, aware that stepping back into the clothes he had been wearing for the last couple of days was taking its toll.

He stretched out on the large bed and watched a news channel which was still buzzing with the deaths of the migrants but had also picked up on the arrest of a serial killer in New Cross and even had some footage of the actual arrest of McCabe, taken by the driver of one of the cars that had crawled past as Jake was kneeling on the prisoner's back. Fortunately, all the faces had been pixelated out.

Then he opened his laptop and transferred the photographs he had taken with his phone of all the documents seized from the flat on Norman Road on to it so they were easier to expand and inspect.

Before perusing them, though, he made a couple of phone calls.

First to Royal Lancaster Infirmary for an update on Diane. There was no change; she was still critical, but the internal bleeding had definitely stopped.

Next he called Rik Dean to update him on progress and asked him to get things together to circulate Darren McCabe as wanted for the murder of Bethany York, Jack Carter and Billy Lane, together with the shooting of DC Diane Daniels. Henry sent him a copy of the photographs he had taken from the flat search.

Rik promised to pull that together and then asked when Henry and his little crew expected to be back in Lancashire.

'Tomorrow sometime. Going to chill tonight, see where we are up to in the morning, then head back. Late afternoon, I suspect.'

'That's fine . . . Hey, look, come round for tea, will you? Get dropped off and I'll ensure Lisa makes that chicken casserole – you know, her signature dish? After that I'll drive you up to RLI to see Diane, then take you home. Lisa needs to see you, I need to catch up with you . . . What d'you say? You haven't even seen the new house yet.'

'OK, but what if I bring Flynn along too? Then I can do the RLI thing without bothering you and he can take me home because he's bedding down at The Tawny Owl anyway. I promise he won't trash your house, and if I have to, I'll make him wear a bib and feed him myself.'

'If you must.'

'OK, speak tomorrow.'

Henry returned to the photographs and documents from the search. Although he had sent Ted Sandford a copy of the photograph that Flynn had found of the happy couple and baby, so far nothing had come back about that. He knew Sandford was busy with Cosmo, so he didn't push him about it.

As he skimmed through more documents, he came across one relating to the lease of a car. He hadn't read it at the time of seizure, but now he did and saw it was about the long-term lease of a Rolls-Royce at some astronomical monthly figure; the lease had been terminated when the car was taken back by the lease company for failure to keep up payments. These documents were all dated about four years before.

Something made him frown. Then he remembered.

He picked up his phone, flicked through the contacts, found who he was looking for and made the call. It rang and was answered quickly.

'Jenny Peel here.'

'Jenny? Sorry to bother you. This is Henry Christie. I came with DS Daniels to chat to you about John and Isobel York if you remember?'

'Course I do. What can I do for you, Henry?' she asked.

'You recall mentioning that someone came to see John York, a woman who landed in a Rolls-Royce? A woman with a driver?'

'Yes, the hunky driver. I remember him well,' she purred.

'Do you mind if I text you a photograph just to see if it's the same people who turned up to see John?'

'No probs.'

Henry did and a few minutes later Jenny Peel came back with a reply via text. *These are the ones.*

Henry thanked her by text, then slowly closed his laptop, sank back on the bed and closed his eyes, unable to stop thinking about Diane Daniels. He did something he rarely did: he prayed for her.

NINETEEN

There were worse places in the world to spend an evening than Greenwich, which was bustling and pleasant. They ate at the Cutty Sark pub which, understandably, had a good view of the *Cutty Sark* itself, the old tea clipper preserved forever near the Thames, and much bigger than Henry had imagined from his school history lessons.

All three had fish and chips and a couple of pints before strolling to the riverside to take in the spectacular view of the city, then walking back to the hotel where they weakened and had another couple of pints at the wine bar next door before returning to their rooms.

Henry phoned RLI again before sliding into bed: no change with Diane.

He slept well enough, and after breakfast they caught up with the progress of the investigations into the deaths of the migrants and how things were going with Gerald McCabe. The latter, it seemed, could simply not stop admitting offences; with regard to the former, Ted Sandford told Henry that Dunster Cosmo was tight-lipped and hard work; told him to call back in a couple of days to try to arrange an interview, but not before.

In effect, that left the trio with nothing to do in London other than hope the Met did the job properly.

It was a strange feeling for Henry because it made him feel slightly powerless.

Had he been a fully fledged detective super, he would have stayed around, annoying people, butting in, but being a civvy stripped away this right. It was hard to accept but he had to go with the flow. Not only that: a big part of him wanted to get back up north now, work the cases from that end – because capturing Darren McCabe was his priority now – and also be in a position to be by Diane's bedside when she woke up. Or didn't.

They ate a leisurely breakfast.

Flynn was feeling better, though still sore.

Jake just wanted to get home. Some sort of domestic crisis was now going on between his wife and son, and there was a stack of jobs on the rural beat that needed his attention.

When they jumped into the cars, they were all glad to be on the road.

Henry travelled with Flynn in the Audi, sharing the driving.

And it was a tedious journey to say the least.

Traffic in London was horrific due to a combination of a terrorist incident in Westminster – which had an enormous knock-on effect of completely blocking traffic flow on every road north and south of the river – and the normal volume of traffic. So, having looped out of Greenwich around on to the A202, they found themselves in standing traffic by the Kennington Oval; Henry's off-the-cuff plan to head west towards Wandsworth to try to link up with the M25 instead of crossing the Thames at Vauxhall was just as much a dead end.

They finally crawled on to the M40 just before noon but hit more standing traffic in the Midlands, so that by the time they were on the M6 north of Birmingham it was three o'clock, with at least another couple of hours' travel remaining. To turn on to a service area for the loo and a brew was a relief for the pent-up stress they were feeling.

It was here Henry had a call from Rik Dean.

'So, where are you?'

'Don't ask,' Henry said. 'I could have walked quicker. More importantly, where are you up to?'

'McCabe is circulated as wanted,' Rik told him. 'When we've spoken face-to-face, I'm thinking we get a team together and head down to the Met to root him out . . . What do you say, Henry?'

'That sounds good. What's happening with the prison job – Tommy Costain?'

'Well, one thread of it is obviously Dunster Cosmo, as you know, but we are being held at arms' length by the Met from speaking to him regarding his involvement; at least the guy isn't going anywhere fast.'

'Good. And Diane?'

'We've managed to contact her brother at last. He's in Uganda on some charity project or other and he'll be flying back in two days.'

'That's brilliant. If he's struggling for somewhere to stay, I'll put him up at Th'Owl for as long as necessary.'

'Right . . . uh . . .' Rik hesitated.

Henry sensed it. 'What?'

'Erm, you and Diane? I know you work well together . . . but is there anything more I should know about?'

It was Henry's turn to hesitate. 'Possibly.'

'You old dog!'

Henry just grinned. 'Friends with benefits.'

'Henry, you don't work that way. You fall in love . . . that's always been your problem, mate.'

'Might be some truth in that . . . anyway, never was your problem.'

Henry was referring to Rik's wild days as a serial womanizer up to the point where he met Henry's equally wild younger sister, Lisa. Despite an often tempestuous relationship, the two of them had lived happily ever after in some sort of marital bliss.

'No, it wasn't . . . hey, talking of which, I'm looking at the clock now . . . that chicken casserole's in the slow cooker, mate – with enough for Flynn, too – and we can't wait for you to land. Rice, potatoes, peas – you know it makes sense.'

'Sounds great. We'll be there,' Henry promised and hung up.

The three men dawdled and chatted over their coffees. Henry decided that he probably did not need Flynn at his back any more. He told him he would pay him as promised and release him, which suited the big man who needed to get back to Gran Canaria as he'd had some enquiries for his fishing charter and did not want to let anyone down.

The rest of the journey should have taken a maximum of two hours, but as they rejoined the M6 it was pretty much a car park and it took four hours, by which time all three men were tired and irritable.

Henry really wanted to get home – via a visit to see Diane – but he felt obliged now to visit Rik and Lisa. He toyed with the idea of taking a rain check, but wimped out, not wishing to incur their ire.

Henry and Flynn left the M6 at junction 32 and picked up the M55 to take them towards the coast while Jake stayed on, flashing his headlights as he passed. At the end of the M55, Henry and Flynn came off and headed to Lytham.

For Lisa Dean, née Christie, Henry's once flaky sister (as he used to describe her) and now Rik Dean's wife, that day had begun well. After Rik had gone to work, she had prepared the chicken casserole and chucked it in the slow cooker, feeling quite excited about seeing Henry who had become a bit of recluse recently. To be fair, she and Rik had been focusing on their new house on the front at Lytham, and she had concentrated a lot on her own business, making bespoke jewellery for clients who were willing to pay outrageous prices for one-off pieces. Her average price was in the £3,000 area and she tended to make a couple of items each month, so between them, their income was pretty healthy – Rik earned around £73,000 – which is why they'd splashed out on the house.

Once the chicken was in, she made her way upstairs to the bedroom at the front of the house, overlooking Fairhaven boating lake, which was now her work room. She settled at the desk, adjusted her hands-free magnifying glass and began work on her latest creation which was something different and unusual for the wife of a local millionaire and had been quoted at £10,000.

It was coming along well and would be worth the money.

The work consumed her, as she delicately built up the frame, shaped like the wings of an egret, and then added and set into place the tiny diamonds. A real work of art and she was proud of it.

Two hours later, with aching eyes and an aching spine, she leaned back in her chair and stretched, deciding she needed a break. Glancing outside, the weather was blustery but she quite fancied getting her hair windswept and maybe calling in for a milky coffee at the café by the lake.

She went down to the kitchen and checked the casserole (without removing the lid) and then looked for her duffel coat under the stairs, at which point someone knocked on the front door.

'Coming,' she called, pulling on her coat. She opened the door to find a woman standing there with a baby in a sling clutched to her chest. She did not recognize her and immediately thought that although she looked quite well turned out, she was probably a Romanian beggar on the con. Rik had told her that there had been a few incidents recently in the area with people thought to be from Romania and that the women involved often used babes in arms as a distraction technique. 'Can I help you?' Lisa asked.

The woman smiled. 'I am really sorry to bother you . . .'

The woman looked to be on the verge of tears, but Lisa was wary of being drawn into any kind of trick. All that changed in an instant when the woman's right hand, which had been hanging down at her side just out of sight behind her, appeared in view.

There was something in the hand which Lisa thought was a mobile phone, but the hand came up quickly towards Lisa's upper chest and whatever she was holding touched her.

The pain was incredible as the compact handheld stun gun – which *was* disguised to look like a phone – released its electroshock charge into Lisa's body, jerking her backwards into the hallway, momentarily paralyzing her with the electrical discharge which overrode her muscle-triggering mechanism.

The woman bustled into the house followed by a man whom Lisa hadn't noticed and must have been hiding. The man slammed the front door, grabbed the stun gun from the woman and applied it once more to Lisa's neck for good measure.

Moments later, Lisa had been flipped over, her hands bound with plastic ties, and dragged through to the kitchen and flung roughly into a corner. A piece of tape was thumbed into place over her mouth by the woman, who patted her face and smiled down at her.

'Hello, Mrs Detective Superintendent Dean,' she said.

Lisa was convinced the two people were here to rob her of the diamonds she had upstairs in her work room which were probably worth around £20,000.

She was wrong.

Marcie Quant and Darren McCabe glanced at each other and smiled. They were here for much, much more than that.

Rik Dean finished work around five, a short day by his usual standards, but he wanted to get home more or less in time for Henry (and Flynn), just to chill and catch up and make up with someone he had known for all his police service and to whom he had a great deal to be grateful for, even if Rik had ended up stepping into Henry's shoes when he retired.

He was pleased by the progress made on the murder investigations and felt it would only be a matter of time before Darren McCabe was arrested. The guy's name and photograph were now all over the news media, and unless he was already abroad, which was possible, he would soon be in custody. Rik was looking forward to interviewing that bastard and putting him down the hole for a long, long time.

There was no real shortcut from Lancaster to Lytham, so Rik settled himself for the journey via the motorway, settling back and listening to Sinatra again.

He was surprised that Henry's car wasn't at the house when he arrived home and pulled up in the drive, parking behind Lisa's car. But Henry had said that traffic was bad, so no doubt he would be here in due course.

He climbed out of his car and looked proudly at his new house. He and Lisa had worked hard for it.

He slid his key into the lock and pushed the front door open, announcing, 'Honey, I'm home . . . the eagle has landed,' as he did every time he came home at a civilized hour.

The stun gun brandished by McCabe, forced into his neck, dropped him to his knees instantly.

* * *

'You are out of your fucking minds,' Rik said, staring sullenly up at Darren McCabe. 'You need to let us go now and you need to start running fast because your time is running out, mister.'

Almost as soon as Rik had entered the house and been incapacitated by the stun gun, three more men had arrived on the driveway in two small vans and joined McCabe and Marcie, helping to drag Rik into the dining room which overlooked the back garden. The curtains had been quickly drawn. Rik's hands had been tied together, as had his feet, and he'd been heaved into one corner of the room and had watched with bile rising inside him as Marcie brought a clearly distraught Lisa in and placed her on one of the dining chairs. Rik's wife looked beyond exhausted, her eyes sunken with dark rings around them, and Rik knew she'd had a terrifying day at the hands of this pair of monsters.

On Rik's words of warning, McCabe said to Marcie, 'Zap her.'

Marcie touched Lisa's neck with the stun gun again and the shock spun her off the chair. She fell to the floor in a writhing heap. Marcie screamed with laughter, and Rik could tell that both she and McCabe were on drugs – speed or cocaine or both.

Rik moved in fury. 'You bastards – leave her be.'

'One thing you don't do,' McCabe said, leaning into Rik's face, 'is even think about telling us what to do.' McCabe had the Browning in his hand and he touched it to Rik's cheek. 'Any idea what this can do?' he asked. 'Any idea of the damage it can do?'

'I've seen what it can do,' Rik said coldly.

'Ah, right . . . so you know?'

'I know a lot about you, McCabe.'

McCabe's mouth twitched. 'Anyway . . .'

'Anyway what? I can't help you. You might think I can, but I can't.'

A laptop had been set up on the dining-room table. Marcie pressed a button and the screen came to life. She turned the device around so Rik could see the screen. She pressed play and ran a news item from BBC North West showing Rik Dean talking to a reporter. In the background was a table displaying the vast amounts of money that had been seized from Hawkshead Farm and the subsequent police raid on a travellers' site in Blackpool. Millions of pounds, dollars and euros were stacked up. Two uniformed constables stood either side of the table guarding the cash.

'Remember this?' Marcie asked Rik. The baby was still in the harness.

'Obviously.'

'Where is this money now?' she demanded.

'It's locked away in secure storage.'

'On police property?'

Rik hesitated. 'Yes, headquarters. There's a special storage facility for this sort of money.'

'And you have access to it?'

This time he did not speak. Suddenly, he knew where this was going.

'Well, this is very simple, Detective Superintendent,' Marcie said. 'We are going to have a very civilized evening and night, and then, tomorrow morning, Mrs Dean will stay with me – not here, somewhere else, of course, somewhere you won't know – and you will go to police headquarters and wherever this money is stored, and you will fill in the necessary *genuine* paperwork to authorize its transfer to the National Westminster Bank in Preston. I'm sure you'll be able to do that. A genuine-looking security van will then turn up, be allowed access to headquarters and collect the money, and then your job will be done. After this, and as long as I am satisfied, I will release Mrs Dean unharmed. If this money transfer does not happen, or you do something stupid, brave or decent or unnatural, then I'll cut her tits off and stuff them into her mouth, I'll shove a knife up her cunt and then I'll stab her to death and throw her out of a moving vehicle on to the motorway.' Marcie grinned. 'Is that clear?'

Lisa made a terrified squeak.

One of the other men poked his head around the door and said, 'Those pizzas are here.'

'So you've never been to your sister's new house?' Flynn said to Henry. 'Never once?'

'Nah . . . I know I should have done, but I don't know . . .' Henry couldn't really explain it, didn't even want to try really. Not to Flynn, anyway.

'Other than you're an antisocial, anti-family kinda guy?' Flynn teased him.

'Hit the nail on the head there,' Henry conceded. He was in the passenger seat, lounging back. He sighed; he couldn't be bothered.

'You've only got one family, you know,' Flynn went on.

'Let it go, pal.'

Flynn chuckled. He got a lot of pleasure from winding Henry up. It was a good sport.

The evening was drawing in as they drove east down Squires Gate Lane towards the sea, with Blackpool airport on their left. When they reached the point at the end of the road where the choice was right into Blackpool, left to St Annes or straight ahead into the sea, Flynn went left. He turned off after about a mile so that he was driving along the sea front at St Annes, eventually reaching Lytham, the affluent, genteel resort, passing the café on the beach which Henry had used occasionally during his police career to meet informants. He'd been a few times since just to enjoy its good food and drink. They passed King Edward VII and Queen Mary School on the left, then Fairhaven Lake on the right, where, looking across, Henry spotted the Spitfire memorial – a full-size replica of a Spitfire warplane stuck on a pole next to the lake.

Henry said vaguely, 'The house is just along here on the left somewhere,' and turned his attention to finding Rik and Lisa's house, straining his neck to look at the numbers. Then his eyes narrowed. 'I think this is . . .'

Flynn was slowing down to a crawl.

'Keep driving, keep driving,' Henry said urgently. 'Right, right, pull in here.'

Flynn complied with the rushed instructions, parking maybe another hundred yards past the house.

'That was their house for sure,' Henry said. He had recognized Rik's and Lisa's cars in the driveway, but not the two scruffy vans parked behind them, clustered into the drive. Nor had he recognized the man standing at the open front door.

'Problem being?' Flynn asked, slightly perplexed.

'I thought we were on chicken casserole for tea, not pizza.'

Apart from seeing the stranger at the door, Henry had also seen a pizza delivery van on the road and the stack of pizzas being handed over to the man.

He picked up his phone from the footwell and called Rik.

* * *

Rik's mobile phone and the rest of his belongings from his pockets had been dumped on to the dining-room table. The phone began to ring and McCabe picked it up to look at the screen.

'Who's "HC"?'

'Brother-in-law. You want things to be natural, so I should answer it. He's supposed to be coming round this evening.'

McCabe pointed the Browning at Rik's face and gave him the phone. 'Anything stupid, I'll blow your wife's head off, OK? Now put him off and tell him not to come.'

Rik nodded.

McCabe pressed the answer button, turned on the speakerphone and held the phone at an angle in front of Rik's face so he could speak into it.

'Hi, HC, you're on speakerphone . . . how's it going?'

'Hi, Richard.' Henry's voice came over the phone. 'Sorry, we're running a bit late, traffic and all that. I reckon we're a good half hour away. Hope nothing's spoiling . . . how's that casserole coming along?'

'Casserole's doing all right . . . but, hey, mate, I'm really sorry about this, but can we cancel? I know it's short notice, but Lisa's feeling really rough – got some sort of vomiting bug. I'm really sorry, was looking forward to see you.'

'Hey, Richard – can't be helped. I'll just head off back home, no problem.'

'Right, see you.'

McCabe ended the call and stared hard at Rik, who said, 'What?'

McCabe turned away, walked to Lisa and with a brutal blow smashed the Browning across her face, knocking her off the chair. Then he looked ferociously at Rik.

'That is for telling him he was on speakerphone.'

'Why would he tell me I was on speakerphone?'

'To warn you not to speak out of turn?' Flynn ventured.

Henry thought about it. 'And he called me "HC". Which he never has done, ever.' He looked at Flynn. 'Am I reading too much into this? Maybe they really don't want me around.'

'And they're having a pizza party instead?'

'Maybe they've got workmen in?' Henry guessed.

Flynn looked squarely at him. 'Tell you what, just to make you feel better, let's go and have a look.'

Flynn switched off the engine, and both men got out and crossed the road to the boating lake and trotted down the steps to the lake itself. They walked quickly around it, cut across the skateboard park and came up on the grass verge directly opposite Rik's house, keeping down low behind the concrete cast wall that surrounded the park in which Fairhaven Lake was situated.

Henry peered through a crack in one of the fence panels, from where he could see the entrance to Rik's drive and the rear number plate of one of the two vans parked behind Rik's and Lisa's cars.

The light was going quickly now as night drew in, and although the road was well illuminated by the streetlights, Henry struggled to make out the registration number of the van.

Flynn's eyes were better. He could see the number.

'So much easier when I could just call these things in,' he said, dialling Jake Niven's mobile number. Jake answered quickly, and from the echo and delay, Henry could tell he was still in the car and using a Bluetooth connection. 'Jake? Get a PNC check done for me, will you?' Henry said without preamble. He'd decided that calling Jake would get a quicker result than trying to contact the actual police; even if he got through, which would have been a miracle, there would be the rigmarole of explaining who he was and what he wanted; doing this via Jake, he knew, would be simpler.

Jake didn't even ask why, just said, 'I'll get back to you.'

Henry and Flynn waited with their eyes looking through the slit.

There was no movement at the front of the house now.

'Just odd, is all,' Henry muttered. 'Probably nothing.'

His phone rang. 'Hi, Jake.'

'Henry, what the hell are you looking at?'

'I'm looking at a Renault van of some sort, parked in Rik Dean's driveway.'

'Actually, you're looking at a vehicle that was stolen in London about six weeks ago and has been used in several robberies across the Midlands since – that's what you're looking at.'

'Shit. Where are you, Jake?'

'Almost home . . . but I'm going to spin the car round.'

'Yeah – start making for here, will you? Inner Promenade at Lytham, opposite Fairhaven Lake.'

'I'm on my way.'

Flynn had overheard the conversation. He said, 'Are we going to take a chance and check this out?'

They were three guys McCabe had known a long time, trusted and would be glad to share some percentage of any takings with. In his younger days, following his dishonourable discharge from the army for toasting his sergeant's fingers, McCabe had come across the trio in Redditch when he was drifting around building sites looking for labouring and security work. They were working the sites as well, mainly as security guards. He had fallen in with them for a while and tagged along, helping out with some of the security issues they had been tasked to deal with – mainly breaking bones and warning people off – and also a couple of cash-in-transit robberies they had committed.

McCabe had drifted away from them eventually, but knew they had continued to make their living from robbing anyone and anything that had money in it, from simply using JCB forklifts to ripping ATMs out of walls to quite complex jobs that needed careful planning and logistics. He knew they had a couple of Ford Transit vans that had been resprayed to look like genuine armoured security vehicles and had used them as decoys in a couple of their robberies. One of those vehicles was now parked in a side road close to Rik Dean's house with the fake security company logo covered by removable stick-on signs that related to a bogus utility company.

When Dunster Cosmo had released him and Marcie and demanded his money back, Marcie had proposed her scheme to steal the money that had been seized from the Yorks' farmhouse. She'd had to convince him that it was feasible if done the right way – by holding a hostage – and when he had eventually nodded that it could be done, he knew they would need some help and turned to the three robbers he knew: Dagger, Santer and North. He also knew these guys would use any amount of violence necessary and were not remotely intimidated by cops. They were only interested in money, spending that money, then accumulating more, and when McCabe promised them a bumper payday, they were more than happy to run with him and Marcie.

It was a fairly straightforward plan. Simply force Rik Dean to do their bidding by holding his wife hostage and under threat of death, move the money into the back of the mocked-up security van provided by the three villains and then disappear with it – and probably murder Dean's wife, but that was by the by.

When to move in had been an issue for discussion, but it had been decided that it would be easier to get into the cop's house during the day and hold the wife hostage until he arrived home from work, then hold them both until the next day when the wheels would be set in motion to acquire the money. It would be a long night, admittedly, but with five of them, they could share keeping watch.

Dagger, Santer and North were not privy to the discussions between Marcie, McCabe and their captives. They weren't interested in that side of things, just in the excitement of committing the crime and then spending the money in Spain afterwards. They had ordered pizzas after devouring the chicken casserole and were now sitting around the kitchen table with five half-eaten pizzas in their boxes in front of them. Also on the table were three handguns.

North folded a whole slice of pepperoni pizza into his mouth and stood up, wiping his hands down his jeans.

'Going for a fag.'

Leaving the other two guzzling the pizzas and half watching the TV that dropped down from under a kitchen cabinet, he picked up one of the guns and slid it into the waistband of his jeans at the small of his back, went to the back door and stood on the patio, where he lit up and blew smoke up into the night sky. He wasn't too worried about being seen because the large garden was surrounded by tall trees on all sides and not overlooked by any of the adjoining properties.

As he smoked, he walked to the edge of the patio and down the steps on to the back lawn, strolling across the nicely cut grass to the border where he put his cigarette between his lips and decided he needed to piss.

Henry and Flynn scurried across the road and slithered over the corner of the front garden wall, dropping into a flower bed and keeping low, using the cover of overhanging bushes and trees as they sneaked down the side of the house, taking a chance to try to peer through the side windows as they crept along. The first one gave a view into the entrance hallway behind the front door; next along was a smaller frosted window which could have been for a downstairs loo. Then there was a much larger window, again with the curtains pulled across and just the smallest gap between them. By twisting his head to alter the angle at which he looked through, Henry could make out the people in there. He could see Lisa, strapped to a chair, the side of her face bleeding badly. He saw Marcie Quant with the baby on the sling and then he saw Darren McCabe standing up, talking down to someone – that would be Rik – whom Henry could not quite see.

Henry drew back to allow Flynn a look.

'What's going on, Henry?' Flynn whispered.

Henry shook his head, incandescent with a burning rage. 'I don't know, but Lisa's badly hurt, and Rik could be, too.'

Flynn jerked his head and they moved on to the next window at which there was a blind drawn, but Henry and Flynn could just about see underneath this into the kitchen beyond where the three men sat at the table with the pizza boxes open in front of them. And three handguns.

'Hired help,' Flynn said.

One stood up, took a gun, walked to the back door.

Flynn edged along to the corner of the house, flattening himself against the brickwork, with Henry just behind him. With one eye, Flynn watched the man light a cigarette and, after a few drags of it, set off down the steps and left towards the edge of the lawn where his urination started.

Flynn had no compunction about taking a man halfway through a piss.

The man was about twenty feet away. Flynn moved silently at first, but after that there was no grace, just accuracy and astonishing power as he drove a superbly aimed punch with his big right fist into a point on the side of the guy's head by his left ear where the jaw hinged on to the skull.

The guy went down instantly, his knees buckling. Flynn caught him and eased him to the grass, then grabbed his collar and dragged him out of sight around the corner of the house from where Henry had watched.

Flynn pulled the handgun, a snub-nosed revolver, out of the guy's waistband, checked it was loaded – it was – and handed it to Henry.

'We have a plan?' Henry asked.

'This guy will start to come round in about four minutes. He'll start moaning and groaning and alerting everyone else. So before then you need to be knocking on the front door with that' – he pointed at the gun – 'hidden behind your arse. I'm going to go for the two guys in the kitchen as soon as I hear you knocking.' Flynn paused. 'We've started, Henry; we either run away now or finish whatever's happening. This is our play at the moment.'

Henry nodded, split off and crept quickly back to the front of the house.

Flynn hauled the guy under a bush in the flower bed, then edged his way to the back door where once again he flattened himself against the wall and waited.

At the front door, Henry knocked.

'Who the fuck is that?' McCabe demanded.

'I don't know.'

'You said you weren't expecting anyone.'

'I'm not.'

The doorbell rang, followed by another impatient knock.

Rik said, 'We need to answer it. It's obvious someone's home, isn't it? Our cars are in the drive, yours too, and the fucking lights are on.'

Flynn twisted into the back doorway and stood on the threshold. The two men at the table had risen cautiously on hearing the knock at the front door, putting down their pizza slices and picking up a gun each. They were facing away from Flynn into the house.

Flynn then did something he had always had a hankering to do.

The men were not of a big build, not tall, but quite wiry. Each had a shaved head and they were standing shoulder to shoulder, both about the same height.

He went for them in a rush.

His hands reached out, one on either side of each man's head, and he did the thing that a chemistry teacher had once done to him and another miscreant at school – he banged their heads together. Hard. The noise was an incredible hollow 'thuck' as their skulls collided, but he did not stop there, because he readjusted his hold so that his large hands gripped the top of each man's head as if he was holding two bowling balls and he then slammed both heads face down into the table top, busting each man's nose into their pizzas.

Flynn then swept their feet from under them, one to the left, the other to the right, and, unconscious, they fell on to the hard tiled kitchen floor with blood spouting from their faces.

Flynn grabbed the guns, one in each hand, crossed to the kitchen door, sidestepped into the hallway and sidled behind a grandfather clock.

Rik Dean stumbled out of the dining room, pushed in the back by Darren McCabe who growled, 'Answer it and tell 'em to fuck off.'

Rik walked unsteadily to the front door and unlocked it while McCabe kept a step back, pointed his gun at Rik's head, then turned slightly and shouted towards the open kitchen door, 'You guys! What the fuck are you doing?'

Flynn had ducked back against the wall, hoping not to be seen, but McCabe saw the movement.

'Shit!' McCabe spun and fired twice at Flynn, splintering the highly polished woodwork of the old clock. Flynn darted back into the kitchen just as the front door opened to reveal Henry standing there with the gun in a firing position.

McCabe pivoted just as Rik dived across the doorway, leaving Henry with an open shot of McCabe who swivelled back, bringing his weapon around towards Henry.

Who fired twice. One slug tore a huge chunk of McCabe's neck away, the other ripped his left ear off.

McCabe dropped his weapon and crashed to his knees, clutching the neck wound from which huge amounts of blood poured through his fingers.

'Cunts!'

Henry looked up from what he'd done to see Marcie – with the baby strapped to her – frogmarching Lisa out of the dining room with one hand holding the collar of her blouse and screwing a small revolver into her right ear.

Henry kept his position, with one eye on Flynn at the kitchen door.

'Drop your gun,' Henry told her.

'Cunts! You fuckers!' she screamed, shaking the terrified Lisa and waking the baby who began to scream deafeningly.

'I said drop your gun. You're not going to get out of here, Marcie.'

The use of her name jarred her for a moment, then she shoved Lisa aside and screamed, 'Are you going to shoot a mother with a baby?'

She raised the gun to fire at Henry just as Flynn stepped out of the kitchen and, aiming low with the handgun he was holding in his right hand, shot Marcie Quant twice in the upper legs.

Henry watched her drop to her knees, screaming and clawing at her legs, but he ignored her and walked over to McCabe who had blood gushing out of his neck wound. Henry stood over him, pointed the revolver at his head and thumbed back the hammer.

TWENTY

Henry spoke to her for a long, long time.

He brought her up to date with everything that had happened since she had been shot. He told her that they – he and Diane – had been on the right path with the investigation. Chasing the money trail found at Hawkshead Farm and also going to the travelling community had been the way to go. It would have led them to bring people to justice.

Then – bollocks – she had to go and get shot.

He had smiled at her at that point. Smiled at the unmoving, unresponsive figure of Diane Daniels in the bed in the critical care unit.

'You silly arse,' he chided her. His eyes were moist and he swallowed. He folded his hand across hers.

He went on and told her all about Tommy Costain's murder at Lancashire prison and the link to a big-time gangster in London called Dunster Cosmo who had sanctioned the hit, just as he'd sanctioned the death of the two lads whose bodies had been found up at Hawkshead Farm. He told her that Tommy's murder was yet to be solved, though, and that he had since learned that Conrad Costain, the boss of the Costain crime clan, had been found dead in his cell at Manchester prison from a massive heart attack.

He told her about his trip to London with Jake Niven and Steve Flynn, where they had 'brilliantly' (his word) arrested a serial killer and prodigious sex offender, and then managed to lead the cops down there to a huge people-trafficking operation run by Cosmo – whom the police up here were still waiting to interview.

'So, I've been pretty busy,' he said. 'I think you would have wanted that, wouldn't you?' he whispered, hoping there would be some response.

There wasn't. But the monitors still kept showing that her heart rate was fine, blood pressure low but OK, and the drips kept on feeding her vital medicines through tubes.

He lost track round about then. He'd wanted to tell her about the completely nuts idea to hold Lisa Dean hostage while Rik Dean went to work and handed over the millions seized from the Yorks, and that Marcie Quant – who Diane did not yet know anything about – was in custody. And that Henry had been forced to shoot Darren McCabe – the man who had killed and wounded so many, including her – and that he was now dead, having bled out in the entrance hall of Rik Dean's fancy house in Lytham. And that he, Henry, had to be prevented by Rik and Flynn from putting even more bullets into him as he lay there bleeding.

'Long story,' Henry said to Diane.

Then he blabbed on for much longer, saying that the legal implications of what had happened would stretch from here to eternity – him having shot dead someone, Flynn having shot someone, too. Both were things that had to be done, but the judicial fallout would be 'fucking awful' (his words).

He went on talking about more inconsequential subjects then: The Tawny Owl, about Ginny and her boyfriend, and, 'Oh, I probably need to tell you about Maude Crichton, too. That's if we – you know, me and you – are more than a one-night stand, as discussed. Because I'm up for it. Kinda hope you are too, because one thing I know – you came back into my life at just the right time, lass . . . the bad guys came in at the wrong time, obviously, but you, your timing couldn't have been better . . . Thing is, I knew it as soon as I watched you walking up the field towards me after I'd found Beth York's body by the lake . . . pretty romantic setting, eh? Yeah, so I knew it, but I sort of fought it . . .' He ran out of words there.

He winced and sighed and then experienced a strange surge in his body as Diane's fingers tightened ever so slightly on his hand. Just a twitch. Hardly anything. An involuntary muscle spasm?

He looked up at her and saw her lips moving.

'Oh, God,' he gasped, rose slightly from the chair he was on and leaned over her. She was saying something. A whisper, hardly audible.

Henry's heart began to ram in his chest as he leaned in, angling his ear close to her moving lips.

Then he heard.

'What . . . what do you need to tell me about Maude Crichton?'